NO SAFE
SECRET

Books by Fern Michaels

Sweet Vengeance
Holly and Ivy
Fancy Dancer
No Safe Secret
Wishes for Christmas
About Face
Perfect Match
A Family Affair
Forget Me Not
The Blossom Sisters
Balancing Act
Tuesday's Child
Betrayal
Southern Comfort
To Taste the Wine
Sins of the Flesh
Sins of Omission
Return to Sender
Mr. and Miss
Anonymous
Up Close and Personal
Fool Me Once
Picture Perfect
The Future Scrolls
Kentucky Sunrise
Kentucky Heat
Kentucky Rich
Plain Jane
Charming Lily
What You Wish For
The Guest List
Listen to Your Heart
Celebration
Yesterday
Finders Keepers

Annie's Rainbow
Sara's Song
Vegas Sunrise
Vegas Heat
Vegas Rich
Whitefire
Wish List
Dear Emily
Christmas at
Timberwoods

The Sisterhood Novels

Need to Know
Crash and Burn
Point Blank
In Plain Sight
Eyes Only
Kiss and Tell
Blindsided
Gotcha!
Home Free
Déjà Vu
Cross Roads
Game Over
Deadly Deals
Vanishing Act
Razor Sharp
Under the Radar
Final Justice
Collateral Damage
Fast Track
Hokus Pokus
Hide and Seek
Free Fall

Books by Fern Michaels (Cont.)

Lethal Justice
Sweet Revenge
The Jury
Vendetta
Payback
Weekend Warriors

The Men of the Sisterhood Novels
High Stakes
Fast and Loose
Double Down

The Godmothers Series
Getaway (e-novella exclusive)
Spirited Away (e-novella exclusive)
Hideaway (e-novella exclusive)
Classified
Breaking News
Deadline
Late Edition
Exclusive
The Scoop

eBook Exclusives
Desperate Measures
Seasons of Her Life
To Have and to Hold
Serendipity

Captive Innocence
Captive Embraces
Captive Passions
Captive Secrets
Captive Splendors
Cinders to Satin
For All Their Lives
Texas Heat
Texas Rich
Texas Fury
Texas Sunrise

Anthologies
Mistletoe Magic
Winter Wishes
The Most Wonderful Time
When the Snow Falls
Secret Santa
A Winter Wonderland
I'll Be Home for Christmas
Making Spirits Bright
Holiday Magic
Snow Angels
Silver Bells
Comfort and Joy
Sugar and Spice
Let It Snow
A Gift of Joy
Five Golden Rings
Deck the Halls
Jingle All the Way

Published by Kensington Publishing Corporation

FERN MICHAELS

NO SAFE SECRET

ZEBRA BOOKS
KENSINGTON PUBLISHING CORP.
http://www.kensingtonbooks.com

ZEBRA BOOKS are published by

Kensington Publishing Corp.
119 West 40th Street
New York, NY 10018

Copyright © 2016 by Fern Michaels

Fern Michaels is a registered trademark of KAP 5, Inc.

All Kensington titles, imprints, and distributed lines are available at special quantity discounts for bulk purchases for sales promo-tion, premiums, fund-raising, educational, or institutional use.

Special book excerpts or customized printings can also be cre-ated to fit specific needs. For details, write or phone the office of the Kensington Sales Manager: Attn.: Sales Department. Ken-sington Publishing Corp., 119 West 40th Street, New York, NY 10018. Phone: 1-800-221-2647.

Zebra and the Z logo Reg. U.S. Pat. & TM Off.

First Kensington Books Hardcover Printing: April 2016
First Zebra Books Mass-Market Paperback Printing: April 2018
ISBN-13: 978-1-4201-3589-3
ISBN-10: 1-4201-3589-9

eISBN-13: 978-1-4201-3590-9
eISBN-10: 1-4201-3590-2

10 9 8 7 6 5 4 3 2 1

Printed in the United States of America

Part One

Nothing weighs on us so heavily as a secret.
—Jean de La Fontaine, French poet
(1621–1695)

Prologue

Prom Night
Blossom City, Florida

Maddy Carmichael pushed the rusty-red 1964 Mustang's accelerator to the floor, the instant surge of speed charging through her veins like an unexpected bolt of lightning under a clear-blue Florida sky. Hot tears spilled from her eyes and rolled down her cheeks as she made the familiar turn onto the main road. She should've stayed home. Her dream from three nights ago still haunted her, *taunted* her.

She was naked and standing in the middle of the gymnasium while her entire class examined her. A nightmare she wanted to forget, yet it wasn't all that far from what she'd just experienced. Actually, the dream was much better.

Just hours earlier, she'd slipped into the beautiful, emerald gown she'd purchased on sale at Belk's department store last week. The main reason she'd bought the gown, other than the sale price, was that the dress had pockets. Pockets solved the problem of not having a date to carry her evening bag.

As she swiped at the tears flowing down her cheeks, she remembered how she had ignored the nagging sensation of foreboding she felt as she finished hemming her dress for tonight's prom.

She had purchased a wrist corsage just this morning at Fiona's Floral Designs. Cheap white carnations dipped in teal, with teal ribbons, three shades lighter than the gown for contrast, streaming from her wrist to her elbow. She'd smiled at her image in the small mirror she'd hung inside her closet door. At that moment, she had promised herself to put all negative thoughts aside. Just for tonight. Tomorrow, she knew, real life would come rushing back at the speed of a hurricane, and her real life was rarely pretty.

Tonight was special. Tonight was her senior prom. Her last year of high school. The beginning of a new, and better, way of life. She had prayed for this daily since she'd been old enough to pray.

She had a bit of savings from her various after-school jobs; the usual babysitting; cashiering Wednesday nights at All Bright Cleaners; waitressing three nights a week at Tony's BBQ Pit. Every Sunday, after the last morning service, she helped Pastor Royer gather the hymnals and any debris the parishioners or their children had left behind. For this she was paid a flat twenty dollars. Many times she'd refused the pastor's offering, but finally she'd relented after he had insisted rather harshly that it would be stupid of her to refuse. This embarrassed her, but she'd learned long ago that pride truly wasn't as tasty as a hot meal. With a great deal of reluctance, she had accepted these acts of charitable kindness whenever they were offered.

She shared a small trailer on the edge of town, within smelling distance of the local tomato-canning factory, with her mother, Lenore, and twin brother, Marcus. Marcus, the golden boy. The boy all the girls wanted to lay claim to. The boy with the golden eyes. When she was younger, Maddy often wondered why their eyes didn't match since they were twins. Once she'd asked her mother about this, and her reply had been a lightning-fast slap to her face. She never asked again. In fact, she rarely saw her mother. Though Lenore shared the beaten-down trailer with her and Marcus on occasion, it was rare for her mother to make an appearance. As long as her man of the moment had a place where she could spend her days in a drunken stupor and her nights with him, and as long as he was willing to provide her with enough money for her daily intake of booze and whatever drug she currently craved, she stayed away.

Her mother's reputation caused Maddy a great deal of humiliation. She'd learned to ignore the wry comments and the suggestive glances from the group of guys Marcus hung with at school. Maddy wanted to shout to the world that she was not like her mother, that she worked very hard to pay the rent on the dumpy tin box she called home. She worked even harder to keep her grades up. Hoping for a scholarship that had yet to materialize at this late date, Maddy still studied in her spare time, which there wasn't much of these days. She was determined to have a better life.

In six weeks, both she and Marcus would graduate. As far as she knew, Marcus's plans were to attend Florida State on a football scholarship. His grades were horrible, but everyone knew that didn't matter as long as you could handle yourself on the football field. Marcus excelled at the sport. He also excelled at being a jerk. Maddy was sure the latter trait wouldn't help him one little bit, if, or rather when, he received the expected scholarship. Some of the not-so-cool guys didn't like him. Brett Lynch, her best friend since seventh grade, said that a lot of the guys made fun of Marcus behind his back. Thought he was all grit minus a brain. Maddy secretly agreed but didn't say so. He was her brother. Her twin, if that counted as extra points. She supposed she owed him at least a touch of familial loyalty, even though he'd just totally and completely ruined her life.

Unable to hold back any longer, she screamed silently in the car, her tears rivering from her eyes in big, angry splashes on the bodice of her prom dress, making the emerald color appear black. Blinking back another round of tears,

Maddy sniffed, and without taking her eyes off the dark dirt road, reached inside her clutch purse on the passenger's seat, feeling around for the wad of tissues she'd stuck inside right before she left the house. She remembered thinking, as she had crammed them in her bag, that perhaps tonight wasn't going to be special, and she might end up crying. She had intended to leave the bag on the seat of the car until she returned after the prom was over. She just knew she was going to cry all the way home. Just knew it.

She blotted her eyes, keeping one hand on the steering wheel. She blew into the tissue she held in her free hand, then rolled down her window and tossed the used tissue out, not caring that she was littering. The warm air hit her like a blast furnace. She hated Florida, hated the heat, the humidity, the crazy wildlife she always seemed to come upon. Just last week, she'd been trapped inside the trailer by a coyote that had refused to leave until she called 911 and the city sent a trapper out in hopes of catching the creature. Already, her neighbor had lost three cats and one small dog. Yes, she thought as she rolled the window up, she couldn't wait to leave this place. Maybe she would move to Alaska, someplace cold. A place where they had four seasons. Not hot, hotter, and hottest. Why her mother had ever brought them to this state remained a mystery to this day.

Maddy would bet her savings it had something to do with a man, possibly her father, but he, too, remained a mystery. Her mother had refused to talk about him the one time she'd been brave enough to bring up the subject.

Her thoughts were all over the place. Anything to avoid thinking about what had just sent her running out of the gymnasium to her beat-up Mustang. She hated Marcus and his perverted gang of thugs right now; more than anything, she wished someone would beat him within an inch of his life so he would never, ever play football again. At the very least, she prayed that someone would knock some sense into him. But right now, this very second, she could not care less if they killed her brother. Truly, she wished they'd beat his brains out. Only, in light of what she'd just gone through, that would be a kindness. Way too kind.

Maddy made the wide turn onto Carroll Road, which was really just a large group of curves surrounded by groves of orange trees, but the road was narrow and unsafe. Blinking back yet another round of angry tears, she slowed down to thirty miles per hour, knowing this road was as dangerous as ever, even more so tonight since it was prom. Lots of booze, weed, and coke had been passed around earlier. Most of her classmates were idiots and wouldn't stop to think about drinking and racing around in their cars after prom. At least Marcus didn't have a car. That was almost a blessing. Almost, because she still hated him. Any emotions for Marcus were wasted as far as she was concerned. Her big, tough football player brother who'd laughed at her, humiliated her as his friends, and possibly he, too, had ruined her for life. He'd set her up for the right price to anyone willing to pay. He was a bully. And a coward. A worthless human piece of flesh.

Her mother should have aborted him, but then she wouldn't be here either, but she could still wish. And now she wished that he would die. Not necessarily by her hand but by someone else's hand. She wouldn't shed a tear, either. She rather thought she'd probably dance a jig on top of his grave.

Hands clenched, knuckles white and tight as they gripped the steering wheel, Maddy mentally replayed what she could recall of the nightmare she'd just escaped. She should do something, but she wasn't sure what that something was. She needed to pay attention to her driving.

She needed to think.

Crime. Her brother and his group of friends had just committed a terrible crime against her. They would *not* get away with this. She went through the events of the evening again. From beginning to end, mentally naming her suspects. Ricky Rourke, the leader. Dennis Wilderman, Ricky's cousin and best friend, who did whatever Ricky asked of him. Kevin Marsden, recently voted most likely to succeed, a superior student and football player. Troy Bowers, another top football player, but as dumb as Marcus, maybe even more so. And, of course, there was Marcus. Her brother. Her *twin.*

When, how, and most of all *why* had they

planned this? To humiliate her? Nothing else to do on prom night? The money? None of it made sense. There was no excuse for the criminal acts they had committed against her.

Her mind returned to the beginning of prom. The evening had started out better than she'd anticipated.

Entering the gymnasium alone on prom night hadn't been nearly as much of a nightmare as she'd imagined. In fact, if anything, several of the popular kids greeted her. Karen Clark, captain of the cheerleading squad, and Karen's best friend and cocaptain, Elizabeth Mirro, with their boyfriends, Randall Harris and Andrew "Big Andy" Wiley, who stood six-foot-seven, had smiled at her as she stepped inside the glittery gymnasium. They were the cool group that everyone wanted to be a part of. She returned their wave, a slight smile on her face.

Tiny white lights strung from the ceiling created a glow above the polished floor. Card tables with gold paper tablecloths were placed in a U shape around the gymnasium floor. In the center of each table was a small vase with a single gardenia that Maddy knew had been donated by Karen Clark's grandmother, whose gardening skills were known throughout the county.

Their theme song, "Can You Feel the Love Tonight" by Elton John, played in the background. It was one of her favorite songs. When she learned this was to be the theme song for senior prom, she took it as a sign of good things to come.

Love conquers all.

She couldn't have been more wrong.

After returning hellos to Karen and Elizabeth and their current loves, she saw Brett and his girlfriend, Carla, serving themselves from a punch bowl that was most likely spiked with rum. She'd heard talk of this just yesterday. Making her way across the gym, she saw that Brett was watching her. She gave him a quick wave, then hurried over to the table with the punch.

He held out a paper cup full of cherry-red punch. As she reached for the cup, she stuffed her small clutch, which she had decided to bring with her at the last second, into her pocket. She smiled. *Perfect,* she thought.

"Before you ask, yes, it's spiked. Vodka. It's gross, but it was all they could come up with," Brett explained. Maddy and Brett had been friends since seventh grade. He'd been a bit stumped with a math assignment. Mrs. Crawford, their math teacher, had suggested Maddy tutor him, and they'd been best friends since. Brett, too, had a screwed-up family, so he never questioned why Maddy and Marcus lived virtually on their own with no supervision or anyone to answer to.

Maddy accepted the paper cup of punch, took a sip, then grimaced at the bitter taste. She observed the group hitting the dance floor for the first fast song of the night. Cyndi Lauper's "Girls Just Want to Have Fun" blared from the speakers onstage.

The senior class had wanted to hire a band, but their fund-raising projects hadn't produced enough cash, so they'd settled for a local disc jockey to play popular songs throughout the evening. She thought this was better because the music sounded as it should, not some half-baked band trying its best to mimic the latest tunes.

Maddy watched several of her classmates, all decked out in their best finery, as they swirled and swayed to the music blaring from the giant speakers onstage.

"You want to dance?" Brett asked.

She laughed, tossing her long blond hair over her shoulder. "No, I do not. You and Carla should, though."

Maddy knew Brett was trying to make her feel comfortable, but at this point, she was okay. She was actually enjoying watching the couples dance. "Go on," she urged Brett. "This is your last prom."

Carla, petite, with gorgeous wavy black hair and eyes to match, looped her arm through Brett's. "Maddy's right. We're at the end of the road here, and I don't want to miss a single mile of it. Come on."

Carla led Brett to the center of the gymnasium. The girly sound of Cyndi Lauper was replaced with the slow, soft music of Luther Vandross's "Always and Forever." The couples danced as close to each other as they could without being admonished. Too close, and the chaperones were instructed to remove the couple from the dance floor. Maddy watched with a touch of sadness. Here she was at her senior prom and about to turn eighteen and graduate in a few weeks, and she'd never had a real date. So much of her free time was spent studying and working. And trying to survive. A normal social life was something she'd often dreamed about, but her lifestyle forced her to be a realist. It was not going to happen for her. Marcus, yes. His only interests were football and girls, in that order. He'd never bothered to look for a part-time job because most of his free time was spent on the football field or with whoever happened to be his girl of the week. Where he got all the money he threw around—and she'd seen him do this more than once—remained a mystery to her. It was possible their mother supplied him with funds. She'd made it very clear from as far back as she could remember that Marcus truly was her golden boy. Eyes and all.

Maddy felt a tap on her shoulder. She turned to see who was behind her and felt her heart miss a beat when she saw Ricky Rourke. He was the most popular guy in school, next to Marcus. He was beyond good-looking, with blond hair and blue eyes, and he knew it, and for Maddy, that ruined all the good things she knew about him. He made good grades, was respectful to the teachers, didn't brag too much when his father had given him a brand-new bright-yellow Camaro for his sixteenth birthday. But all in all, he was an ass, just like Marcus. Tonight, he wore a white tuxedo, with a pale blue shirt and cummerbund that matched his eyes.

"You look hot tonight, Maddy. Wanna dance with me?"

She felt his warm breath on her neck. Suddenly she felt helpless as chills traveled down her spine. She cleared her throat, turning around so that she could see his face. "Did Marcus put you up to this?" she asked, not caring. She'd known Ricky forever and didn't really like or dislike him. However, his asking her to dance set alarm bells ringing. He rarely spoke to her. Why would he bother asking her to dance?

The invitation reeked of Marcus's work. The fine hairs on the back of her neck moved. A warning. She should pay attention to. She really should.

Ricky gave a short laugh. "No, Marcus has nothing to do with it. You look unbelievably pretty tonight, that's all. I just thought you might want to dance. I like the curls in your hair."

Maddy drew in a breath, unsure, because she was not used to compliments from one of the hottest guys in school. Maybe Ricky truly was being sincere. Marcus didn't rule everyone. The hairs on the back of her neck were still moving, however. She ignored them. What the heck, she thought, maybe he was being truthful; she didn't know him to be a liar. Because it was prom night, and she doubted she would have another opportunity to dance, she decided to throw caution to the wind.

"I," she stammered over her next words, "would like to dance." Then she added, "Sure," hoping she didn't come off as desperate, "what the hell?" As though she used this kind of language regularly. She didn't. She instantly regretted what she'd said. "I'm sorry, that just slipped out. What I meant was, yes, Ricky, I would love to dance with you."

Surprise registered on Ricky's handsome face. His dark eyes glinted with a trace of humor, and his perfect smile revealed that the many years of orthodontics his parents had paid for were worth the cost. He reached for her hand. "This is going to be the best night of your life. I promise."

A bit hesitant, Maddy took Ricky's hand, then suddenly stopped as a cloud of darkness swept over her, a sense of foreboding, the feeling coming on so suddenly it was disturbing. "I . . . I changed my mind, Ricky. I don't think dancing with you is such a good idea after all." She tried to pull her hand away, but his grip was stronger. He squeezed her hand a bit too hard, pulling her toward him.

"Let go of me! I said I don't want to dance!" Maddy's raised voice could be heard over the slow love song oozing from the speakers. She felt several couples turn to stare at her. She took a deep breath. Not wanting to cause a scene, she quickly relented.

"Never mind. One dance." She would dance with him, then she was out of here. She didn't need a remake of that scene in Stephen King's novel *Carrie*. Ricky actually acted as though she'd hurt his feelings. "Hey, I'm not that bad, am I?" He grinned, and Maddy gave him a halfhearted smile. Jerk.

"Well?" he persisted as he guided her toward the exit of the gymnasium.

Maddy didn't answer. "Where are we going?" she asked as he led her to the exit door.

"I'm just gonna have a smoke first. That okay with you?" His voice suddenly sounded curt, almost as if he were daring her.

"Sure." She was lying, and she knew that he knew it. She didn't care.

Once outside, he fumbled inside his jacket pocket and whipped out a package of Kools. He stuck one between his lips, then swiped a match on the cement wall. He held the flame to the cigarette, drawing deeply, all the while his eyes never leaving her. She averted her eyes and wished she'd stayed inside. He was a jerk, just like Marcus.

Outside the gym, the night air was thick with humidity, leaving her skin clammy and damp. The curls in her stick-straight hair that had taken forever to style were now drooping, despite all the hair spray she'd used.

She was uncomfortable while she waited for Ricky to finish his cigarette and felt weird standing next to him, so she took a few steps away, then turned her back to him, pretending to gaze at something that wasn't there.

"Stay here," Ricky said.

For the second time that evening, Maddy felt a slight prickle of fear, a bit of apprehension. Not wanting Ricky to pick up on her sudden anxiousness, she turned to face him. "Who says I'm going anywhere?" She tried to sound tough, and unafraid, but she knew she came off as a wimp and slightly on edge.

Ricky dropped his cigarette on the cement, then crushed it out with his shiny, black-leather dress shoe. "You promised you'd dance, remember?"

This was getting beyond creepy. Unsure whether she should run back inside to the safety of the gymnasium or show Ricky Rourke that he didn't intimidate her in the least, she decided on the latter, figuring she had nothing to lose. One dance, then she would go home.

She nodded and started walking toward the door when she felt strong hands grab her from behind. "What the heck . . ."

The words were barely out of her mouth before a second pair of hands reached for her, cramming her mouth full of what felt like T-shirt material that reeked with dried perspiration. She gagged, then yanked her arms as she tried to free herself, trying to shove the nasty cloth from her mouth with the force of her tongue. Suddenly, another pair of strong hands squeezed her wrists even tighter, yanking them so high they almost reached the top of her shoulder blades. Hot shards of pain rippled in her arms and neck.

She heard the sound of tape ripping, the deep, gushing sound of her heart beating wildly in her ears. Quickly and efficiently, her wrists were bound securely behind her back. She tried to scream, but her effort was useless, snuffed out by the gag they'd jammed in her mouth.

Shaking uncontrollably, she did her best to focus on the hushed words coming from the guys as they dragged her all the way to the darkened football field, stopping when they reached the bleachers, pulling her under them for protection just in case there were any prying eyes, then dropping her like a sack of potatoes. Her silver sandals hung loosely around her ankles, her heels raw and bleeding from being dragged along the gravel path leading from the gymnasium to the football field, which was at least two hundred yards behind the school.

Through blurred vision, she saw slats of lights coming through the bleachers, and then she heard another spurt of laughter coming from her attackers.

"Ain't no one gonna come lookin' for ya, Maddy," one of the guys said in a hushed, phony voice.

Focus. She had to concentrate if she wanted to get away from these freaks. This was her only hope of seeing that they didn't get away with whatever they were planning. If she could identify the harshly whispered words of her attackers, she might be able to put names to the voices. For sure, Ricky Rourke could be named. He'd duped her into thinking he wanted to dance with her. And she'd been a complete and total fool, playing right into his dirty hands.

That bastard, she thought. Just wait. These pieces of scum would regret the day they ever whispered her name.

One of the boys—she couldn't make out his features, as it was dark under the bleachers, and what bit of light shone through wasn't enough for her to identify him—gave her breast a hard pinch. Someone grabbed her hands, which remained bound behind her, and pulled her away from the bleachers to a spot where the lighting was better.

"What the hell are you doing?" one of the guys whispered harshly.

He gave a bitter laugh. "I wanna look at her, you stupid ass! What do you think I'm doing? Isn't this why we snatched her? Get with the program, bud."

Maddy tried her very best to identify the voices but couldn't because the boys were all whispering, trying to disguise their voices. Straining to make out their features, she also realized that they were covering their faces with some kind of cloth, the way the bandits did in the old westerns she and her friend Cassie used to watch. Except for the eyes. They needed to see. Bastards. Tears clogged her throat. Fearful that she would choke, she focused her attention on the sounds, hoping she might hear her brother, Marcus. None of them even remotely sounded like her brother. Was it possible that he wasn't behind this, after all?

Before she could answer her own question, she felt the front of her gown being pulled down to her waist, exposing her breasts. More tears spilled, and her nose stopped up, making it even more difficult to breathe. She tried to speak through the nasty piece of material stuffed in her mouth, but she only managed to produce garbled noises.

This made them laugh at her.

"The bitch sounds like a retard."

"We need to get back to the gym before we're missed."

"Yeah, we know. We better get our money's worth after what we paid Marcus."

Maddy stiffened in shock. She seethed with an anger unlike any she'd ever known. And humiliation. So this was how Marcus kept his cash flowing. Fire burned deep in her gut.

One of the boys grabbed her breast, squeezing so hard that it brought tears to her eyes. "Yep, Marcus was right. They're real."

More laughter, then another set of hands took turns touching her breasts, pinching her. Then what she feared most happened next. Someone pulled her long dress up around her waist. Knowing what was about to happen, Maddy did her best to try to scream through the gag in her mouth, but she only sounded more garbled than before.

"Hey," someone shouted, "Marcus said all we could do was look at her boobs. Man, this is not right. Come on, back off *now!*"

Maddy heard the words and prayed that they would be struck down by some unknown force, some superhero or whatnot, that silently protected girls like her. She wished she believed in a higher power, anything to get her through what she knew would define her for the rest of her life.

"Crap!" said one of the boys, "She wears granny panties, and they aren't even silk! What a downer! Man, from the way Marcus talked, I thought she'd be wearing a pair of those sexy crotchless things from Victoria's Secret. I'm going to make Marcus give me my frigging money back."

Seething with a mounting rage so intense she felt as though her head were about to explode, she tried to swallow another round of sobs as they pushed their way up her throat. Wishing she'd told Ricky no when he asked her to dance was useless at this point, she thought, as a slimy hand reached for the waistband of her white-cotton panties.

A round of laughter, from at least four boys, Maddy guessed. She heard Ricky Rourke sneer, a sound she knew from science class with Mr. Bledsoe. Every time Ricky was asked a question, he'd give that particularly unattractive sound, a sort of gush of breath followed by a low growl. The son of a bitch.

As she lay on the dew-soaked grass at the edge of the football field, partially beneath the bleachers, her arms twisted behind her at an unnatural angle, the backs of her feet raw and burning while the group of boys took turns looking at her most private area and touching her, Maddy prayed that one of the chaperones had seen her step outside with Ricky and, hopefully, would come outside to look for her. Squeezing her eyes tightly shut and allowing another round of tears to trickle down her dirt-encrusted face, Maddy reluctantly accepted the fact that no one was going to come looking for her.

She'd made it a point her entire life to do her best to go unnoticed, to remain as anonymous as one could in such a small town, despite the circumstances of her family life and living conditions, which the entire town of Blossom City—population 3,742, according to the sign at the city limits—was quite aware of. She'd heard the whispers, and jeers, observed the faces of the townspeople when they crossed paths. You would've thought she'd committed a crime by name alone, or that she had an infectious disease. And for this, she hated her mother beyond belief. If she knew who had fathered her, she was sure she would hate him, too.

A sweaty hand grabbed the waistband of her panties and yanked, the sound of ripping cotton bumping up her level of fear so high, she thought she might pass out. Again, she tried to scream, to yell, anything to prevent what she knew was about to happen, but all she did was gag on the built-up saliva from her inability to properly swallow.

Closing her eyes as tightly as she could, she forced her mind to another place, a safe place, where girls like her were wanted and needed. And loved and cared for. But there was not a single happy recollection she could call up to help her. She tried to remember a pleasant experience from her childhood, a trip maybe, but couldn't. She tried to recall a time when her life was happy and carefree, when she lived without fear. She couldn't.

Next she felt a hot, searing pain in her most private area, then pounding against her thin body. Over and over. Again and again. She silently prayed for a quick death, an end to the physical and emotional trauma she was suffering before she thankfully blacked out.

Later, she didn't know how much time had passed, only that it was still dark outside, and she sensed she was alone, though the smell of sweat and fear still clung to her in the humid night air. She discovered that her arms had been freed of the heavy-duty duct tape. Someone had made a halfhearted attempt to pull the bodice of her dress over her breasts and cover her from the waist down with the torn remnants of the prom dress she'd carefully chosen for this night, which should have been special, memorable. Memorable, yes, but not in the way she'd hoped for. Tears fell freely from her eyes, and she tasted the saltiness as they fell to her mouth. She had awakened from a real nightmare. She would never forget this night as long as she lived.

Carefully, she moved her hand down to her genital area and realized that her panties had been removed. With a hesitant hand, she touched herself, felt dried blood and something else she was not even going to put a name to. Slowly, she pushed upright into a sitting position. She was still under the bleachers, but the few lights that had given her attackers a better view were no longer shining on the football field. Surrounded by total darkness and not knowing if her attackers were still lurking nearby, she stood up, her legs weak and shaking. An unfamiliar ache throbbed between her legs, and she cringed knowing why.

Her silver sandals were long gone, and she didn't care. Her heels were bloody and raw from where they'd dragged her down the rocky path, but she was still able to walk. It was then she remembered her clutch purse. She reached inside the deep pocket of her ruined dress and removed the clutch. With shaking hands, she opened it, saw that all the cash she'd brought was still there, along with the dolphin key ring that held two keys. One to the trailer, and the other to the Mustang.

"Thank God," she whispered, surprising herself. Maybe some of Pastor Royer's sermons had seeped into the deep recesses of her mind. She was thankful, whether it was to God or someone else, it didn't matter. She had to get out of here. She didn't know where her attackers were. For all she knew, they could still be watching her, waiting for another chance to pounce on her like wild animals. Quickly, she ran, stumbling as fast as she could over the rough gravel, not caring that her feet were torn and raw. She gripped the dolphin key ring so tightly in her hand for fear of losing it that she cried out in pain before she realized that the end of the key had punctured the soft fold of skin between her thumb and finger.

As she neared the exit to the gymnasium,

she stopped, held her breath, and listened. Crickets, a frog's croak, and the shrill cry of a whippoorwill could be heard in the grove of trees opposite the gymnasium. A mosquito buzzed above her head. Night sounds all.

The prom must have ended hours ago. The music that had cheered her as she'd entered the gymnasium—so full of hope that, for just one night, she could just be seventeen—could no longer be heard. But she'd had those foreboding feelings, and now she knew they had been a warning. She would never ignore feelings like that again.

Never.

As assured as she could be, given her circumstances, that none of her attackers were still inside the gym, she ran past it, the track, and the teacher's parking lot. Out of breath and trembling, she stopped when she reached the northeast corner of the school building, where only hours ago, she'd fooled herself with hopes of an exciting prom night; she'd even believed she would receive a scholarship to college. She realized now that was just false hope. Scholarships weren't given out during prom week. For some odd reason, she'd had this in her head and dreamily imagined the evening ending with her education secured. What a fool she was. After she caught her breath, she ran the length of the high school, rounding the end of the building where the student parking lot was located. Spying her beat-up Mustang where she'd parked earlier, she sprinted so fast across the blacktop parking lot that she almost lost her footing. Slowing down just long enough to catch her balance, she had the key ready to unlock the door.

Her hands shook like dried leaves on an autumn tree preparing for winter, but she managed to unlock the door and crawl inside the safety of her car. She tossed her clutch purse on the passenger seat as she'd done before, then locked the door. With shaking hands, she slid the worn key into the ignition, and the old Mustang roared to life. She shifted into DRIVE, and the tires squealed as she stomped on the gas, turning onto the main road.

Her tears had completely soaked the bodice of her prom dress now, but she didn't care. She planned on burning the dress as soon as she got home.

Home!

Did she really think she could go back home after what had happened tonight? No, she had to go away. She could never go back to that hotbed of hell. *Never!*

She was glad she'd crammed all of her cash, around six hundred dollars, into her purse as a precaution because both Marcus and her mother, when that upstanding woman bothered to be around, were known to rummage through her room when they were low on cash. Thankfully, she'd had the forethought to bring it with her tonight and nobody had touched it. Again, she hadn't listened to her other warnings, but at least she'd had the good sense to bring her hard-earned cash with her.

As she came to the last winding curve on Carroll Road, she gave a sigh of relief when the road straightened, both lanes expanding to four at this newly constructed part of the highway. She saw this as a sign that she should get away from the nightmare she'd just lived through and stomped down on the Mustang's accelerator. She watched as the speedometer climbed from forty to fifty, then sixty, steadily climbing to seventy-five, the speed freeing her from the bonds of a life she no longer wanted to be a part of. It was almost like the car had a mind of its own and was doing its best to take her as far away from that miserable life as she could get, as quickly as possible. She gripped the wheel with one hand, then decided that at this rate of speed, she'd better fasten the seat belt. She took another glance at the speedometer and saw the bright-orange needle struggling to reach eighty-five. She'd never driven this fast in her life, but tonight it was warranted.

She rolled down the window, the night air drying what was left of the tears on her cheeks. She used the back of her hand to swipe at her nose, which felt bruised and sore. Maybe she'd been hit by those perverted scumbags when she'd blacked out? She didn't know, and quite possibly, she'd never know exactly what those sick-ass creeps had done to her. All she cared about now was putting as many miles between her and Blossom City, Florida, as possible, and as fast as she could.

A bit calmer than moments before, Maddy

didn't have time to react when she saw the group of guys ahead, gathered in the middle of the road.

"What the . . . ?" she cried out.

Unable to slow the Mustang down fast enough in order to bypass a party of what appeared to be a group still living it up on prom night, Maddy's heart nearly blew out of her chest when she saw a bright-yellow Camaro parked on the side of the road.

Later, she would try to recall what happened, and she would have several theories, but what she was one hundred percent sure of: she had run over at least three of the guys who'd attacked her, and she didn't stop to check to see if they were dead or alive.

Chapter One

Molly stood in her spotless, newly remodeled designer kitchen and checked her shopping list one last time before driving across town to Gloria's, her favorite market, which specialized in organic produce, freshly caught seafood, and everything in between. She had ten people coming over tonight for yet another one of Tanner's dinner parties.

This morning, as he was leaving for the dental clinic, he'd said one word to her: "perfection." He'd winked to soften his sharp command.

It was her warning that the outcome of this dinner party would determine their future. Everything must be perfect. Tanner was a true perfectionist. *A bit harsh*, she thought as she reached for the keys to her silver Mercedes, Tanner's gift to her on their fifteenth wedding anniversary. Now, nearing their twentieth, she continued to drive the same car. It had seemed like only yesterday that she'd gifted him with a photograph of the three children in an exquisite silver frame, an acknowledgment of the best part of their life together. The children. Holden and Graham, twins Tanner had from his first marriage, boys she'd raised since they were toddlers. Their mother, Elaine, had died in a tragic accident just months after they were born. To Molly, they were different than Kristen, her biological daughter, who was five years younger than her big brothers.

She remembered Tanner the day she'd given him the picture, all those years ago. He had been preoccupied with something and had only glanced at the framed photo, tossing it aside as though it were merely a flyer advertising a window-washing service or someone who was hoping to cut their grass. If he'd only known how hard it'd been to schedule the photographer and get all three kids in the same place for the scheduled appointment, maybe he would have actually appreciated her thoughtful gift.

She hadn't wanted or needed a new car then, didn't really like it all that much now. Her eight-year-old Range Rover had suited her just fine. She'd carted all kinds of sporting equipment when the boys played hockey, followed by football, stinky pads and all. Kristen had insisted on taking French horn lessons that she'd never quite got the hang of, but having such a large instrument was cool at the time, and she could fit it in the back of the

Range Rover without a problem. Yes, she thought as she pulled out of the garage in her sleek and shiny car, her old Range Rover held many good memories, as did the other car, the one she'd had restored, which was now tucked safely away in a place where it belonged.

She glanced in the rearview mirror as she backed out of the driveway, aware that she looked older than her actual age. She put her foot on the brake and brought the car to a sudden stop, pulled the visor down, and looked into the vanity mirror. Her blond hair was more gray than blond, and her green eyes were lusterless. Her eyelids had begun to sag, and her once-full mouth drooped in a permanent frown. She traced the web of wrinkles around her eyes, then quickly raised the visor.

Shifting into PARK, she wondered when she'd begun to look so old. She had turned thirty-eight last month, had been dreading the big four-oh, but at thirty-eight she already looked much older than the ghastly forty. She was aging faster than Tanner, who at forty-eight looked much younger. Why hadn't Tanner mentioned this to her? He always critiqued her. What she wore, too much makeup, not enough makeup, too tan, too pale, too fat, too thin, and on and on it went. At least she had good teeth, she thought as she pulled onto Riverbend Road, the most exclusive neighborhood in Goldenhills. She ran her tongue across her teeth. They were as smooth as the mother-of-pearl necklace Tanner had given her on her thirtieth birthday. Of course, her perfect teeth were courtesy of Tanner's expertise; he was one of the top cosmetic dentists in the state.

Which brought her back to the reason for tonight's dinner party. Tanner owned three dental clinics, one here in Goldenhills and two in Ocean Orr, and wanted to open a fourth in Boston, near the Harvard School of Dental Medicine, his alma mater. Tonight's guests were potential investors.

Molly knew that tonight was very important to her husband. She truly appreciated his hard work and dedication, but there were times when she thought he took his business drive to the extreme. Tonight's dinner, for example. He didn't need these investors any more than she needed a snake for a pet, yet for Tanner, having a clinic that actually drew in investors was just another way to feed his already huge ego, though she would never say anything like that to him. Tanner strove to be a good husband and father most of the time, as well as a dedicated medical professional. A tiny thought crept into her head, a truth she rarely acknowledged: in point of fact, he was neither a good husband nor a good father. Right now, she chose not to consider those truths.

Forgiveness. She must remember to forgive thy neighbor.

Isn't that what Father Richard Czerwinski, or Father Wink, as he preferred to be addressed, had shared with her just last week when she'd stopped by the church to light a candle? Religion was a very important part of her life. There was a time when she hadn't believed in any formal religion or a higher power, and she felt guilty about that to this very day. But she reminded herself that she'd never really had an opportunity to seriously explore any religion. Her own day-to-day survival had been her top priority. Of course, when Tanner and his twin boys came into her life, all of that had changed. She rarely thought of her life before Tanner and the kids, and when she did, it angered her. For days afterward, she would be in the most dreadful mood.

Chapter Two

Maddy, After the Prom

Maddy drove as fast as she could, keeping an eye on the odometer. Shaken and unsure if she was making the right decision, she told herself that she really didn't have much of a choice. But hanging around Blossom City was not possible. She drove through the night and pulled into a rest area when she crossed over the Georgia border.

Maddy got out of the car and walked around it, looking for any damage that might have resulted from the accident. The car was so old and banged up that it was difficult to tell if any of the dents and scrapes were new. She got back into the car and sat for a few minutes thinking about what her next move should be. Her eyes were swollen from crying and felt gritty and dry. She longed for a cool shower but had to put first things first. She needed to find a place to stay and get some rest. More importantly, she needed to rid herself of the disgusting teal dress that only a day ago she had worn with so much promise. As soon as she could, she planned to burn the dress, and hopefully that simple act would erase the traumatic events of the previous night. She realized that she was being naïve in the extreme, but she didn't care.

She would never forget last night as long as she lived.

As she pulled back onto I-95, the traffic was light at this early-morning hour. She wished the radio worked now. She was so tired that maybe a loud rock song would keep her awake. She drove several miles until she saw an exit for Brunswick. She used her signal as she switched lanes, then followed the exit ramp to a traffic light. She waited for the light to turn green. Unsure if she should turn left or right, she took a right. Just the word "right" was enough. Slowly, the old Mustang crawled along Main Street.

"Main Street, how original," she said out loud. Her words were hoarse, broken, unrecognizable, as if they came from someone else. From this moment forward she would do her best to act as if she were someone else. Start over, put the past behind her. Forget last night. Forget Marcus. Forget her mother. Forget her life in Blossom City.

"Right," she said aloud.

Above the stretch of tall pines, the sun rose, bathing the early-morning sky in shades of pinks, purples, and various hues of deep blue. Off in the distance, clouds darkened in rich shades of slate and silver.

Rain, she thought as she slowly drove down Main Street. She came to a halt at a four-way traffic sign but didn't come to a complete stop. There were no other cars on the road this early in the morning, so she saw no reason to. Ahead, a bright-green neon sign, flashing MOTEL VACANCY, grabbed her attention. Increasing her speed, though not exceeding the posted limit of forty-five, she pulled into the motel's parking lot. Shutting the engine down, she leaned her head back against the seat, the events of last night still spinning crazily in her mind. Even though she'd just given herself a new beginning, she realized it wasn't going to be quite as simple as she thought.

Did her mother know what had happened last night? Had Marcus told some off-the-wall story, one that her mother would believe just because her golden boy told it to her? Usually, she believed every lie that rolled off his tongue. Knowing it would only cause her pain, but doing it anyway, Maddy flashed back to that second when she raced away from the school, coming upon the group of guys standing in the center of the road, the sudden impact as their bodies slammed against the grill, then the thwack as the Mustang's tires crushed flesh and bone. In a blind daze, she'd been too shocked at the time to realize the true significance of what remained on the road behind her, but she'd increased her speed in spite of

this. Now, she fully realized, it was very probable that she'd committed a crime after she'd
been the victim of a nightmarish crime herself.
If she had decided to turn back, would she
have spent the rest of her life behind bars for
vehicular homicide, or, if no one was killed,
just leaving the scene of an accident? Maybe
whoever she hit would tell the police they saw
her car? She was the only one in Blossom City
who drove a battered red 1964 Mustang. At
least to her knowledge she was the only one.

"No!"

She would not allow this one mistake to tor-
ture her for the rest of her life. With that
thought in mind, she grabbed her purse, which
was still lying on the passenger seat, tucked it
in her dress pocket, again, and realized once
more that she desperately needed a change of
clothes. She got out of the car, minus her silver
heels. Holding the skirt of the long dress with
one hand, raking the other through her stiff
hair, and not caring what anyone thought, she
entered the motel lobby.

A woman who appeared to be in her late six-
ties, judging by her graying hair and stooped
back, looked up when she entered. "Can I help
you?" she asked in a kindly voice.

For a moment, Maddy didn't know what to
say. She'd never stayed in a motel. Other than
what she'd seen on television, which involved
signing a guest book and a taciturn desk clerk
sliding a single key across the counter, she wasn't
sure of the protocol. Licking her lips and tast-
ing a bit of dried blood, she regretted not

checking her appearance before coming inside.

"May I help you?" the old woman asked again, showing just a hint of impatience.

Nodding, Maddy reached into her pocket for her clutch purse and pulled out her wad of cash. In a soft voice, she said, "I, uh . . . need a room." She chewed her bottom lip again.

The woman nodded, then asked. "Single or double?"

Swallowing, she spoke a bit louder this time, "It's just me, so a single."

"And how long will you be staying with us? There is a discount if you stay at least three days."

Taking a deep breath, she decided she'd stay. This would give her time to plan, time to make a decision about what to do. "Yes, I'll, uh . . . I'll stay three days."

"Good choice. We offer free cable TV, and there's coffee available from six to ten every morning." She motioned to the corner.

Maddy glanced over her shoulder, where she saw a small table with a Mr. Coffee machine, paper cups, and a container of powdered cream, plus a basket filled with little packets of sugar.

"Thanks," she replied. She didn't drink coffee, but maybe she'd start.

"If you will just fill this out." The woman slid a form, along with a pen, across the counter, just like Maddy had seen on TV.

Turning her back to return to her former task, the old woman flipped through a stack of papers. "Oh, and I'll need to see your driver's license, too," she added nonchalantly.

Maddy quickly scanned the form. With an empty feeling in the pit of her stomach, she realized she'd have to lie if she wanted to spend the next three nights there. If she let the old woman look at her license, it would open a whole new can of worms. She made a snap decision. If she were going to lie, she might as well make it a whopper. She cleared her throat, dying for a drink, but that would come later, after she'd settled in, and only if the woman believed her and rented her a room. Making a big show of searching through her clutch purse, Maddy removed a tube of cherry-flavored lip gloss, her house key, which she knew she'd never use again, and the stub from her prom ticket. "I think I might have left it," she answered quickly, "at home."

The old woman stopped her task, turning around. "Where is home?"

Before she had a chance to change her mind, she spurted out, "Naples, Florida. I'm here to visit a friend."

When the woman just stared at her, she added, "We're . . . uh, spending two weeks together before we start college."

"Not that it's any of my business, but why aren't you staying with your friend?"

Good question, Maddy thought. "I confused the dates, she's staying with her grandparents and, uh . . . I didn't realize it until last night when I"—was brutally attacked and raped, she wanted to shout—"left in such a hurry."

"Is that why you're wearing that?" She pointed at Maddy's prom dress. "You didn't have time to change?"

God, why was this woman making this so frigging complicated? She just wanted a room. It wasn't like she was applying for a job. A dozen lies whirled in her brain. Before she thought too long, she said. "Uh, yeah. Well, last night after the prom, I had a fight with my boyfriend. I was packed for the trip"—Maddy pointed to her car in the parking lot—"but I was just so upset, I didn't bother to go home and change." Thank God the woman couldn't see her bare and bloodied feet.

"Your parents are fine with this, I take it?" the clerk asked.

"Uh, yes. They're out of . . . the country. They took a cruise. To the Bahamas. For their twenty-fifth wedding anniversary, and well, I just left, and here I am," Maddy explained sheepishly.

"Well, go on, just fill out that form. You look like you could use a good night's sleep, though I wouldn't sleep all day if I were you. You'll be awake all night."

Maddy's heart pounded. She couldn't wait to escape this old woman's scrutiny. "Yes," she said, then proceeded to fill out the form before the woman had a change of heart. She wrote as fast as she could, and none too plainly. She made up an address, 2806 Palmetto Way. Naples was a ritzy city, so she figured that if she'd made up something like 123 Elm Street, it would be a dead giveaway. She decided it was best if she didn't use her real name either. If the police in Blossom City were looking for her, well, she wasn't sure how lying about her name would matter, given the fact that her Mustang was easily identified as belonging to her. She'd lied about everything else, so why not about her name? She put Molly where the form asked for her first name. She didn't dare add Ringwald, her favorite actress from the cult favorite movie *Sixteen Candles*, so she put Hall as her last name. Michael Anthony Hall, the geeky actor from *Sixteen Candles*. She liked her new name. Molly Hall. *It sounded quite nice,* she thought, as she slid the registration form across the counter for the woman to view.

A chain with a pair of glasses hung around the woman's neck. The old woman put them on before reading the form.

Maddy leaned forward, trying to see if she'd added something she shouldn't.

"Okay, Molly. I'll put you in 108. It's at the end of the building, and it's our last room."

Finally, she thought as she offered up what she hoped was a thankful smile. "I appreciate this, Mrs.—" Under her current circumstances, she'd completely forgotten her manners and hadn't asked for her name.

"Mrs. Wilkins. My family has owned the place for close to fifty years."

"Mrs. Wilkins, uh, thanks." She turned around, anxious to get out of the office, when Mrs. Wilkins called out to her.

"Aren't you forgetting something, young lady?" She'd put extra emphasis on her last two words.

Maddy, Molly, turned around. "I don't think so," she said because she truly didn't.

"The fee for the room," Mrs. Wilkins stated.

Crap! How could she be so stupid? "Oh." She gave a false laugh, like something Scarlett O'Hara would have done in *Gone with the Wind.* "I'm sorry. How much?" She'd almost walked out and left her cash on the desk. She grabbed her money, stupefied that she'd forgotten it.

"Thirty dollars per night, which comes to ninety dollars, plus tax, but since you're spending the three nights, it's a flat seventy-five dollars."

Seventy-five dollars! Maddy almost choked. Quickly, before Mrs. Wilkins noticed her shock, she took three twenties, a ten, and five one-dollar bills from her wad. "Here," she said, holding the money out in a fanlike position so the old woman could see she wasn't trying to cheat her.

Mrs. Wilkins took the money, then handed her an old blue key ring, the numbers so faded that they were barely discernible.

"108," she called out as Maddy/Molly turned to leave.

She nodded, waving as she hurried back to her car. Had she known the cost of a motel, she would've slept in her car, but she needed a shower, and a night to rest in a real bed. Maybe she should've opted for just one night. Too late now. If she asked Mrs. Wilkins for her money back, explaining she'd changed her mind and only wanted to stay one night, it would draw even more attention to herself. She started her car, driving slowly until she found the parking space for Room 108. She glanced around before getting out of the car, fearful that Ricky, Marcus, or whoever else had been in the group she had plowed into were just waiting to grab her. And God forbid that the police, alerted to what she had done, were watching her, intending to arrest her and return her to Florida.

She wondered if she'd hit Marcus last night. Wondered if he had been one of the guys standing in the middle of the road. Telling herself she was being overly paranoid, she got out of the car, locked the door, then took the key, preparing to insert it into the lock. The key was worn and thin, and the brass doorknob looked like something out of the fifties, but the key slid smoothly into the lock, and the knob turned effortlessly.

Closing and locking the door behind her, Maddy walked across the room and turned on the TV in search of any news about the accident. Finding none, she perused the room that had cost her a large chunk of her savings. A full-size bed, bigger than any she'd ever slept in, was in the center of the room. The bed was neatly made with a brown chenille bedspread and two pillows tucked in neatly. Maddy walked the few feet to the inviting bed, where she traced the spread and touched the pillows. They were soft. Curious, she pulled the spread down, exposing clean white sheets that appeared to have been ironed. She lifted the sheet to her nose, inhaling sunshine and fresh air. A night table was placed on each side of the bed, near the head. One held a lamp; the other, on the right side, toward the door, had an alarm clock, a small pad of paper, and a pen with the motel's name spelled out in large dark-green letters:

WILKINS MOTEL. FAMILY OWNED AND OPERATED FOR OVER FIFTY YEARS.

Original, for sure. She hadn't even realized the motel had an actual name. She thought it was just MOTEL because that's what the neon sign read.

She sat down on the bed, then lay against the soft pillows. Her eyes were gritty from crying and lack of sleep. Wanting to close her eyes and forget about her life, instead she pushed herself off the bed and peeked inside the bathroom.

Tiny brown-and-beige diamond-shaped tiles covered the floor, their coolness soothing against her raw and bloodied feet. Above the sink, which matched the beige-colored tiles, was a mirror. She pulled on the latch at one corner, and a door opened to reveal a medicine chest. She quickly opened the mirrored door, then closed it, keeping her eyes down. She really did not want to see what she looked like just then. Not noticing the glasses on the little shelf above the sink, she turned on the spigot, filled her hands with cold water, and drank until her thirst was quenched. She quickly turned away, frightened of what she'd see if she dared a glance in the mirror.

The shower-bath combination was much larger than the one in the trailer. On a small shelf above the toilet, white towels and wash-cloths were stacked in a neat pile. They, too, smelled of fresh summer air and sunshine. Beside the sink were two tiny bars of soap. Maddy couldn't wait to soak in the tub, but right now, she needed to purchase some clothes. Before the bed tempted her further, she took her purse and the room key, and hurried out to her car.

Unfamiliar with Brunswick, she returned to Main Street, only this time she drove in the opposite direction, away from the motel. It was almost seven-thirty, and she wasn't sure if she would find a store open this early. Since it was Sunday, she assumed most decent folks were preparing for church. Briefly, she thought of Pastor Royer. Would he miss her this morning or just attribute her absence to a late night at the prom? Either way, it didn't matter because she would never return to Blossom City, no matter how desperate she might be.

She wasn't so foolish as to think that life would be easy. She was a few weeks shy of eighteen, and all she had were the clothes on her back, a beat-up, very old car, and the cash in her purse. That wouldn't last long. She would have to find a job, then a place to live. After that, well, she hadn't thought that far ahead. For now, she simply needed a few items to get her through the next three days. That was as far ahead as she would think.

She continued driving down Main Street for a couple miles. When she spied a giant Walmart sign, she almost cried with relief. There wasn't a Walmart in Blossom City, but Fort Myers had one, and she was familiar with their brands and prices. It wasn't like she had much of a choice. She certainly wasn't going to shop at Macy's. No way did their prices fit with her meager budget.

She pulled into the parking lot, where dozens of vehicles were already parked. She saw people entering the store and gave up a silent thank-you.

Inside, she removed a blue basket from a stack by the door, turning around just in time to see an older couple staring at her, shaking their heads. She wanted to laugh but couldn't. She might stare, too, had she been in their position. She instantly spied the sign to the juniors department, where she picked out a pair of Lee jeans in a size 5 and three T-shirts that were on sale. From there, she went to the lingerie section. With jittery hands, she selected a packet of white-cotton panties. Without warning, memories of the night before attacked her. She threw the pack of underwear on the floor, then kicked it with her tender foot, not caring if anyone observed her fit of rage. Wobbling, she reached for the shelf to steady herself.

"Stop!" she whispered as she scoured the shelves, wishing she could erase the vile image from her mind. Spying a packet of pastel-colored panties with the days of the week on them, she crammed them in her basket. Anxious to get this task over with, she chose two pairs of white socks, then hurried to the shoe department, where she grabbed a pair of plain white tennis shoes in size 7. Before she forgot, she returned to the lingerie section, grabbed a long pink nightgown made of soft cotton and a cream-colored bra that looked like something an old woman would wear.

She had pushed her hair away from her face and was preparing to check out when it dawned on her that she would need toiletries. In the health and beauty department, she located a toothbrush, a tube of toothpaste, a hairbrush, and a bottle of shampoo. As an afterthought, she removed a small bottle of gardenia-scented lotion from the shelf, putting it in her basket. She raced to the front of the store, mentally adding up her purchases, and decided that she would be broke if she didn't get out of there soon. Shopping for herself was still a new experience. Most of her earnings had gone toward food and the rent on the trailer. Clothing was purchased at Goodwill and the Salvation Army. She suddenly realized she would be wearing her first pair of brand-new jeans, as all the outerwear that she'd owned had been second-hand.

At the register, she felt the stares of other customers, heard their angry whispers, but didn't care. She didn't know these people and didn't plan on sticking around Brunswick long enough to make friends. The cashier, a short, chubby girl around her own age, said, "That'll be thirty-seven dollars and ninety-three cents."

Maddy took two twenties from her pocket and gave them to the cashier. She held out her hand, waiting for her change. The second her purchases were bagged and her change placed in her hand, she almost ran out of the store. She needed to get back to the motel, needed to remove all traces of what had happened the night before, even if it was just physically. The psychological damage would remain, forever etched deeply inside that part of her brain where memories were stored.

Chapter Three

Gloria's Organic Market had everything a lover of gourmet foods could dream of. It was Molly's favorite place to shop when she had a special dinner party planned. Located in downtown Goldenhills, in the historic district between the public library and Dr. Laird's family practice, Gloria's was always packed with shoppers, no matter the time of day. Crates of fresh fruits, vegetables, and herbs lined the sidewalk in front of the store. Huge tubs of rosemary flanked the entrance. Molly inhaled the piney, minty scent as she entered the market.

One could find fresh, grass-fed beef, free-range eggs and chickens, and a variety of homemade preserves supplied by local farmers. Spice rubs, salsas, and chutneys, along with an array of homemade breads, muffins, and crackers, crowded the shelves. Gloria's always had the best bay scallops and cherrystone and little-neck clams in the Boston area. Molly took in the smell of freshly made pesto, which brought a smile to her face; Gloria's was indeed a smorgasbord for the senses. She reached for a bright-yellow basket from a stack piled neatly at the entrance. Gloria must've stripped her basil plants out back in order to make the pesto. The last time Molly was here, the aromatic plants had little spikes of white flowers, indicating they were ready to pick. She spied Gloria at the back of the store behind the large wooden counter. "The pesto smells divine. I'll have half a pint," said Molly.

"You want pasta, too? Chelsea made some fresh this morning."

"You know I do," she said. "I'll pick it up on my way out."

Chelsea, Gloria's daughter, had inherited her mother's natural love of cooking and her ability to prepare just about anything connected with the human consumption of food and drink.

Mindlessly, Molly walked up and down the narrow aisles, searching for a new, unique gourmet item, anything to impress Tanner and his guests at tonight's dinner. She wound her way through the aisles, stopping in the refrigerated section. Glass jars filled with a shrimp-colored liquid caught her attention. Spicy tomato gazpacho with freshly ground horseradish, Gloria's handwritten label stated, along with a lengthy list of organic ingredients. This would be a perfect start to tonight's dinner. She placed four jars in her basket, thinking how refreshing it would be, given that it was smack-dab in the middle of summer. They'd had un-usually high temperatures this year. A cold soup to start was ideal.

She took three pints of blackberries for the blackberry-rum shrub she planned to make. According to digital drinks.com, this was the hottest drink of the summer. She'd made it last week. It was to-die-for scrumptious, if you could call a drink scrumptious. A bottle of rum and a good balsamic vinegar completed her cocktail ingredients. Molly hoped tonight's guests were up for her fabulous blackberry concoction.

She bought a dozen and a half fillets of black sea bass for the main course, and fiddle-head ferns as a side dish. She planned a simple Caesar salad, with her special homemade dress-ing. She usually made this tableside in the formal dining room when she was casually entertain-ing friends, but tonight she'd prepare it in the kitchen. She didn't want to embarrass Tanner if she forgot an ingredient or, God forbid, dropped something.

She'd forgo the bread since she planned on serving baguettes with a cheese platter. She'd be serving five cheeses: smoked Gouda, Dan-ish Havarti, pepper jack, a sweet ricotta, and a soft goat cheese. She always liked to add both sweet and dill pickles, three or four varieties of mustards, cappicola ham, and a good salami. She picked up two jars of preserves—apricot and strawberry. To her, this was a meal, but when dealing with such a large group, as she knew from experience, one could never have too much food.

She took a red velvet cake from the enclosed glass case. There wasn't enough time to make something from scratch.

She finished her shopping and stopped to chat with Gloria before heading to the checkout. "I'll use the pasta and pesto for tomorrow night's dinner. I've already got enough food here to feed a small army," she explained, gesturing at the small cart she'd exchanged for the basket she had picked up when she first arrived.

Gloria laughed. "You love every single minute of the prep, right down to the last detail, and don't try to tell me otherwise. As I've said in the past, anytime you want to come and work for me, a job is yours."

Molly laughed out loud, the sound foreign to her ears. She didn't have much to laugh about these days. "I don't think Tanner would approve, but thanks for the offer. I have that fancy kitchen, you know. We just remodeled last fall. I'm still searching for some of my pots and misplaced gadgets." She and Gloria always made small talk, but other than the fact that they shared a love of cooking and each had a daughter, Molly knew virtually nothing about the woman she'd been acquainted with for at least fifteen years. Looking at her watch, she realized she had lingered much too long. She would need at least three hours to prep and prepare dinner. Maybe she would enlist Kristen's help tonight, though she felt sure her daughter had other plans. At seventeen, and it being the summer after her senior year, she rarely spent an evening at home. Tomorrow, Kristen would be leaving for Europe, where she and her best friend, Charlotte, would spend the next two months on a bike-and-barge tour. Tanner didn't approve, but Kristen had begged and pleaded until she got her way. And tomorrow was the big day.

Molly loaded her car with the recyclable bags, careful to arrange them so they didn't topple over. Once she was satisfied, she closed the door. She didn't dare store the fish in the trunk.

Driving back to their house on Riverbend Road, she thought back to the day that she'd first laid eyes on Tanner.

Chapter Four

After three days of rest, Maddy/Molly was ready to get back on the road. She had no clue where she would go, but she hoped to go as far north as her money and the old Mustang would take her. Boston, she thought. She'd often dreamed of attending Harvard.

When the money was gone, then she really would have to settle down and find work, and the Wilkins Motel would be nothing more than a distant memory. She'd packed the clothes she'd purchased at Walmart in the shopping bag they'd provided when she'd purchased them. She put her few toiletry items in a clean wastebasket liner. Promising herself she would burn her prom dress, she removed it from the bottom of the closet and stuffed it in another clean wastebasket liner. She made a promise: as soon as she was settled, she would set fire to that dress. That way, maybe she could burn that night from her memory.

She glanced around the room that had been her home for the past three days, making sure that she had left nothing behind. She scanned the room, then searched the bathroom. The only sign of her was the small sliver of bath soap placed neatly in the soap dish. She'd soaked in the tub twice daily and used her shampoo as bubble bath. She'd loved staying at the motel in spite of the circumstances that had brought her here. Mrs. Wilkins's cleaning crew changed the sheets daily. Fresh towels were given out to all the guests whether they needed them or not. And just as she'd told her when she'd registered three mornings ago, there was fresh coffee from six in the morning until ten. What she hadn't said was that there were also pastries, bagels, muffins, jams, and jellies. The first morning Maddy/Molly had been reluctant even to enter the office, but she needed something in her stomach besides tap water, having spent the entire day and night sleeping. She remembered the coffee and found several guests milling about, with cups of coffee and small paper plates filled with all sorts of goodies. Her stomach growled, and she took two blueberry muffins and a cup of black coffee back to her room. She'd spent the next half hour savoring the muffins, which, she later learned, were prepared by a local bakery and delivered promptly at five in the morning, seven days a week. They were to die for. She didn't remember seeing any type of pastry when she'd checked in, but later she learned that if you didn't make it to the office by six-thirty, there would be nothing left but crumbs. So, for these past three days, she'd stuffed herself with pastries and coffee in the morning, then lounged in her room, enjoying being alone without the fear that Marcus or, as she thought very occasionally, her mother would barge in on her.

She watched television to her heart's content and read the copy of the *Brunswick Times* that was placed outside her door each morning. She had scanned the HELP WANTED section and noticed several possibilities, but this was too close to Blossom City. She wanted more than a few hundred miles between her and her attackers. And, of course, the law.

She put her bags in the trunk before going to the office to return her room key. As usual, Mrs. Wilkins was busy with paperwork. She wore her glasses and looked up when she entered.

"Have you decided to stay longer?" she asked the young woman. Maddy/Molly had told her how much she had enjoyed staying here yesterday as she'd waited her turn for a pastry.

If only, she thought. "No, I'm heading to my friend's for two weeks, remember?" Why she'd brought up the story that Mrs. Wilkins had probably figured out was a lie, she wasn't sure. Maybe she wanted to be like all the other guests who had a clear destination. "I came in to give you back the room key, and to thank you. This is the nicest motel I've ever stayed in." Her heart fluttered when she realized what she'd said. Not wanting to listen to Mrs. Wilkins's probing questions, or see that look of suspicion in her eye, she said, "On this trip. Of course I have stayed in fancy hotels, but this was . . . uh nice. For this town."

Mrs. Wilkins smiled and shook her head. "That's good to know. Make sure you spread the word. Now, young lady, if you wish to stay with us at another time, the front desk will be open all night during the summer months."

Maddy smiled, and said. "Thanks, but I'm off to college in two weeks. I'm staying at the dorm." Before she spurted out another lie, she turned around and walked out the door, giving a quick wave to Mrs. Wilkins. Yes, this had been a nice place to stay when it was the only motel you'd ever stayed in. In the future, she would have to be very careful, watch every word she said, because if she didn't, her freedom could be taken away in the blink of an eye.

Before she pulled out onto Main Street, she counted her cash again. She had four hundred and fifty-five dollars left after paying for her motel room, clothing, incidentals, and gas. She figured gas averaged about a dollar twenty a gallon. The Mustang didn't have the greatest record as a gas saver, but she'd been getting around twenty miles a gallon on the open road. She roughly calculated that she had enough money to get her to Boston. She'd always had Harvard on her brain and thought this would be as good a place as any to start her new life. Once she'd had dreams of attending the esteemed university. Now she knew that that would never happen, but nothing said she could not live nearby and dream, did it?

In the beginning, she planned on getting some kind of menial job, save her money, and sleep in her car. If she didn't like the town or the job, she would move on. With this sketchy plan in mind, she pulled onto Main Street and headed for the interstate.

Wednesday-morning traffic on State Road 25 was minimal. She'd filled the Mustang up in Brunswick, then grabbed a large black coffee and two blueberry muffins in a cellophane package. She munched on one as she drove along at a safe speed of fifty miles per hour. If she'd expected these to taste like the muffins at the hotel—which she hadn't, but if she had—she would have been greatly disappointed. These tasted like the cellophane in which they were wrapped. Still, she ate the second one, too. Not because she was particularly hungry but because she wasn't wasteful.

She remembered what hunger was like.

Driving down the long stretch of open road, memories of her life in Blossom City came to her in flashes, like random bits from a movie reel. It seemed she had always been hungry. Maddy recalled the gnawing feeling in the pit of her stomach the times when it had been empty, the many times when even a cracker would have sufficed. How a mother could allow her child to suffer like that, she still hadn't figured out. But one thing she did know: when and if she ever had a child, she vowed to be the best mother she could be.

She'd been driving for a few hours when she made a quick stop in Florence, South Carolina. She liked the name, but still, it wasn't far enough. She filled her gas tank, bought a soda and a pack of peanut-butter crackers, then returned to I-95.

She cruised along, staying in the right-hand lane, carefully following all the traffic laws. Again, her thoughts returned to Blossom City and her sad life there.

She recalled a time years ago—she had to have been around eleven or twelve—when her mother had decided to take her and Marcus to Texas, telling them she had come into a large inheritance. Florida to Texas had been a long, boring car ride, she recalled. Her mother stopped only when they needed to gas up or use the restroom, but that was it. Not once had they stopped for a meal. Not even a quick stop at a fast-food restaurant. Maddy remembered being so hungry she'd rummaged through her mother's purse when she'd been given instructions to keep her eye on it while her mother went to the restroom. Her mother's purse was always off-limits to her. If her mother had caught her even looking at her purse, there would have been hell to pay. She never knew why, maybe she'd been hiding drugs or something equally bad, but she knew she'd be in a heap of trouble if her mother caught her rummaging through her purse.

She'd looked in the front seat to make sure Marcus was still slumped against the passenger door sleeping. He was. Drool dangled from his chin, and his mouth hung open like a door. He was out like a light. Quickly, she crammed her hand inside her mother's purse, using her fingers to feel around for the loose change her mother always tossed in her purse when she was in a hurry, which seemed like most of the time on this trip. She scooped up a handful of change and quickly sneaked inside the service station, where she saw a vending machine. She dropped thirty-five cents in and pulled on a knobbed handle. A package of Chuckles dropped to the bottom, and she grabbed it and hurried back to the car before her mother returned. She'd tucked the candies inside her shorts. Her heart was beating so loudly, she was sure her mother would hear it when she returned, but she'd ignored her as usual, grabbed a cigarette from her purse, and continued their long drive to Texas.

Years later she would learn that her mother, Lenore, which is what she preferred Maddy to call her, had learned that her own mother, Maddy's grandmother, had passed away. A life insurance policy had listed Lenore as the sole beneficiary to the tune of a measly five hundred dollars. Her mother had thrown a hellacious fit when she'd left her grandmother's attorney's office. She'd raised hell the entire ride back to Blossom City. Scared to utter a word, Maddy had focused on allotting herself one Chuckle every four hours. If she could keep this up, the jellied fake-fruit squares would ward off the hunger pains until they reached Blossom City. There, she knew she would get at least one meal a day at school.

She didn't care that she was on the free lunch program and that several of her classmates whispered behind her back when she held out the pale-green meal card for the lunch lady to punch. Everyone knew the pale-green cards were for the poor white trash. She'd been humiliated when she was old enough to realize her family life was very different from that of most of her classmates. But when your stomach kept you awake most of the night, and drinking well water from the bathroom sink didn't cure your hunger, humiliation was a small price to pay for a full stomach, even if it was only one meal a day. Sometimes her friend Cassie, who got free lunches, too, would save a roll for her and slip it to her, wrapped in a napkin, beneath the table in the cafeteria. She'd always thanked her, and Cassie and she had been best of friends until Cassie's family moved away when they were in sixth grade.

After Cassie left Blossom City, there were no more yeast rolls to stave off the hunger at night. It wasn't too bad, really. She hardly ever saw her mother, had no clue if she even had a job, or why she only occasionally made an appearance at home, but Marcus always had a pocketful of money, and he never complained about being hungry. She suspected he stole from various people, but if she were to tell this to their mother, again there would be hell to pay.

By the time she was thirteen, Maddy had started offering babysitting services to a few families in the trailer park. Word got around. She was good to the kids, they all seemed to like her, and she could change a diaper like a pro and never complained when it was messy. With this job, she earned enough money to keep a few nonperishable food items hidden in her closet-size bedroom. If she had any cash left over, she would hide it, knowing the day would come when she would need it.

That day came at the beginning of seventh grade. While the junior high school provided textbooks for all of her classes, three of those classes—English, math, and science—required the students to purchase the accompanying workbooks. These were sold in the school bookstore. Maddy knew she had enough money stashed from her babysitting to pay for the workbooks, so she didn't think too much about it until the next morning when she pulled out the small jewelry box hidden inside a shoe box at the back of her tiny closet and saw that it had been emptied. She cried, and for the first time, she wished she were someone else, someone who belonged to a loving, kind family.

She recalled the humiliation she'd felt when her homeroom teacher, Mrs. Swan, took out a supply of last year's workbooks and gave a set to her after she had erased a former student's answers. She'd been thankful but still wished for a real family. A mother and a father. Parents who paid for her school supplies. Parents who made sure she never went to bed hungry, and parents who loved her.

More than anything, Maddy wished that her mother loved her. The other things really weren't all that important, but she guessed that if she had a mother who truly loved her, having things she needed would be taken care of. She'd had neither, and she accepted her life, though as she grew older, she became more aware of her mother and her mother's actions.

Put simply, her mother was a whore and a drug addict. She only cared about the next man, and it didn't matter who he was as long as he could provide her with drugs, alcohol, and a place to flop when she needed one.

By the time Maddy was fifteen, she had three part-time jobs as well as continuing with school, studying as hard as she could, and making straight As. It was then that she'd started paying rent on the trailer. She'd thought her mother owned the tin box, and she had at one time, but she'd sold it to some guy for a wad of cash on the condition her kids could live there, explaining to him that her daughter would pay the rent. It was a great deal for her mother. It was a terrible deal for Maddy, but she didn't really have much choice.

But now, she thought, as she continued down I-95, she had a choice. And she was not going to live like white trash ever again.

She'd arrived in Boston at four o'clock the next morning. Exhausted, she'd driven through the city, stopping in Cambridge, just north of Boston, at an all-night diner near Harvard, a place called Lou's. It reminded her of the diner on *Happy Days*. She and Cassie had spent many hours laughing at the characters' antics, both secretly wishing for the normal and often silly lives of the characters they admired so much.

Inside the diner, the floor had large black-and-white-checkered tiles, the booths were red faux leather and the tabletops a pale-gray Formica.

Even though it was still early, the place was pretty full. *Students*, she thought, as she glanced at the diners. Some had piles of books on their tables, with notebooks and cups of coffee beside them. Others were dressed in business suits, and some wore what looked like hospital scrubs. *Quite a mix*, she observed, as she found a seat at the long counter that stretched across the entire restaurant.

She sat down on a high stool at the counter. A young girl about her age asked, "What'll you have?" She quickly ordered black coffee, two scrambled eggs, toast, sausage, and a side of bacon, with home fries and a large glass of milk. When the food was placed in front of her, she focused her attention on eating every single morsel she'd been served. This wasn't going to be an everyday thing, she told herself. But as a reward of sorts, she'd decided to start her new life with a good, hot meal.

"I don't think I've ever seen a girl eat that much in my life," the man seated two seats down from her commented.

Maddy looked at him, her eyes doubling in size. Had he followed her? Were they on to her already?

"I'm Tanner. Dr. Tanner McCann. And you are?"

Maddy wanted to faint, but instead, she held out her hand, offered a slight smile, and said, "I'm Molly Hall." It was then she realized how she must look and realized how stupid it was to give him her name, even if it was fake.

Dr. Tanner McCann was older than she, but not so old that she didn't appreciate his good looks. His coal-black hair and compelling blue eyes, the assured set of his shoulders, the way he held her hand when she'd offered it—all left no room for doubt: this guy was somebody, and she had no business pretending she'd fit in with his kind.

"Well, Molly Hall, what brings you to Lou's this hour of the morning?" He let go of her hand, but not before giving it a slight squeeze.

Chapter Five

Molly returned home, unloaded her purchases, and for the next three hours, she chopped, mixed, chilled, and sautéed. When she finished, she set the formal dining-room table with her best china and the eighteen-karat gold utensils that Tanner had insisted on purchasing years ago when he'd decided that their dinner parties needed a touch of class, that having the best of the best would impress his colleagues. Personally, Molly thought they were just a bit gauche. But if Tanner wanted her to use gold utensils at their dinner parties, she would. She removed crystal flutes from the hutch and put one at each place setting. For the next hour, she decorated the dining table. She'd used her newest cloth napkins, white linen with tiny, hemstitched crosses done by hand, given to her as a gift after Tanner's hygienist, Regina, had taken a trip to Italy. Sure that they'd cost her a small fortune, Molly remembered being shocked when she'd received them but was reminded that all of Tanner's employees, right down to the receptionist, knew of his immaculate taste in every aspect, so she'd accepted the napkins.

Tonight would be the first time she'd actually used them. Maybe Tanner would take notice and appreciate her extra attention to detail in order to make everything perfect, just as he'd commanded this morning before he left.

As Molly adjusted each place setting, straightening a knife here and there, making sure each plate was perfectly aligned with the matched set on either side, she took a deep breath, stepped back, and viewed her work. She could not see anything out of place. Not even a speck of dust reflected off the highly polished china. Taking her time, she slowly circled the formal dining table that could seat as many as twenty guests. Tanner had said ten, so adding herself and Tanner, there would be twelve. Earlier, she had removed the eight extra dining chairs to the large walk-in pantry in the kitchen. Had Graham or Holden been at home, she would've asked them to take the chairs to the basement. Molly felt sure that their guests, all of them in the medical profession—at least this was what Tanner had told her last night when he'd said he wanted to host a dinner party for his new investors—would not be visiting the pantry. She straightened another knife, made sure the calla lilies were centered and that the white creamy flowers were all in full bloom. A droopy calla lily could bring on an evening of Tanner's rage.

Satisfied that all was as perfect as could be, she had an hour to bathe, do her hair, and dress. She'd called Sally, her weekly house-keeper and occasional cook, to assist her to-night. Sally quickly agreed, knowing Molly would stuff an extra hundred-dollar bill in her pocket. Tanner said these extra duties were part of Sally's job, and he saw no reason to pay her any more than her normal hourly wage. Molly thought otherwise. Tanner, for all his wealth, could be a stingy curmudgeon when he wanted to be, which was most of the time.

Molly hurried upstairs. She'd wanted to soak in the tub and shave her legs, but she'd taken too long prepping and had to settle for a quick shower. She didn't have time to wash her hair either, which Tanner was sure to com-ment on later. The smell of basil clung to it.

As she dried off in the elegant master bath, Molly felt uncomfortable. Why did they need such a bathroom if she never had time to enjoy such a luxury? A deep-set tub was positioned in the center with a view of the beautiful city park that was, in her opinion, one of Goldenhills' most scenic views, but Molly couldn't remem-ber the last time she'd actually had a chance to soak in the tub and enjoy the view. She had a fleeting thought about the marble fireplace in her bedroom that was flanked by two antique club chairs and a tea table. To her knowledge, the tub and the chairs had been used only a handful of times since they'd remodeled the master bedroom in the home they'd purchased shortly after their marriage.

Tanner had insisted they periodically re-model and update the kitchen and baths so that they would always look up to date, pris-tine, and *perfect*. About the time she became comfortable with the rooms, a team of con-tractors and decorators would storm through the house, making swift changes as per Tan-ner's ideas. Only once had he bothered to ask her opinion on any of the changes: did she have a preference on the type of wood to use for the custom-built cabinets? She truly didn't care if they were made out of cardboard. She didn't enjoy spending time in the kitchen as much as she had in the early years of her mar-riage. With the twins and then when Kristen came along, she'd loved preparing healthful meals for them and was totally thrilled when they would ask her to make them their favorite cookies and cakes. Her children had *never* gone to bed hungry.

Where did that come from, she thought as she brushed her graying blond hair into a sleek chignon.

Shaking her head to focus on the here and now, she turned her attention back to her hair. She took a hand mirror and turned around so she could view the back of her handiwork in the large mirror mounted on the wall. Decid-ing it wasn't going to get any better, she misted a light hair spray to ensure there wasn't a hair out of place. Tanner would be sure to notice that, too. She applied her makeup, hoping to take off at least a couple of years, but when she looked into her magnifying mirror, she saw her foundation had settled into her fine lines, and the light pink lipstick she'd applied moments ago had fanned out just beyond her lip line. She removed the lipstick with a tissue, then lined her lips with a matching lip pencil, assuring herself that she wouldn't look like a clown within minutes of greeting their dinner guests.

She heard Sally downstairs in the kitchen. Thank goodness she'd arrived on time. Molly had already wasted way too much time at the market. She slipped into one of the slinky black dresses she reserved for dinner parties. A pair of low-slung black heels, and she was ready. She stood a few feet away from the mirror to view her reflection. Not bad from a distance, but hideous up close. Maybe it was time to start thinking about an injection or two of Botox or possibly a face-lift. Tanner hadn't mentioned this to her yet, but something told her he would in the near future. Of course, he would find a way for one of his colleagues to perform the surgery or inject the botulism for a reduced rate, of that Molly was sure. Again, she was reminded of his stinginess, at least when it came to her.

More and more lately, Molly tried to recall exactly when and why she'd fallen in love with Tanner and couldn't come up with an exact moment when she knew he was *the one*, or an event that defined the moment as special, life-changing. Had it been gradual? Like a slow-burning flame? No, that wasn't her at all. Why *had* she fallen in love with her husband of almost twenty years? Why she was having such strange thoughts bothered her, but not so much that she would consider making a change. She had a good life, one that most women would envy. A handsome husband. And a doctor at that. Three beautiful children. Their home, which was probably worth more than the average person would earn in a lifetime. Yet she couldn't help but feel unsettled. Possibly it was the realization that she was growing old. She shouldn't have looked in that damned vanity mirror this morning. Natural sunlight didn't tell lies. She was aging, and to her, it didn't appear that she was aging gracefully. She took one last glance in the mirror before going downstairs. *I am what I am,* she thought, as she plastered a smile on her face when she saw Sally in the kitchen.

Sally looked up from the cheese tray she was arranging. "Why, Miss Molly, you look absolutely stunning! What I wouldn't give to have a figure like yours."

Molly gave a wry laugh. "Thanks. I sure don't feel very 'stunning' today."

She took an apron from a drawer and tied the straps around her waist and neck, then spoke. "What can I do?" Although she already knew what needed to be done. She'd planned the dinner party herself. However, after getting to know Sally, she had determined it made the little woman feel better about herself if Molly played the role of the helpless wife. From what she had gathered, Sally's home life was lacking. She knew her husband drank, and occasionally Sally would show up with a black eye and would do her best to try to convince Molly how clumsy she was at home. Molly didn't believe her, but had never once considered telling her so. She liked Sally. Sometimes she liked to think of her as a surrogate mother. She was certainly old enough. Molly felt an extra layer of protection when Sally was in her house.

With iron-colored hair and matching eyes, Sally was short and round like a beach ball, and just as colorful with her use of the English language. She said, "That shit over there"— she nodded to the counter indicating several unopened jars—"needs to be opened and gussied up a bit. Maybe one of those fancy china bowls you have."

Molly laughed, an honest-to-goodness laugh. Sally was just what she needed to perk her up for the boring evening ahead. "Consider it done." She removed three small crystal bowls from the bottom of the hutch. Carefully, she filled each dish with the contents of the jars of jams and mustards she'd purchased from Gloria's. She hoped this wasn't too casual for Tanner. He did like his dinner parties to be formal, a bit on the uppity side. Cheese trays were quite popular now. She would remind him of this if he complained. He liked keeping up with the latest trends.

"I'll let these chill for a bit." Molly placed

the bowls in the refrigerator. She glanced at the clock on the stove. "I don't think I'm going to have enough time to sauté these fillets," she said, eyeing the small mound of white fish on the platter when she opened the refrigerator. "I'll broil them."

"Absolutely, give you more time with your company," Sally said while she arranged the platters.

That was the last thing Molly wanted, but Sally didn't need to know that. "I doubt they'll even know that I'm here. After dessert, I'm sure they'll do their doctor thing. Tanner wants to open another dental clinic." She wanted to ask Sally to not mention this to Tanner but decided against it. Doing so would just call more attention to herself, and she didn't need that. His dinner parties were always stressful. As much as she enjoyed spending time in the kitchen, she detested his dinners on demand. If she dropped a fork, if the meal didn't meet his expectations, later there would be an argument and possibly more.

Molly jumped when she heard pounding footsteps, followed by a door slamming. "Mom? You home?" Kristen called out as she made her way to the kitchen. "I guess you are," she said, entering the kitchen and reaching for a slice of cheese.

"No!" Molly said, then caught herself. "That's for tonight. Appetizers. Now, hands off," she said, smiling.

At seventeen, Kristen was the spitting image

of her mother, with thick blond hair and bright-green eyes. Molly thought her daughter quite stunning at seventeen. Often when she looked at her, she would travel back in time to her youth and thank the high heavens Kristen didn't have to live like she had. She never spoke of her past to her children, and they never asked about her life before she married their father. Their lives were too full, and for this she was grateful. She'd dedicated her life to her family. Unlike her benighted mother.

"Dad at it again?" Kristen asked as she yanked the refrigerator door open. She pulled out a carton of orange juice, then closed the door with her hip.

"Careful!" Sally called. "Your momma's got those crystal dishes in there. You break 'em, and she'll have your ass, kiddo."

Kristen looked at Molly, raising her perfectly shaped brows. "Oh. Sorry."

Molly shook her head at Sally's words. "Dad's having dinner guests tonight."

"Figures," Kristen said as she reached for a glass. "He's always having his stupid cronies over for something."

"Kristen! Don't let your father hear you say that," Molly admonished, a bit too harshly.

"Or what?" she asked.

"Yeah, or what?" Graham said. "I'm starving. What's to eat?"

Molly jumped, then calmed herself a bit when she saw Graham. He sounded exactly like his father. Almost twenty-two, Graham stood six-foot-two and weighed a perfect two hundred pounds. With black hair and blue eyes, he was identical to Tanner. Though she'd raised Graham and Holden since they were toddlers, she'd always felt something was missing. The maternal bond she'd felt when she gave birth to Kristen just wasn't there. She loved both boys dearly but often felt as though they only tolerated her because of Tanner. They had no memories of their mother, but Tanner was always quick to remind them that she was only their stepmother. As if in saying this, he meant she didn't deserve the respect that their biological mother deserved, had she lived.

Molly had always suspected that there was more to his first wife's tragic death than Tanner had shared with her, but she wasn't willing to risk an argument by bringing up the topic. The few times she had brought it up, Tanner had gone into a rage. His blue eyes glazed over, and the muscles in his neck bulged with rage. She recalled a time when she'd actually watched the skin on his neck dancing up and down as it pulsed with anger, his heart beating so fast that, for a moment, she'd feared he might suffer a heart attack. If the topic was brought up, she always let Tanner tell his version of the day that Elaine had fallen down the stairs and broken her neck. She would listen, but she always kept her opinion to herself. She had learned. The hard way.

"I said, what's to eat? Didn't you hear me?" Graham repeated impatiently. He stretched his arms out in front of him, lacing his fingers together, then knowing how Molly detested it, he cracked his knuckles one by one. The smirk on his face said it all. "Earth to Molly? I *said*, 'What's to eat?'" The twins had never called her Mother, or Mom. Just Molly.

Kristen tossed the remainder of her orange juice in the sink, then slammed her glass down on the counter. "Are you helpless? Can't you see *my mom* is busy?" Kristen said, her voice raised a notch.

"Both of you calm down," Molly said before their verbal slashing worsened. "Graham, your dad is having guests tonight. I didn't think you would be home, so I . . ."—*didn't plan on serving you dinner*—"figured you guys would eat before you came home. Or I can order a pizza, if you like." Molly had begun to feel intimidated by the twins when they were around fourteen. The sweet little boys she'd raised had turned on her. She had complained to Tanner, and he had done nothing. In fact, once she'd brought it to his attention, it seemed that he actually encouraged their disrespectful behavior. If she served them a dish they didn't like—the two seemed more connected to one another's likes and dislikes as they got older—they would make a big show of their dislike: dumping their food on the floor, pretending they were going to throw up. Their antics knew no bounds. Once Graham took his plate and tossed it into the deep ceramic sink, causing the plate to shatter. When he'd grabbed a piece of the broken plate and cut his hand, requiring stitches, Tanner had flown into a rage, telling her she was a horrible stepmother, and if it weren't for Kristen, he would contact the authorities and report her for abusing *his* son. She remembered being shocked at Tanner's accusation. When she'd tried to point out Graham's deliberate act, he had slapped her in front of the boys. They'd laughed at their father. Grateful that Kristen hadn't been home to witness that horrible night, from that moment on Molly felt as though she had to tiptoe around them when they were in the house.

Both boys had just graduated from Harvard with business degrees. But they hadn't moved out or bothered to search for a job. She feared their expensive education had been nothing more than a waste of money.

Sally placed a dishcloth over the cheese platter, her way of saying what lay beneath it was now off-limits. Kristen leaned against the refrigerator door, watching and waiting.

"I hate pizza. You'd know that if you ever paid attention to me," Graham said, his man voice firm and decisive, just like Tanner's.

Holding back the urge to scream and remind him of the hundreds of times she'd served him pizza, she took a deep breath before she spoke. "Graham, now isn't the time. I'm busy. If you'd like a sandwich, I'm sure Sally would be more than happy to make one for you." She hated dragging Sally into their arguments, but Molly felt Graham needed to be reminded that they were not alone in the kitchen.

"You're an asshole, Graham," Kristen said before turning her back on them and opening the refrigerator. She grabbed a package of turkey, a jar of plain mustard, and a package of processed cheese slices. She closed the door with her hip and took a loaf of bread from the cabinet. "Here," she said, holding the food out in front of her. "Make your own goddamn sandwich."

"Kristen!" Molly gasped. Her insides turned to water. For a second, she thought she might be sick. She took a deep breath to steady herself. Tonight wasn't a good night for a fight between brother and sister. *But was there ever a good night for a fight?* she thought, as she formed her next words. "Graham, make yourself a sandwich," Molly said as Kristen plopped the food in the center of the kitchen's large island.

"I'm going upstairs to finish packing. I can't wait to get out of this hellhole," Kristen shouted as she stomped out of the kitchen.

Kristen was right. Their home had become a hellhole, at least when the twins were home. *And their father*, Molly thought, but knew it was best not to share this with her daughter. Tanner was her father, too.

Without so much as an apology, Graham hurriedly made two sandwiches and grabbed a can of soda; then he, too, stormed out of the kitchen.

She breathed a sigh of relief. She would be so glad when the twins moved out. They made everyone miserable. Except for Tanner. He actually thought their hateful, childish behavior comical. Afraid to challenge him, Molly kept her opinions to herself. It was enough that the twins turned the house upside down whenever the urge hit them. She wasn't going to add to the chaos. She kept telling herself that when they moved out, things would be different, like they used to be when they'd first married. She and Tanner would have the house to themselves. She would try harder to make their evenings more romantic. They'd have dinner, spend more time making love and relaxing with one another. They would discuss their day together as they lay in bed, hips touching, his hand lightly touching hers. She would tell him about Gloria's constantly asking her to come to work, and he would tell her about the frightened, cavity-filled patients he'd seen during the day.

Right. She knew full well that this was an absolute fantasy. She might as well wish that she and Tanner could hop on a rocket and fly off to the moon for some sightseeing.

"Miss Molly, you all right?" Sally asked in a much softer tone than normal.

Was she?

She cleared her throat. "Sure, I'm good. Those kids just love to annoy me," she said. Her words sounded as though she were including Kristen, but she wasn't. *Those kids*, in her mind, referred to the twins. How had two adorable toddlers turned into such cruel, hateful young men? She knew the answer but didn't want to go there. She was so tired of trying to be a good mother to them and a good wife to Tanner. Her yearning for the perfect family had become nothing more than a fantasy from long ago, one born out of the hellish existence she had lived through as a kid. The fight to turn that fantasy into reality left her the night Tanner had slapped her in front of the twins.

Sally removed the cloth from the cheese platter and added more brie. "Kristen's a good girl. She don't ever annoy me. Now, those two grown boys, well, you know as well as I do, that's a completely different story."

Molly wanted to agree but refrained. These days she never knew when they might be lurking around the corner.

"Kids are challenging," Molly offered. A flimsy answer, but she wasn't taking any chances with their overhearing what she said.

"Yep, they are. Especially when they ain't your own," Sally whispered.

Molly knew this was her way of saying what she herself wouldn't. Holden and Graham didn't share her genetic makeup. They were spoiled, mean, and beyond immature. She had tried her best to be a good mother to both of the boys, and truly, she did love them, but not with the same all-consuming, to-the-death kind of love that she felt for Kristen. When they were toddlers, she had loved them, cared for them as if she'd given birth to them. The change had been abrupt and hurtful.

At first, she had berated herself over and over for her lack of motherly feelings, told herself she wasn't normal. Then she decided it was just a phase. The boys were in their early teens, at an age where even biological parents might question their feelings for their children, even if only in thought. This was when she really began to notice how Tanner encouraged them to disrespect her. She made excuses. Boys will be boys. They were hormonal teenagers. They would grow out of their hatefulness. One excuse after another, but their behavior only worsened as they got older. She took most of it, swallowed it, and occasionally choked on it. When the plate-shattering incident happened and Tanner accused her of physical abuse, she knew both her husband *and* the boys were not acting normally. It was at this time that Tanner's abuse took a turn and became more than she wanted to admit. She couldn't even think about the state of her marriage. Not now. If she did, she was afraid of what she might do.

Molly took a deep breath. "I love them, Sally, but sometimes they make it hard."

Sally moved the cheese platter aside and began working on the meats. "Yep, I can see that. I just don't understand why Mr. Tanner doesn't discipline them."

Molly removed lemons, garlic, and Worcestershire sauce from the refrigerator. She took a knife, a cutting board, and a garlic press from a drawer and began prepping the Caesar dressing. "It's difficult at their age. They're adults, remember?" She popped a clove of garlic into the press. "I'm sure once they're out on their own, they will mature and settle down."

Did she really believe that? No, not even for a minute.

"I sure hope so, Miss Molly," Sally said, her tone doubtful and unconvinced.

"I think it's a guy thing that they'll grow out of."

Again, she didn't believe her own words. Dreading the evening ahead, Molly chopped and sliced, anything to erase the twins and their father from her thoughts, even if it was only for a little while.

Chapter Six

Summer, Boston

On her first day in Cambridge, she'd learned about Mrs. Garner's Boarding House for single women from an ad in Harvard's newspaper, the *Crimson*. For twenty dollars a night, she shared a small attic room with three other girls who weren't much older than she. The twenty dollars included one hot meal per day, the use of a large bathroom with a time limit of ten minutes per shower, and you had to provide your own bath towel. Sarah, a shy girl not much older than she, had loaned her a clean towel. Molly was thankful and planned to wash it and return it to her as soon as she was able to purchase one of her own. She found the streets of Cambridge filled with tiny shops, selling everything from homemade candles to rosary beads that claimed to be blessed by some pope she'd never heard of. So far, she hadn't located a Walmart or a discount department store she could afford that sold bath towels.

Molly stepped off the city bus, amazed that she'd mastered the Massachusetts Bay Transportation Authority's system so quickly. Florida had no public transportation system. If you needed to get from point A to point B, you either drove, walked, or hitched a ride. She'd decided it would be best to use the public transportation system. In the first place, she feared the police would be looking for her Mustang, and second, the parking situation in Boston and the surrounding towns was very tight, so that off-street parking was way too expensive. Finally, Mrs. Garner allowed free parking. She was immensely grateful that her parking space was located behind the giant old Victorian that, for a while, would be her home. For the past three mornings, she'd been stunned upon opening her eyes and realizing that she was no longer in her tiny room in the trailer in Blossom City, Florida. Being surrounded by others somewhat like herself reassured her that she wasn't the only girl to have suffered in a way that had brought them all together in the small attic room. They shared two large chests of drawers, where they stored their meager clothes and any personal belongings.

Molly used one drawer for clothing. In her second drawer, still inside the wastebasket liner from the hotel, was her prom dress. She had promised herself she would burn it. So far, she had yet to find an ideal place to do this, so she had been forced to hang on to the dress until she found a way to destroy it without attracting attention. There had been much talk on the news lately about something called DNA and how it could identify people and solve crimes. From what little she'd gathered between reading the newspapers and listening to the occasional bits of news, this stuff had helped O. J. Simpson get away with murder. She didn't understand the science behind it but stored the information for another time.

As she hurried along Bayline Street, she rehearsed what she would say when she entered the diner. Molly had spent the past three days searching for a job. She scoured the *Boston Globe,* the *Boston Herald,* and *USA Today* searching for work. Having had no luck, she returned to Lou's Diner for a quick bite and with a plan in mind. Secretly, she was hoping to see the doctor again, if only to see if he recognized her. She'd had an idea that she wanted to work at the diner, and if luck was on her side, she was about to do something so out of character, it truly scared her. She reminded herself she wasn't Maddy anymore. She was Molly. Molly was smart, secure, and unafraid. Yeah, sure you are, she thought as she entered the diner.

The smell of coffee brewing and bacon frying wafted throughout the diner. Molly found a seat at the counter, her hands trembling as she picked up the plastic-covered menu. She'd calculated her money, and the figures weren't very promising. If she didn't find a job in the next few days, she was going to be in trouble. Hence her decision to make another visit to the diner. She'd waitressed at Tony's BBQ Pit and had plenty of experience, so that shouldn't be a problem.

An older woman—she guessed her to be in her mid-forties—placed a glass of water on the counter in front of her. "What'll it be?" she asked in a thick Boston accent.

Should she order first, then ask for a job? Or wait until after? Taking a deep breath, she said, "I'll have the number three, over easy with bacon."

"You's want the toast that comes with it?" the waitress asked. Beneath her long brown hair, Molly could see part of a name tag, but only the last few letters. Pastor Royer always said it was nice to be personable with his parishioners and, whenever possible, use their name. He said it made people feel comfortable. She wanted to take his advice now, but the waitress's hair prevented her from seeing the rest of her name.

"Uh, sure. I need to ask you . . . ," she stumbled over her next words. "Would it be possible to speak to the owner?" She paused, swallowed, then went on. "I am searching for a job, and"—she motioned to the crowd of diners behind her—"it looks like you all have a lot of customers." There. She'd accomplished what she'd set out to do. Well, not really, she thought, as the waitress scribbled something on her pad.

"Call this number, ask for Louise. She's out sick, but between me an' you, girl, we need plenty of help here. School starts in August, and we ain't prepared, if ya know what I mean."

Molly nodded her head. "Yes, I do." She thought she sounded way too southern and made a mental note to practice speaking without her twang, just one more thing that would draw attention to herself. Maybe Sarah would help her. She'd offered the bath towel, and she hadn't even asked for one. She would ask her tonight.

"Tell her Teresa told ya to call," the waitress said before turning away to place her order on a round metal wheel with clips attached to it. Tony's had used this simple but efficient system, so at least she knew how to use one. Simple is all she could handle now, she thought, as Teresa slammed a cup of black coffee in front of her. Molly took a sip, liking the hot, bitter taste. Three days spent drinking it at the Wilkins Motel, and she was already craving a cup of the stuff in the morning. It didn't take long for habits to take root.

A few minutes later, she tucked into her breakfast, wishing she could have this every day, but until she secured a job, she'd settle for the one meal a day provided by Mrs. Garner and write this breakfast off as an investment. It wasn't as though she wasn't used to being short on food. She'd gone way longer than a day without food when she was younger, and her body had adjusted just fine as long as she had water.

Molly felt a presence come up behind her. Hesitant to turn around, fearing it could be the police or, God forbid, one of the guys who'd attacked her, she almost jumped out of her skin when she heard his voice.

"Do you eat like this every day?"

Feeling heat rise to her cheeks, she kept her gaze on what was left of her breakfast. Feeling the desire to be hip and testy, she replied, "So what if I do?" She said the words slowly, forcing herself to speak as much as she could without her southern accent.

He slid onto the empty stool beside her. "You'll get fat. Men don't like fat women."

Molly turned to stare at him, not caring if she appeared to be shocked. It took her a few seconds to gather her thoughts. When she did, her words were honest, something she hadn't practiced the past four days. "That was an incredibly rude thing to say." Just to prove herself, she took a piece of toast, slathered it with butter and jelly, then took a huge bite. She felt his eyes on her, watching her, and for some odd reason, she liked the idea that she had his full, undivided attention. She wasn't used to feeling this way since she almost always tried to avoid being noticed. Maybe her newfound courage came from the name change, and the new city. The beginning of a new way of life.

"I'm being truthful. Men like women who take care of themselves."

Was this true? Her mother certainly hadn't taken care of herself, and men swarmed around her like flies on a sticky tape, but she certainly would not tell this to the doctor. For that matter, she would never tell this man, or anyone else, about her past. From this day forward, she was Molly Hall. Maddy Carmichael no longer existed. So she continued to eat, deciding not to reply to his comment. She buttered another slice of toast and took a bite, waiting for him to comment. When he didn't, she raised her coffee cup in the air as she'd seen the other diners do, in hopes that Teresa would refill her cup. Anything to break up this uncomfortable silence between herself and the doctor.

"Patience, kiddo," Teresa yelled from the opposite end of the counter.

Molly felt like crawling into a dark hole. Kiddo? That certainly wasn't the impression she'd hoped to make. Maybe Teresa thought she was a student. She could live with that. Yes, being called kiddo, someone who appeared to be, at the very least, old enough for college was okay. It didn't hurt that Harvard was right around the corner.

Teresa appeared with a coffeepot in her hand. "Hey, why don't you stick around for a while? We're super shorthanded today. I'll call Lou myself. You seem like a decent enough kid."

Did this mean what she thought it meant?

She must've had a strange look on her face. Teresa's next words, "Yeah, I think we can give ya a test run today. I'll show ya the ropes, then you can help out with the lunch crowd. Whatever tips ya make are yours." She spoke fast, and Molly had to strain to understand, as Teresa's Boston accent was extremely strong.

All she could say was, "Today?"

"Yep, if ya can. I'll go call Lou now while I have a minute." She poured coffee for the doctor and immediately disappeared through the swinging doors behind the counter.

"You're really looking for a job? Here?" the doctor asked, incredulously.

The new Molly spoke. "Yes and yes."

"Ah-ha, I see you are a woman of few words. Just what I like," he said, then took a sip of coffee.

Molly felt her face turn red again. Did this mean he thought she was attractive, that he liked her? She had no experience with older men. Or any man, other than her perverted brother's friends, the ones who'd sent her running.

"I might have a job for you," he said.

She looked over at him. "What?"

"A job. You're looking for a job, right? I might have something for you. It's much better than serving greasy diner food."

"Why do you come here if you don't like the food?" Molly asked, curious as to why the doctor would frequent a place if he didn't like the food.

"It's convenient to my office," he replied. "And really, the food isn't bad. I wouldn't be here if it were."

"Oh," she said, at a loss for a witty and clever reply.

"Don't you want to know what the job is?" he questioned her.

She placed her fork across the top of her plate, wiped her mouth with the paper napkin, then turned to look at him. "Not really." She couldn't work for a doctor! She didn't even have a high school diploma! He must think she was older than Teresa had. She wasn't sure if that was good or bad.

"Are you joking with me?" he asked her.

"No. Why would I do that?" she replied.

He smiled and shook his head. "You are an original, I'll give you that much."

Molly tilted her head and stared at him. "What do you want from me? I don't even know you. Do you always speak this way to strangers?"

"I'm sorry. You're right, I don't normally speak so bluntly to strangers. Please accept my apology. I didn't mean to offend you."

Now she felt guilty. "It's okay. You didn't offend me. I'm just not used to . . ."

"What?" he quickly asked.

Men. But she wasn't going to tell him that. "I . . . I'm new in town. I guess what I meant to say is most of the people I've met aren't quite as outspoken as you are."

"Wait a while. You'll find that most Bostonians are quite friendly and mean you no harm."

Teresa pushed through the double doors. "I talked to Lou. She says if I think you're waitress material, then she says, welcome aboard."

Molly's heart raced. For once, something was going her way. "Thank you so much. I . . . where do I start?" She stood, picked up her clutch purse and tucked it under her arm, and raked a hand through her hair. She was glad she'd shampooed her hair last night. At least it wasn't hanging in greasy strands, and her clothes were new and clean.

"Come with me," Teresa said. "I'll find you a

uniform." She glanced down at Molly's feet. "Those shoes will work for now. Long hours on your feet, you'll need a good shoe. Trust me on this, kiddo. First time I spent twelve hours on my feet, I went home and cried. Sharps has the best shoes in town. Tell 'em you work for Lou, they'll give you a ten percent discount. Isn't much, but it beats nothing."

Molly nodded. A new pair of shoes was the last thing she needed, but maybe later, when she settled in and had put aside extra money. For now, her sneakers would have to do.

Without saying another word to the doctor, whose name she couldn't recall, Molly followed Teresa through the swinging doors, leaving the doctor sitting at the counter.

Lou's kitchen was huge, ten times the size of Tony's. It had a prep area where three people chopped, diced, and sliced. There was a huge grill next to a stove top that had at least eight gas burners, all with pans of various sizes and shapes sitting on them. It was attended to by a short woman with a long black braid hanging down her back and a man who was at least a foot and a half taller than the woman. Two sets of fryers were attended to by a middle-aged man. Activity buzzed throughout the kitchen as she followed Teresa. A giant dishwasher hummed in the background, and a young girl around her age quickly stacked thick white dinner plates beside the grill.

"In here," Teresa said, opening a door at the very back of the kitchen.

Molly stepped inside what appeared to be

an employee break room. A shabby brown sofa
shoved against the wall held scattered newspapers, and three card tables with chairs sat in
the center of the room. On the right side was a
long counter with cabinets above it. A micro-
wave, a sink, and two coffeemakers were placed
on top of the counter. A variety of cups were
upside down in a dish drainer, along with several spoons. "This is where we live when we're
not running our butts off," Teresa said. "Lou
lets us take a break whenever we can. In here,"
she opened a closet, not much bigger than the
one Molly had had at the trailer. Several boxes
were stacked on top of one another. Molly
stepped forward for a closer look.

"I'd say you're a size small," Teresa in-
formed her as she removed a box with a bold
black S on its end. "These uniforms tend to
run large, so don't worry if it hangs on ya now.
After a few washes, it'll shrink up." She removed a starchy white dress from the box.
Crease marks from the folds were clearly visible. "Lou insists on clean, ironed uniforms.
Today you can get away with it because it's your
first day." She held the uniform out to her.
"There's a restroom." She pointed to another
small door Molly hadn't seen when she had
first entered the break room. "It's for the women
only. The guys have to use the restroom in the
kitchen; you know how that is."

She didn't, but she took the white uniform
anyway. "I'll be right back."

She emerged from the restroom a few minutes later, her jeans and blouse carefully folded

in one hand, her purse in the other. The white dress was at least two sizes too big. The hemline hung well below her knees, the shoulders were too wide, and the waist would've fit someone three times her size. She waited for Teresa to notice.

"Looks pretty bad," she said. "But I can fix ya right up."

She rummaged through the back of the closet, then pulled out a small shoe box. "Lou's always prepared." Teresa removed a handful of white cloth belts from the box. "Try this."

Molly tied the belt around herself, cinching it in at her small waist. "This will work," she said. "Thanks." She didn't want Teresa to think she worried about her appearance. Truly, she was glad for the long, baggy-fitting uniform. She did not want to attract attention. This would ensure that no one gave her a second look.

"Okay, it's a bit ugly, but wash it tonight, toss it in the dryer, run an iron over it, and you'll look good as new. Now"—Teresa rubbed the palms of her hands together—"you've waited tables before, right?"

Molly nodded. "Tony's—" She caught herself. The last thing she needed to do was to reveal her former place of employment. "Tony's" would have to suffice. She doubted Lou would check references.

"Don't matter where, just as long as you have. Now, we use the spindle method. Orders are placed clockwise, and Houston, our head cook, hits the bell, then calls the waitress's name when the order is ready. We don't have a set formula for abbreviations. So long as Houston can read your handwriting, you'll be fine. No curlicues or smiley faces dotting your i's, either. Just print normally, and keep your eye on the customers and your ears on the kitchen. We'll have a lunch rush; we always do from noon till around two-thirty. You follow me. You can help with drinks and refills, removing plates when the customer finishes. Once I think you have a feel for it, you're on your own. As I said, whatever tips you earn are yours. We don't split tips. We don't take credit cards or checks; we're cash only. Lou pays us two bucks an hour, and we make up the rest to cover minimum wage, and not one penny extra. You familiar with this method?"

"Yes," she said, even though she wasn't. Her jobs had all been cash under the table, but she didn't feel the need to share this with Teresa.

"Lou'll have ya fill out a W-2 form when she comes back. You got a copy of your Social Security card? 'Cause she don't hire illegals."

Thankfully, her Social Security card was stuck to the back of her driver's license. "Yes, and I have a driver's license, too."

"That might come in handy, in case Lou needs something delivered. Once in a while we deliver lunch to a few of the doctors and professors at one of the colleges, MIT or Harvard. The restaurant has a car for deliveries, so having a license will make Lou happy. I personally don't drive. Never had to, living here."

Molly couldn't imagine not driving but didn't

say this to Teresa. For now, she, too, would use the public transit system.

She had to focus on remaining as anonymous as humanly possible.

Her life could very well depend on it.

Chapter Seven

Sally removed the last dinner plate, and Molly breathed an inward sigh of relief. She couldn't wait for the evening to end. She'd had a difficult time remembering all the names of all the doctors and their wives and had to devise a mental plan in order to do so.

Dr. Wolf was there with his fiancée, Liz, whom she would never forget because she chewed with her mouth open and wouldn't stop talking long enough for anyone to get a word in edgewise, so Molly mentally deleted her from her future guest list, of course with Tanner's approval. Then there was Dr. Marsden, along with his wife, Carolina, who owned three day-care centers in the city. She, too, talked non-stop about how important her work was, and after an hour of listening to the ins and outs of running a day-care center, Molly had visions of

cramming the centers *and* the children down
Ms. Marsden's throat. She'd smiled and com-
plimented her on her choice of careers. Something about Dr. Marsden bothered her, but she
didn't know what it was, or why the thought
even entered her head.

She had listened to Dr. O'Leary and his wife
of twenty years, Megyn, discuss what college
they wanted their son to attend. Both had decided Harvard was not the best college, having
both graduated from the prestigious Ivy League
school themselves. Megyn, who'd been seated
next to her, whispered, "He would never be accepted." Molly nodded and wondered about
Kristen. If this were the case, would she openly
admit that her daughter wasn't as intelligent as
others her age? Probably not, she thought.

While most of the doctors and their wives
were in their late thirties to middle forties, Dr.
Kent and his wife, Dianna, were old enough to
retire. She taught high school English at Boston
Latin Academy. She bragged about her students'
accomplishments, and said how much she would
miss them when she retired.

"Then why retire?" Molly asked, just to be
polite.

Dianna looked at her as though she'd lost
her mind. "Albert's retiring soon. I wouldn't
dream of working after he retired."

These were modern women, married to doctors. Didn't they have careers or retirement as-
pirations of their own? Not knowing what to
say, Molly simply smiled and took a bite of her
fish, trying not to think that, when push came

to shove, she really wasn't all that different from these women. And that led her to wonder if they had secrets, too.

Tanner chose that moment to clear his throat rather loudly. "This investment will be ideal for both of you. Guaranteed to provide you with a good return while you travel the world."

Dianna nodded but deferred to her husband. "Whatever Albert wants to do."

"I think it's time we took a vacation from our hectic lives. It's been so long since I've slept in, though truthfully I'm not sure I can any longer," Dr. Kent explained, laughing. "But I plan on doing my best to try to get used to the idea."

Jill Waters and her husband, Dr. Peter Waters, had barely uttered a word since they sat down to dinner. As hostess, Molly knew it was her job to encourage conversation, to make her guests feel comfortable enough to let down whatever barriers restrained them. "Dr. Waters, do you and Mrs. Waters have children?" This was always a safe question. Or so she thought.

Jill Waters, bland and pale, with white-blond hair and skin to match, shook her head. "It's Jill. Uh, no. We can't . . . we don't have children." She looked to her husband as though he should explain why.

Dr. Waters cleared his throat as Tanner had moments ago. "Jill can't have children, and I do not want to adopt. So, no, we don't have children. And frankly, in this day and age, I think of it as a blessing in disguise. Kids have no respect. Want the world handed to them on a silver platter." He stopped when he realized that all of the attention was focused on him. "Not that I dislike children," he added.

"Of course we love children," Mrs. Waters, *Jill*, added. "We've been blessed in other ways."

"Of course you have," Molly encouraged. "Children are often challenging, and not everyone is suited to parenting." The second the words came out of her mouth, she wished she could take them back.

"But then, there are those of us who are born to become parents," Tanner added none too kindly as he shot her a look that she called "the death look."

It was Tanner's idea of a challenge. She would go with it. He wouldn't dare show his true colors in front of their dinner guests. He should have told her that the subject of children was taboo where Dr. and Mrs. Waters were concerned.

"Yes, and children don't have to be flesh and blood in order to love them as your own." Molly had no clue why she said this since it was certainly not her experience. Maybe it was the truth for some, but it had stopped being true for her a very long time ago. A mental challenge to Tanner? Maybe. She held his gaze across the table's long expanse.

"Some would disagree," he said, continuing to focus his sharp blue eyes on her.

Backpedaling, Molly said, "I'm sure every situation is different."

"Kudos to those who can manage stepchildren or adopted kids. I'd be the first to say it's a mistake. Blood really is thicker than water," Dr. Waters added. "My father never let me forget this. Always told me to keep the bloodline going, didn't want an imposter tarnishing the family legacy."

Molly agreed to a certain point, but now wasn't the time to make her opinion known. Desperate to change the topic of conversation, she stood. "I'm going to serve dessert. Would anyone care for coffee, too?" Scanning the group gathered around the table, she gave a phony smile, and, not waiting for a reply, she headed to the kitchen.

Sally was putting plates in the dishwasher. "You finished with dinner already?" she questioned.

"Don't I wish. No, I'm going to serve coffee, and that red velvet cake I bought at Gloria's. Tanner won't like that since it's not homemade."

Damn! Why had she added that? Sally had enough to deal with in her own personal life. Molly knew she suspected that her relationship with Tanner was far from ideal, but it was very likely comments like this one that had led Sally to that conclusion, or so Molly assumed. Not that she'd ever mentioned her marital issues to Sally or spoke of them to anyone else. She didn't have to. Molly could read Sally like an open book. Sally was in a bad marriage, too. And as the old saying went, "It takes one to know one."

"It's homemade. Just not in your kitchen," Sally said.

She grinned. "I guess you're right. Gloria would tell me the same, I suppose. But . . . ," she didn't finish the thought out loud. *Tanner wouldn't see it that way.* She removed a stack of dessert plates from the cabinet and placed them on a serving tray, along with forks and spoons for the coffee. "You'll follow me with the coffee?" she asked Sally.

"Right behind you, Miss Molly."

She nodded, then hoisted the tray, using the palm of her left hand to carry the bulk of the weight, and her right hand to keep it steady. Old habits, she thought, as she plastered on a smile for her guests.

"I see my magnificent Molly has decided to tempt us with one of her homemade confections," Tanner said when he saw her placing the large tray on the sideboard.

She hated it when he referred to her as his "magnificent Molly"!

Bastard, she wanted to shout, but as usual, she refrained. "Sorry, sweetie pie," she used this term of endearment, knowing how he hated it, "but I didn't bake this. I purchased this at Gloria's earlier. I'm sure it's much better than any dessert I could make." Also, she wanted to add that, given his last-minute dinner demand, he was lucky she'd had time to prepare dinner, let alone dessert. But again, these negative thoughts, which seemed to be appearing more and more frequently in her subconscious, were simply that: thoughts. She would never put them into words.

She watched him. He was so predictable. His Adam's apple was bobbing, and his eyes were darting everywhere but at her. Flustered and ticked. Yes, once again, she'd displeased him. Later, she would hear about it, but now, if only for a short while, she could act as master, and he was her puppet. For a little while. Later, she would question her actions.

"Well, we all know that Gloria's is the best Goldenhills has to offer. Thank you, Molly. I should've suggested this myself."

She smiled and set the dark-red, four-layer cake, with at least an inch of cream cheese frosting, between the other items on the sideboard, where she proceeded to slice huge triangles and place them on the dessert plates. Molly knew it was a bit spiteful, but she wondered if these submissive wives would dig in to the high-calorie cake, or would they claim to be too full? Given her past experience with doctors' wives, she would bet on the latter.

"Jill?" She held out a plate for the vapid woman.

"Leave the dessert on the sideboard, Molly. If anyone wants dessert, they can get it themselves."

Embarrassed, but not enough to care, she nodded and put the plate down. Sally stood by the sideboard with the pot of coffee. "Just leave it there, Sally," Molly said, a very small way of one-upping Tanner. "If anyone wants coffee, they can help themselves to that as well."

God, she could not wait for this evening to end! She'd smiled so much that her cheeks were beginning to throb. She'd developed a headache the minute Tanner returned from the office, shouting commands over his shoulder as he raced upstairs to shower and change. She needed a break. Maybe she would go to Europe with Kristen. They were closer than most mothers and daughters, so she wouldn't mind. An idea to be considered. She'd mention this to Kristen later.

What was she thinking? As close as she and Kristen were, this was her high-school graduation trip! There was no way that she would want her mother tagging along. But Molly really needed time away, time to reevaluate her life. Time to reflect on her past.

Megyn and Dianna both helped themselves to cake and coffee. Bits of conversation flitted past her, but if she had been asked, she wouldn't have been able to repeat a word of what had been said. For some reason, she just couldn't stop thinking about her life. When had it become so frightening? So out of control?

"Molly, did you hear me?" Tanner asked, his voice louder than what was usually considered polite.

She blinked to clear her mind. "I'm sorry, I was thinking about . . . Kristen." She offered up a flimsy smile, hoping he'd soften his tone a bit. She really did not want to have an argument in front of their guests. "She's leaving for Europe tomorrow." She directed her words to their dinner guests, who were now scattered around the large dining room. Some were drinking coffee while others had gotten drinks from the bar. How had she missed this?

"Kristen is perfectly fine. I asked if we have more bourbon? Those silly drinks you made before dinner were disgusting." He said it just loud enough for Dr. Wolf and Liz to hear what he said and the tone of voice in which he said it.

Taking a deep breath, and again offering a smile, lukewarm at best, she replied. "I'm sure we have more in the pantry." With that, she whirled out of the dining room and into the kitchen. Sally was scrubbing the baking sheet she'd used for the fish.

"Sally, is there any more bourbon? Tanner's in one of his moods, says the drinks I made were terrible." Right then, she didn't care if Sally knew she was miffed.

"Of course. In the pantry. Bottom shelf, far right."

"Thank you," Molly said, and meant it. She'd stuff an extra hundred-dollar bill in an envelope for her on payday. Bourbon was Tanner's drink. She should've checked to make sure there was an extra bottle stocked in the bar in the dining room. In her defense, she figured her blackberry concoction would be enough alcohol. They were doctors, and it was a weeknight. Didn't they have patients to care for early tomorrow morning? They weren't all dentists, who worked nine to five. Well, who really cared, she thought, as she grabbed two bottles of the golden liquid. If they wanted booze, they could drink until dawn for all she cared. Molly placed the bourbon on top of the bar, hoping this would be the end of Tanner's stupid tirade, but experience told her that what had come before was just a warm-up for the main event.

He took the bottle, removed the cap, and liberally filled a rocks glass. "Here. This is for you."

She took the drink from him, her stomach knotting up. Tanner knew that she rarely drank, and when she did, bourbon was not her choice of drink. He glared at her, and she pretended to take a sip, just to appease him. She stared at him, then placed the glass down. "You finish it for me."

Molly turned away, felt his icy stare as she walked away. In the kitchen, Sally had cleaned all the pots and pans, the dishwasher was humming, and all traces of their combined dinner prep had been removed.

"Go on home, Sally. I'll take care of the dessert plates," Molly offered.

"I can stay if you want me to," Sally said. "It's not like I have anyone waiting on me at home."

Molly wondered if this was her way of telling her that for tonight she wouldn't be suffering any kind of punishment from her husband. She wanted to ask, but she couldn't deal with someone else's can of worms. Not tonight. She'd opened her own, and she knew it wasn't going to be pretty when their guests left.

"You've been on your feet all day. I'll take care of the rest of the dishes."

Sally dried her hands on a paper towel, then

tossed it in the garbage can beneath the sink. "If you're sure you'll be okay without me," Sally said, though it sounded more like a question to Molly. Almost as though she were asking her if she would be all right if she was left alone with Tanner.

Molly placed a comforting hand on the older woman's shoulder. "Thanks for caring, but really, I'm fine. The kids are here," she added. "I have to make sure Kristen is properly packed. You know how she is. She's likely to forget her undies." Molly smiled, wanting to reassure Sally that she really would be just fine.

"If you're sure, then I'll go on, but if you need me in the morning, just call. I won't be doing anything around my house. Roger is visiting his brother in Maine. He didn't say when he was returning, so I'm gonna enjoy having some time away from the old man."

Molly sighed, wishing she could trade places with Sally. "Then go on and enjoy your time alone. Take the next few days off. Once I get Kristen on that plane, there won't be anything for either of us to do here. I plan to catch up on some reading, maybe watch a few movies."

Molly hoped she sounded surer of her plans than she felt. Something was nagging at her and had been all evening. And it wasn't just Tanner's usual hatefulness. No, it was something more. She needed to think. She wanted to be alone with her thoughts. "Now, go on before I change my mind." Molly gave her a hug and walked outside with her to the old clunker parked in front of the house.

"Thanks, Miss Molly. You need me, I'm here," Sally reminded her.

Molly nodded, smiled, and closed the driver's door. She waved at Sally. A feeling of sadness overwhelmed her as she watched her taillights fade into two small pinpricks of red light. She stood at the edge of the lawn a few more minutes, then went inside, where she found Tanner waiting in the kitchen.

"Where in the hell have you been? You can't just walk out of here when we have a houseful of guests. Who the hell do you think you are?" Tanner grabbed her arm, squeezing so tightly she knew there would be bruises tomorrow.

Taking a deep breath, not wanting him to see how frightened she was, she replied, "I walked Sally out to her car. She was nervous. It's dark outside." She wanted to lie, to tell him Sally was frightened of her husband, too, but she didn't. She'd already stirred the pot one time too many tonight. "Please let go of me, Tanner," she said in as calm a voice as she could summon.

He released his grip and stepped away. "Get back in here and help me convince these men to invest their money in me. In us, Molly. Our future. The kids' futures." His glance softened when he spoke. "Please."

He was crazy. Of that Molly was certain. One minute he was about to twist her arm off, and the next, he looked like a little boy on the verge of crying. "Why?"

He clenched his teeth, his jaw tightening. His facial expression instantly went from sappy to angry. "Don't you ever ask me that again. Do you understand?"

Molly backed up against the sink, more frightened than she'd been all night.

"Sure, Tanner. Whatever you want."

"Let's go back into the living room together. It'll look better," Tanner suggested. In an amiable tone, he whispered. "I'm sorry, Molly."

She simply nodded and wondered who he was sorry for. He wrapped his arm around her waist and guided her into the living room. Their guests appeared content, gathered in small groups in the formal living room. At the end of the room was yet another bar. Molly was sure this one was fully stocked, as she'd done it herself a few days ago when Sally was dusting the shelves. She saw Tanner's favorite bourbon. The bottle was almost empty. Molly hoped Tanner hadn't consumed that much. He was already acting like a beast with the booze she'd seen him drink. Add more, and the beast became more like a barbarian.

Feeling like a guest in her own home, Molly saw Carolina Marsden and Dianna Kent huddled together in a far corner of the room. Knowing Tanner wanted her to mingle and make the wives happy, so they could convince their husbands to invest in Tanner's clinic, she walked over to the women. "Can I get either of you a drink? Maybe a soft drink or an iced tea?" She guessed that both were probably teetotalers.

"Thanks, I would love a Coke if you have one," Carolina said.

Molly turned to Dianna. "Mrs. Kent?" God,

she hated this evening and couldn't wait for it to end. She felt like a waitress.

Going back to her roots.

"A Coke sounds good," the woman finally said.

Molly smiled. "It does, doesn't it? I'll be right back." Before she had to indulge in any more useless chatter, she hurried to the kitchen. In the refrigerator, she removed three cans of Coke, filled three tall glasses with ice, placing them on another serving tray. Again, she was playing the role of waitress, servant, hostess, whatever one called it these days. She hoisted the tray on her shoulder as she'd done all those years ago at Lou's. In the past few weeks, she'd begun to think of her time spent at Lou's as "the good old days." Odd, how one's perspective can suddenly change. *Almost at the speed of light,* she thought sourly.

She set the tray down on the table in front of the two chairs where Dianna and Carolina were now seated. She pulled the tab on one of the cans. The liquid hissed as it met the ice. "Here you go," she said, placing two glasses on the table. She poured her own, then took a big drink. Her mouth was dry from nerves. She glanced at her arm, where Tanner's fingers had dug into her skin. Thankfully, there was nothing too visible, except for the red marks his fingers had made. "So, tell me about the trips you have planned." Molly directed her remarks to Dianna since she and Dr. Kent were retiring soon. Just making conversation. Didn't matter. As long as she obeyed. Out of the corner of her eye, she spied Tanner. He was watching her.

"I think we're going to start with a cruise. Albert says it will be relaxing, and we need to get used to that first." Dianna took a sip of her Coke. "I'm not crazy about spending four weeks on a ship. Hearing about all those people that turn up missing, well, I would rather do something else. Maybe a safari."

"Then you should," Molly encouraged.

Dianna stared at her incredulously. "I wouldn't think of it. Albert deserves this. He's worked his entire life."

"And you haven't?" Carolina joined the conversation.

One for the team, Molly thought as she waited for Dianna's response.

"Yes, but . . . my job. I was just a teacher."

"*Just* a teacher? That's one of the most important careers, bar none. Without good teachers, we wouldn't have doctors, dentists. I think you should tell your husband you don't want to go on a cruise. I'm sure he would take your feelings into consideration," Carolina continued, though her tone was softer and quiet. Almost caring.

"I think you should, too," Molly added as a show of support for something she truly didn't give a rat's ass about. If Dianna wanted to kiss her husband's royal rear end, then let her do it to her heart's content.

Then a little voice inside her piped up. *Isn't this what you've been doing for almost twenty years?*

No, she thought, *it was more than that.*

Survival. She'd had to survive.

Dianna shook her head. "I'm sure a cruise will be just as relaxing as Albert says. He's rarely wrong." She smiled and took another sip of her Coke.

"You must take lots of pictures then," Molly suggested. She was in the same club, so she might as well participate.

She'd no more had the thought when a crashing noise from above silenced everyone in the room.

"What the hell?" Tanner shouted as he ran upstairs. Molly followed behind, not caring that their guests were instantly hushed.

At the top of the stairs, Graham was huffing; his thick black hair stood wildly on end, and his eyes were almost double in size. He wore nothing except a pair of tattered jeans. His breathing was loud, labored.

"What in the hell is going on?" Tanner whispered harshly.

Graham turned his back on them. Tanner followed him into his bedroom, with Molly trailing behind, her heart beating so fast she feared she'd have a heart attack.

Dirty clothes were tossed in piles all over the room. The floor was barely visible. Books, magazines, beer bottles, and an empty pizza box added to the array of filth. A laptop lay open on the bed with an explicit sexual image so disturbing, a jolt from the past hurtled through her brain. Molly closed her eyes, stopping in the middle of the room.

"I asked you what's going on?" Tanner said, his voice rising a notch.

Graham had yet to answer, though this time he walked to the side of the bed that wasn't visible from where they stood and pointed to Holden, who was lying on the floor. "He's stoned."

"Damn!" Tanner said, then stooped down to lift Holden, another perfect match of himself, and tossed his limp body on top of the unmade bed. He placed a fingertip to his neck to check for a pulse.

"What's he on? What was that noise?" Tanner yanked Graham's arm. "Speak up, goddammit!"

Molly remained silent but assumed Holden was alive since Tanner hadn't started CPR or called 911.

"What the hell, how should I know?" Graham finally answered. "Get your goddamn hands off me!"

Tanner released his grip and turned his attention to Holden, who was, incongruously, wearing black dress slacks and a pale blue shirt. If one didn't know the circumstances, one would believe Holden to be a young businessman who'd simply fallen asleep. Tanner rifled through his pockets, tossing his wallet and keys on the floor. In his front pocket he removed a bubble packet of tablets. "What's this?" he asked, turning around to look at Graham.

"You're a doctor, Dad, figure it out."

Tanner squinted at the packet, then whirled

around and slapped *Molly* in the face. Stunned at the unexpected blow, she barely felt the sting. At a complete loss for words, she stood in the center of Graham's room, silent, too shocked to do anything but stare at what was going on around her.

"What kind of mother are you? Didn't you teach my son anything about drugs? Dammit, Molly, these could've killed him. If he dies, it's on your hands." Tanner crammed the packet into his pocket, then proceeded to arrange a limp, unconscious Holden into a semi-upright position.

Molly remained rooted to the floor. She placed her hand on her cheek, where she now felt the sharp burn from her husband's hand. Tanner generally did his best not to leave marks on her, but this time there was no doubt in her mind that there would be a bruise covering her entire cheek.

"Go downstairs and tell our guests Holden fell and is unconscious. Get them out of the house, and when you're finished doing that, bring up a glass of hot milk," he ordered. To him, she was just another piece of property. Something to use when needed. Like her mother had used her so many years ago.

Why had it taken over twenty years, including the months spent as the nanny for the twins, for her to realize that?

In a stupefied daze Molly turned around, ready to comply with his demand, when Kristen appeared out of nowhere, earbuds tossed over her shoulder. "Mom, are you okay?" she cried out when she saw her mother's face.

Molly had to clear her head. She took a deep, yet shaky breath and nodded. "Go back to your room," she whispered, barely aware of her own voice. "Please."

"No!" Kristen said, her voice masterful and commanding. "I'm not going to my room. Dad?" she asked in a loud voice.

"Not now, Kristen. Do as your mother said."

Tanner was seated on the edge of the bed, next to Holden, whose upper body he had propped up with pillows. His head was angled to one side, and his mouth was hanging open. Tanner stared at his watch, monitoring Holden's pulse. Then Tanner and Graham dragged Holden to the bathroom and got him to throw up. Tanner was sure this would help Holden to feel a little better. They then helped Holden back to his bedroom.

"No, Dad. I won't! I'm not like Mom!" Kristen's green eyes filled with tears.

Molly mentally returned to the scenario playing out in front of them. "Kristen, listen to your father." She sounded like an automaton.

She *had* taught all of the kids the dangers of drugs while they were in elementary school. She'd been diligent about making sure they all understood the effects of drugs and alcohol. She'd even attended the adult drug-education classes offered at Goldenhills High School, long before the boys were old enough to know about drugs. Kristen was just a baby, but Molly had wanted to learn as much as she could so she would be aware of the signs, if, God forbid, her children decided to experiment. That was so long ago that she'd forgotten about it until now. She'd never observed either Graham or Holden using, but she knew they were quite fond of booze. And now, with the twins almost twenty-two years old, there wasn't a damn thing she could do about it.

Tanner gently eased Holden against the pillows. His blue eyes were as cold as ice, his teeth clenched in suppressed rage. Molly knew this look well.

"Kristen, could you go downstairs and explain to our guests that Holden has suffered . . . a fall." It was all she could come up with. She was still in shock at Tanner's behavior.

"Did you hear what I said?" he asked, his rage mounting even more.

"Tanner," Molly whispered, touching a hand to her cheek. There wasn't time to allow the marks of his slap to disappear. "I'm afraid . . ." She didn't finish as she knew it was useless. Instead, she turned to Kristen. "Come with me." She gently escorted her daughter out of the room before Tanner or Graham could shoot more orders at her.

When they were halfway down the stairs, Kristen stopped and turned to face her. "Mom, are you going to let him continue to treat you this way? He's a bastard, and so are his damn sons." Kristen's eyes filled with angry tears. "I hate all of them!"

"Stop right now! He's your father, and Holden and Graham are your brothers." Molly couldn't let Tanner's and the twins' actions ruin her daughter's relationship with them.

"Mother," she whispered, though the word was harsh. "Don't you realize they've done nothing but bully and batter you your entire life? I don't like them, and I don't care if he's my father, and those creeps are, thankfully, only my half brothers. Holden is a total asshole. If you only knew some of the dirty little secrets he's kept from you, you wouldn't be so quick to defend him."

Molly took a deep breath and touched her cheek. She knew it was still red, as it continued to burn, but she had to put this aside, at least for a while longer. They had guests downstairs, and she needed to take care of them. "I need to dismiss the dinner guests. As soon as they're gone, we'll talk. I promise."

"Really, Mom? 'Dismiss'? That's so screwed up," Kristen stated in a none-too-kindly voice.

"Yes, it is, I know, but as soon as they're gone, we'll talk. Now, go to your room and wait for me," she said, offering up a halfhearted smile. Three steps down, she stopped, and looked up at Kristen, who was still rooted to the stairs. As quietly as possible, she said, "Lock your door."

Chapter Eight

Molly was greeted with ten pairs of curious eyes when she returned downstairs. Dr. Marsden was the first to speak.

"Is everything all right up there?" He nodded toward the staircase.

Taking a deep breath, she nodded in return. "Uh, yes. Holden seems to have had a bad fall. He's in a bit of pain, but Tanner is with him. I'm sure he'll be fine."

Molly could hear the lie in her voice but didn't really care. A million thoughts danced through her head, yet she couldn't focus on them now. She had to do as Tanner said. For now. Their guests had to leave. But how to ask them without offending them? That would be another mark against her in Tanner's mind.

Before she had another chance to speak, from the top of the stairs, Tanner's booming voice shattered the silence. "We need to get Holden to the hospital."

"Then it's worse than I thought. I'm sorry, if you all don't mind letting yourselves out?" she said, knowing that Tanner had no intention of taking Holden to the hospital. This was his way of showing her who held all the power. Just this once, she was actually glad.

Dr. Marsden stood. "If you're sure, then we should leave. Have Tanner call me when he's available. There is something he and I need to discuss." His dark eyes scanned her. Something about Dr. Marsden bothered her, but now wasn't the time to dwell on the matter.

"I'm sorry," she said. "We will do this another time." She walked over to stand by the front door. She felt like one of those doormen who guard the upscale apartments in New York City.

"You will let us know the outcome?" said Megyn O'Leary.

Molly was reminded of the movie she and Tanner had watched a few nights ago. He'd been too tired to see it to its end and had said something to the same effect.

"Yes, I'll make sure of it. Now, if we could get Holden to the hospital." She let the words hang in the air. One by one, the doctors and their wives, and one fiancée, Liz, who trailed behind Dr. Wolf, took their belongings and left. When Molly finally closed the door, she leaned against it, needing a minute to prepare herself for what was sure to be a knock-down-drag-out all-nighter.

"Get up here!" shouted Tanner from the top of the stairs.

Like the obedient wife she was, Molly raced up the stairs, taking them two at a time. Rooted in his position, Tanner hardly moved a muscle when he grabbed her elbow, squeezing so hard Molly was sure he would break it. She was about to scream when he let go. She let out a fearful breath but didn't say a word.

He pushed her toward the door to the master suite. "Stay put," he demanded.

Praying that Kristen had her earbuds in with her music blasting, she focused on her steps. One. Two. Three. She mentally prepared to escape to her safe place because she knew all hell was about to break loose. Drawing in a deep breath, she closed her eyes, giving in to the mental image. Sounds of waves crashing against a sandy shore, the warmth of the sun as it glistened in an azure summer sky. Puffy white clouds one could bounce on. The cool rush of the ocean teasing her toes as she lay on the warm, sugary sand. The moment the image began to soothe her, Tanner crashed through the door, slamming it against the wall so loudly that it caused her to jump.

His eyes were bulging, and sweat was beaded on his forehead and above his lip. He walked toward the king-size bed, where she sat like a little girl waiting to be punished. She looked down, as she couldn't look at him when he was like this. With his index finger, he jabbed beneath her chin, forcing her to look up at him.

"Is Holden all right or did you have to call 911?" she asked.

"He's feeling a little better and will be okay," Tanner replied. "I need an answer, Molly. Okay? I want a clear, concise answer from you. Do you understand?"

She nodded that she did.

"What?" he shouted. "Did you not hear what I just said?"

"Yes," she replied in a soft tone. "I couldn't help but hear you, Tanner." She wanted to add that Kristen, even with her earbuds playing loud music, probably heard him as well.

"Are you trying to be cute with me, Molly?" he asked, his voice hardened, dripping with sarcasm.

"No," she said. After almost twenty years of marriage, she knew that the less she said, the better it would be for her. *How pathetic was that?* she thought. If she were a very good girl, she would only be punished a little bit. But if she were bad, even just a little bit, she knew what would happen. And it was never pretty, though to Tanner's credit, he hadn't actually hurt her too often. Bastard.

Tanner stormed across the room, then back to the edge of the bed. "Do you realize what your lack of parental skills cost me tonight?" He leaned so close, the sweat from his upper lip dripped onto the tip of her nose.

"No, Tanner, but please tell me. I know you want to." If he planned to knock her around, she might as well make it worthwhile. She looked into his eyes. All she saw were two cold balls of steel-blue ice. Whatever humanity had ever existed in him before was nowhere to be found now.

He took a deep breath, then stepped away from where she sat on the bed. Molly gave up a silent thank-you as she watched him pace their room. He raked his perfectly formed fingers through his hair, a sign, she knew, that he was thinking. The thought had no more skirted around in her brain than, before she knew it, he was standing in front of her with his right hand raised above his shoulder. Before she could beg him not to, and for the second time that night, he backhanded her hard on the same cheek that still stung from the previous blow.

"Tanner," she cried out in a whisper, placing her hand on her burning cheek. "Stop it! Kristen can hear us." She hated using her daughter like this, but it had worked in the past. Tanner adored Kristen—most of the time, as long as she did as she was told. Sadly, the adoration was not reciprocated, not in the least. Tonight Molly had learned just how much her daughter loathed her own father.

"I don't give a good rat's ass who hears me! You got that, woman?" he sneered at her.

She hated it when he spoke to her this way as she knew what was coming next. He rarely deviated from his established pattern.

Molly nodded because she knew he expected her to. Just one more time, she thought to herself. One. More. Time.

"If I hadn't taken you away from Lou's, that shit-hole diner you loved so much, you'd still be slinging hash to us Harvardians. You're stupid, Molly. You know that, right?" He stopped criticizing her as he waited for her to answer.

She nodded.

"I can't hear you, Molly. What was that?" he persisted.

"I'm stupid," she whispered. Tears filled her eyes, and she tried her best not to let them fall, but they did anyway. She hated weakness of any kind. And right now, she hated herself for being too cowardly to stand up to Tanner. She told herself it was better this way. The kids were home. Tanner's abusiveness usually took a backseat when Kristen and the twins were around. Briefly, she wondered what recent event had caused him to change his habits.

"Say it like you mean it," he ordered, only this time he placed his hand on the lower half of her face and yanked her head upward so that she had no choice but to look at him standing in front of her.

Her mind was all over the place. Her past. Her present. Her future. Was this it? A life no better than the one she'd left behind so many years ago. The only difference this time around was that she had every material item a woman could want. A beautiful home. A daughter who was not only beautiful but smart and kind. She had designer clothes, purses that cost more than some people made in a month. Shoes that reeked of money. Shoes she rarely wore. A home that was envied by many. Things didn't matter to her, they never had. Had she simply traded one nightmare for another?

Another sharp slap to her face brought her back to her harsh reality.

Tears fell freely now, and she didn't care. She just wanted this to be over with. She prayed that just this once Kristen had her iPod's volume turned to the highest setting possible. To be caught by her daughter would be humiliating. She would never forgive herself. So with that thought in mind, she used the hem of her black dress to wipe her eyes; not caring that the dress cost four thousand dollars, she hiked it up even farther so she could blow her nose.

Tanner had released his grip when he slapped her. Now, he reached behind her and grabbed a fistful of hair, yanking her head back so hard she thought her neck would snap. "I can do this all night, *Molly.*" He said her name as though it were filth. "The question is, can you?"

If she had had a weapon, she would have used it on him now, but since she didn't, the only way out of this sick situation, albeit temporarily, was to give him what he wanted.

In a clear voice, loud enough for him to hear, but not loud enough for anyone listening to hear, she said, "I am stupid."

He released his death grip on her hair, only to place his hand around her neck. Sweat dribbled down his face, and Molly prayed he would keel over and die of a heart attack or an aneurysm. Something quick and immediate, with no hope of saving his life. Or even better, have a stroke that left him totally paralyzed for the rest of his life. At which point, she could put him away somewhere and leave him. She closed her eyes and prayed. Him or her. This could not continue. Her life was out of control. It had always been out of control, from the moment she laid eyes on Tanner all those years ago.

Had she known the path marrying him would lead her down, she might have returned to Blossom City and taken her chances.

Chapter Nine

Christmas, Boston

For the first time in eighteen years, Molly had her very own Christmas tree. After saving every penny she could, she and Sarah, now roommates, found an apartment they could afford, and they shared the expenses. Molly had been giddy with excitement ever since they'd moved out of Mrs. Garner's.

Sarah was only a year older and also came from a bad situation; at least that's the way she referred to it, though she'd never told Molly too much about her past other than it had been a nightmare. Understanding the need to keep the past in the past, Molly hadn't bothered to question Sarah, and it was because of this that they'd become so close in such a short time. And now they were sharing their very first Christmas together, just two young women on their own.

Sarah worked for a professor at Harvard and made a decent salary. Like Molly, she, too, wanted a place of her own, and they'd often spoken of this during their time at Mrs. Garner's. Together, they'd found this little hole-in-the-wall basement apartment that was conveniently located close to Lou's Diner and the university. It wasn't much, but to Molly it was home.

When she learned of Molly's move, Teresa gave the young women an old sofa. Molly was fairly handy with a needle and thread. On her day off, she'd taken the bus to Fabric World, where she'd purchased enough material to make a giant, soft, beige-colored slipcover for the sofa. Sarah purchased throw pillows in a rainbow of colors to brighten it up, and both had spent an entire night sanding and refinishing the hard-maple coffee table Teresa had thrown in with the sofa. Little by little, they were making the basement apartment their home.

Molly took a few steps back to examine the small tree. She'd splurged on a string of lights that were supposed to look as though they were actual candles. When they were heated by the small bulb, the ginger-colored liquid inside bubbled and the tip flickered like a candle. She'd seen them before in stores, but she'd never had the money to purchase her own set of bubble lights. Not a big deal for most, but to her, this expenditure was extravagant in the extreme.

Last night they'd spent the evening making Christmas ornaments out of flour and water. They used Christmas cookie cutters Molly borrowed from Lou's. Tonight they would paint them, then hang them on the tree when the paint dried. Molly thought the tree the most perfect ever with just the bubble lights, but she didn't tell Sarah this. She hadn't told Sarah that her family never had a Christmas tree. No, she could never reveal her true identity, not to Sarah, Teresa, Lou, or anyone else. She was Molly Hall. Maddy Carmichael had disappeared the night of her high-school senior prom, and if Molly Hall could help it, she would never return.

Molly heard Sarah's heels click-clack as she made her way down the steep flight of steps. She opened the door for her, knowing that her hands would be full with the paint supplies she'd borrowed from one of the art students she was friendly with.

"Let me help you," Molly said, taking two huge brown bags from Sarah. "What's in here?" Molly asked before she peered inside the bag. She saw small metal cans with a splash of color painted on each lid, paintbrushes, and several packets of notebook paper.

Sarah put the third bag down, closing the door behind her. She brushed her dark-brown curls away from her face. "This is dinner. It smells divine. I am so stinking hungry, I could eat an entire ham." She gave Molly a sheepish grin. Sarah Berkovitz was Jewish but in name only; she had explained this to Molly one night at Mrs. Garner's. When Molly questioned her, she learned that Sarah knew hardly anything about the Jewish faith.

They had this lack of knowledge of their religious backgrounds in common also, as Molly didn't always understand many of the things Pastor Royer preached. She and Sarah were just young women down on their luck, like a million others. In the past, Molly always agreed with Sarah when she would say that, and she still did. The past was history, and neither of them cared to relive it, much less to reveal their secrets.

"Then let's eat, so we can paint these." She waved her arm at the small kitchen table covered in homemade ornaments.

"Okay, let me change." Sarah disappeared into their shared bedroom while Molly removed the contents from the bag. She'd never smelled anything so delicious.

An aluminum pan covered with foil and a Tupperware container held a giant lasagna and a green salad. Inside a small brown bag were hot rolls, steaming with butter and garlic.

Sarah returned while Molly fixed plates for them.

"Who made this?" Molly asked. She knew what lasagna was, but she'd never had it before.

"Professor Whitton's wife, Ellen. He told me she thinks I need a little 'meat on my bones,' " Sarah said, as they took their plates a few steps into the small living area.

"She's right; you could use a few pounds," Molly said.

Sarah scanned her. "Yeah, well, it wouldn't hurt you to gain a few yourself."

They used the newly refinished coffee table as their dining surface since their kitchen table was covered with baked ornaments. They'd found twin beds for the small bedroom at a secondhand furniture store. The few articles of clothing they owned were stored in plastic bins at the foot of their beds. At the very bottom of Molly's container, now stored in a large brown bag, was the dress that reminded her of the worst night of her life. Soon she had to find a way to destroy it. When the holidays were over, maybe.

"After this meal, I'm sure to gain a pound or two," Molly said between bites. "I don't think I've ever had anything this tasty." She thought back to the nights in the trailer when she'd calmed her hunger pangs by gulping water from the bathroom sink.

Sarah just nodded, and they both finished their dinner in silence.

"I'll wash tonight," Molly said, taking Sarah's plate.

"Okay. I'll get the paints ready."

"This is so much fun," Molly said as she washed their plates and cutlery.

"You think washing dishes is fun?" Sarah asked. "There must've been something funky in that lasagna."

Molly laughed. "I don't mind washing dishes, but that's not what I was referring to. I was talking about painting and decorating the tree."

Sarah laughed. "It is fun. When I was a kid, I used to make ornaments with my grandma. I made the worst mess, but she never scolded me or hit me," Sarah explained, then went on wistfully. "Those were the best days of my life. I miss Grandma so much sometimes, it hurts to even think about her."

Molly nodded, hoping she would continue with stories about her grandma. She craved stories of happy families, of how they interacted. She'd had no real experience with families and values. Lenore, her mother, was so mean and cruel. Now that she'd been away from Blossom Hill for six months, she'd started questioning so many things in her life or the lack thereof. Mostly, she wondered who she'd injured or possibly killed the night she'd raced out of town.

When she thought about that night, she was horrified by what she had done, even though she herself had been a victim. There was no one to call and ask what had happened, no one she could trust. Well, there was Brett Lynch, but she wouldn't dare put him in a position that might possibly force him to lie for her. Because she knew that he would do whatever it took to protect her. He was probably out of his mind with worry. She'd been gone for six months, and as far as she knew, no one had come looking for her. She should have called Brett and told him what had happened. She didn't have to admit to anything more than running away. Even if one or more of those sick SOBs had been maimed or killed, Brett wouldn't know that it was she who was driving the car.

But then she realized that if that group of perverts survived, of course Brett would know she was responsible. She was the only seventeen-year-old girl in Blossom City with a rusty-red Mustang. She needed to either rid herself of that car or have it painted. Lucky for her, their apartment included an enclosed parking space, a rarity in Boston.

Drying the last dinner plate, she stacked it in the dish drainer. Sarah had placed several sheets of notebook paper under the ornaments. "I wondered why you had all that paper," Molly said.

"It was on sale for ten cents a pack. We don't have any newspapers, so I figured this would work just as well."

Sarah, all five-foot-nothing, had changed into a pair of faded Levi's and a burgundy-and-gray T-shirt with HARVARD in big block letters emblazoned across the front. With Sarah's dark, curly hair and whiskey-colored eyes, Molly was surprised when she learned that Sarah didn't have a boyfriend and wasn't interested. For a while she wondered if Sarah was gay, as she never went out on dates, but one night a few weeks ago, they'd had one of their late-night chats.

Sarah told her she wanted to be an attorney and start a career before she married and had a family of her own. Working as Professor Whitton's assistant, she was able to take one course per semester for free. She had to purchase her own books, but she was okay with that. She saved like a miser and told Molly her goal was to pay her own way through Harvard. Molly believed her, too. She was bright and full of ambition. Molly wished she had more of her confidence.

When they'd first met, Molly thought Sarah was extremely shy. And she was, until Molly got to know her. She was a great friend and roommate. She didn't ask questions about Molly's family or her past, and for this Molly was extremely grateful.

"Where should we start?" Sarah asked.

Their little dinette set was neatly arranged with cans of paint and brushes. Sarah had also thought to bring paper clips to insert through the little holes they'd poked through the dough before baking them so that they would be able to use the clips as hooks for hanging the ornaments on the tree.

For the next hour, they painted Christmas trees, bells, stars, Santas, and little gingerbread men. When the ornaments were dry, they placed them on the tree.

"I think this is the prettiest tree ever," Sarah said, with an ear-to-ear grin plastered across her face.

"It is, isn't it?" Molly agreed.

For a few minutes, both girls stared at the fragrant little tree all lit up, each lost in her own thoughts.

"I love it and could sit here and stare all night, but I'm on the morning shift, so I need to get some sleep," Molly said, wistfully.

"Me too," Sarah agreed. "I'll put the paints away. You can have the bathroom first tonight."

Molly grinned. Though they were cramped,

she loved having a place of her own and enjoyed Sarah's friendship.

Could it get any better than this?

Four o'clock in the morning came early, but Molly was used to getting up at the crack of dawn. She'd been an early riser most of her life. In Blossom City, she'd had to wake up early to study and clean the messes that Marcus and his thug pals made after a night of partying. Just the thought of Marcus and his friends made her sick.

She brushed her long blond hair, then tied it up in a ponytail. Her uniform was clean and ironed. She was grateful the basement apartment also had laundry facilities, where the residents could wash and dry their clothes for a dollar per load. She slipped into the work shoes she'd purchased at Sharp's last month and quietly made her way out the door.

The December air was bitter cold. She crammed her hands in her pockets and pulled her beanie down low to cover her ears. She found three others waiting at the bus stop, each bundled up in heavy winter coats, scarfs wrapped securely around their necks, leaving nothing exposed to the frigid air. She didn't have a heavy coat, just the light jacket Sarah had given her. She would look for one in the thrift shops as soon as she could.

At exactly 5:09 A.M., the Massachusetts Bay Transportation Authority bus stopped with a gush of exhaust fumes in its wake, the winding gears and brakes grinding as it came to a full stop. Molly dropped her coins in the slot and sat directly behind the bus driver.

It was a short ride to the diner, and in better weather, she preferred to walk, but it was too cold, and she couldn't risk getting sick. Eight minutes later, she stepped off the bus and hurried inside the diner through the back entrance. She was greeted by the smell of fresh coffee and frying bacon.

"Hey, girl, you look like you could use a cup of this," Teresa said, and handed her a mug of coffee when she entered the break room. Since Molly had started working at Lou's, Teresa had become a surrogate mother of sorts. Molly thought she was hysterically funny and enjoyed working with her.

"Thanks. It's colder than a well digger's you know what out there," Molly said, gratefully taking the mug of steaming coffee from her.

"Listen, kid, that coat you's got ain't gonna get you through a Boston winter. Now don't take offense, but I went through my closet last night and found this." She pointed to a large white plastic garbage bag on the beat-up sofa the employees used when they needed a quick break.

Teresa removed a full-length black wool coat out of the bag and handed it to her. "Think this should fit. C'mere, kid, let's try it on."

Molly was so touched she felt tears in her eyes. "You didn't have to do this," she said, while Teresa held the coat out for her to try on.

"Nope, you're right, I didn't. Frankly, I need

the room in the closet. I still got stuff from my high-school days in there, and I ain't gonna say how long ago that was."

Molly slid her arms into the warm wool coat and shivered, not because she was cold but because it felt so good against her skin. "Are you sure? This looks expensive."

"I'm sure, and it was expensive at one time, but who cares? It doesn't fit me anymore, I'm getting too fat, so it's all yours, kiddo."

Teresa was tough as nails, but she truly had a kind heart. The more time Molly spent with her, the more she cared for her. It was a strange feeling to have an adult looking out for her. If anything, it had always been the other way around with her and Lenore. Or, at least, it was never the case that her mother looked out for her. She kind of liked being looked after.

Molly removed the coat and carefully hung it in the small employee coat closet. "Thank you so much, Teresa. You've already done too much for me. I really can't thank you enough. I was going to see about getting a warmer coat, and now I don't have to. And you're not fat," Molly added, smiling, a real, genuine, from-the-heart smile.

"Glad to be of help, kid. Now, today's the start of Christmas break, so prepare to run your legs off. Tips will be good, and remember, don't let any of those smart-ass Harvard kids give you a rough time. I've heard a couple of them talking to you like dirt."

Molly nodded. She knew the incident Teresa

was referring to, but it hadn't really bothered her all that much. Just two girls her age making fun of her southern accent. She didn't care, but again, it was nice to know that Teresa had her back. She'd dealt with far worse, but she definitely kept that thought to herself. She had been working very hard to get rid of her accent by observing the customers and thought she had made a lot of progress.

She finished her coffee, rinsed her mug, and placed it in the dish drainer. She took a fresh pad from the stack on the desk and made sure she had at least two sharp pencils in her apron pocket. She removed her hair from its ponytail and braided it, then clipped the braid to the top of her head. Hair and food were a bad mix, according to the health department's notice posted in the ladies' room. When she had waitressed at Tony's BBQ Pit, they'd had to wear hairnets, so she was familiar with the rules of restaurant cleanliness.

"You okay, kid?" Teresa asked.

Jolted back to the here and now, Molly shook her head. "I'm fine. I was just thinking about . . ."—she couldn't tell her what she was really thinking about, so instead of the truth she said—"cutting my hair off."

"Don't you dare! That's the prettiest head of hair I've seen in years. And the color is real. Women would kill for your hair. Don't you go cuttin' if off, ya hear?"

"I promise," said Molly. "I'd best make sure my tables are set up. You need anything?"

"Nope. I'll unlock the door in a few minutes," Teresa said.

Six in the morning, come rain or shine, the doors opened for business. Teresa was the only one besides Lou who had keys to the place, at least as far as Molly knew. Once they unlocked the door, the customers practically bombarded the place. Molly liked working the breakfast and lunch shift. Time went by fast, and she really did enjoy the work. Some might think the job unrewarding, but she liked seeing the looks on her customers' faces when she delivered a big plate of steaming hotcakes with butter melting down the side or sunny-side-up eggs with bacon still sizzling on the plate. The smell of fresh coffee permeated the entire restaurant.

Molly now associated the smell of coffee with happiness. She'd never say this out loud, but it was true. For the first time since prom night, Molly had a bit of hope for her future.

She checked her tables, making sure the salt and pepper shakers were full and clean, the little red-and-black square box held packets of sugar and sugar substitutes, the flatware shone, and the napkin holders were filled. She grabbed cups and saucers from a rack and quickly placed them on all the tables. She'd started the four giant coffeemakers and was ready for the early birds the minute Teresa unlocked the door.

For the next hour, Molly took orders, delivered plates stacked high with omelets, hotcakes, sausage, and toast and a dozen other combinations. Glasses of orange juice were free if you ordered the hash special, so when she had an extra minute she stood behind the counter and filled several small glasses with juice so they wouldn't have to stop and pour every time they had an order for the special. Just one of the little tricks she was learning from Teresa.

"Molly Hall."

When she heard her name, she turned around so fast she knocked three of the juice glasses over, sending a waterfall of orange juice across the bodice of her uniform.

"I wish all the girls lost their cool like you when I said their name," came the voice of none other than Dr. Tanner McCann.

Molly rolled her eyes and turned her back to him. For some reason, he gave her the creeps even when he teased her. "I'll be right with you," she said as she tried to wipe the stain from her uniform.

"I really would like a cup of coffee. Now," he said flatly.

Molly tossed the wet towel on the counter, grabbed the pot of coffee, and filled the empty cup in front of him.

"You're going to be miserable the rest of the day, you know that?" he said, eyeing the spill.

"I'll be fine," she answered, though she knew the wet material would irritate her skin. She wore nothing underneath except her bra and panties, with a small half-slip Sarah had lent her. She'd ask Teresa if she could lend her another uniform for the day.

"Excuse me," she said, and headed toward the double doors.

"Wait!"

She stopped and turned around. The doctor looked annoyed. *Crud*, she thought. He really was bossy, but she wouldn't say this either. She had to keep this job, no matter what. She walked back to the counter and gave him her best smile.

"I'm sorry. Did you need something else?" He never ate breakfast lately, only drank black coffee.

"Yes, I do," he said, returning her smile.

He was handsome, Molly would give him that. But he was too old for her and sort of a jerk.

She took her pad from her apron pocket. "What would you like this morning?" She said the same words she used with almost all of her customers.

"You really don't want to know. But I would like breakfast today. What's good here?" He asked as if this were his first time at Lou's, even though he had coffee there almost daily.

She took a deep breath and tried to appear as if she were really considering his question. Everything was good at Lou's, but he was picky. She knew because he'd refused his coffee more than once when Teresa waited on him, telling her the cup was dirty. Molly knew better, but Teresa knew how to handle customers like him.

"The hash is good," she said, trying to push the special because that was always the fastest.

"No, I hate that. When I was in foster care, one of the homes I was sent to had a crappy version of hash every day, and I swore I would never eat it again. Now, tell me what you like?"

Had he really been in foster care? And now he was a doctor. *Pretty impressive*, she thought. "You've seen me eat, remember?" She saw someone at one of her tables motion for a refill. "The blueberry pancakes are the best, with bacon."

"Then I'll have that," he said.

She quickly wrote up his order, placed it on the spindle, and hurried to the table in need of a refill. The good doctor didn't seem to realize she had other customers. Teresa usually took the entire counter, but one of the part-time girls, Nancy, needed some extra hours, so she'd let her take the counter, and Molly was to handle whatever customers Nancy couldn't get to. She wasn't the most experienced waitress, but Molly liked her. Too bad she hadn't got to the doctor first, she thought, but hey, this is what she was paid to do.

Conversations droned in the background, with the occasional hoot of laughter. Silverware clicked against plates. The cha-ching of the register was almost nonstop.

"Order up, Molly," shouted Houston, whose voice was loud enough to be heard outside.

Hurrying to the window, she saw the doctor's order waiting for pickup. "Thanks," she said to Houston.

She placed the hot plate in front of the doctor. She pushed a bottle of maple syrup next to his plate. "Enjoy," she said, then hurried away before he could say anything more to her.

For the next fifteen minutes, she delivered orders, refilled coffee cups, chatted with her customers, and cleared off tables when Mike, their busboy, was too busy. She liked the fast pace because she had to stay alert, and this kept her mind off the secrets and lies that had brought her to the Boston area in the first place.

As she finished cleaning off one of the tables, she was carrying a tray of dirty dishes in one hand and an empty coffeepot in the other.

"Molly Hall," said the doctor, who stood by the door as he was leaving.

Startled, she dropped the tray, sending egg-covered plates smashing to the floor. "Oh my gosh," she said, then dropped the empty coffeepot. Her hands shook. She scanned the area to make sure the glass hadn't flown into anyone's plate or where someone might step.

Teresa came to her rescue. "Oh, kid, this stinks, but don't you worry. We've all had it happen at one time or another." She had a broom and dustpan and began sweeping up the broken glass.

"I'm sorry, I jumped when . . ." She was afraid to tell her why. "I'm clumsy today."

As Molly stooped and picked up the large pieces of glass, Teresa whispered in her ear. "You dropped the dishes because that dingbat doctor practically screamed your name. I heard it, kid. Something about that man I can't put my finger on. He's a bit odd."

Molly could have kissed her for saying that, but she didn't. "Well, he is quite a character," she said, even though she agreed with Teresa's version. He *was* somewhat of a dingbat, she thought, but there was a part of her that felt sorry for him. Maybe he was lonely. He obviously didn't have a family, or he would be with them at this early hour. Didn't doctors keep weird hours, though?

"Hey, I didn't mean to get you into trouble," Dr. McCann said.

Molly felt her face turn a dozen shades of red. Teresa stood up, the broom in one hand, and a glass-filled dustpan in the other. "Look, mister, I don't appreciate your hollering at my girls. That is why she dropped the tray. If you need something in the future, be patient, and one of us will get to you as soon as we reasonably can."

Molly didn't know what to do, so she stood next to Teresa, waiting for instruction. "Molly, tend to your tables."

Thank goodness, she thought as she rushed away from the mess. Behind the counter she grabbed a dishcloth and began scrubbing the nearby surfaces. She didn't need any attention drawn to herself.

"I'm really sorry, Molly. If you'd work for me, you wouldn't have to clean up people's leftovers."

She jerked her head up to stare at him. Momentarily at a loss for a reply, it took a few seconds for her to gather her thoughts. "I like my job here. I don't want to work anyplace else."

He smiled at her. He had the most perfectly even, white teeth she'd ever seen. He was good-looking, but she knew firsthand that looks were deceiving. Ricky Rourke had been one of the best-looking guys in her school.

"Not even for a thousand dollars a week?" he asked.

Hunger and her future were at stake. "Doing what?"

"My wife recently died, and I have twin boys who need to be cared for."

One thousand dollars a week. She'd never earned that much money in her entire life!

Quickly, before she could change her mind, she said, "I'll need to give Lou a month's notice."

Dr. McCann held his hand out to her. "You're hired."

Part Two

Seeking what is true is not seeking what is desirable.
—Albert Camus

Chapter Ten

It was after three in the morning when Tanner decided to call it quits. He'd refused to let her leave their bedroom and had spent the last several hours telling her how stupid she was. He'd gone downstairs once, and she'd tried to sneak out of the room, but the bastard returned carrying a bottle of bourbon just as she was trying to slip away into Kristen's room.

"Uh-uh," he said, and caught her by the arm, practically dragging her back to the master bedroom.

"Tanner, I'm tired, please stop. You need to rest," she said, her tone void of all emotion. Her life was a disaster.

"Then let's go to bed," he barked, loud enough to wake the dead.

Knowing it would be useless to argue, she nodded. She took off her ruined black dress, tossing it on the floor. She didn't bother with a nightshirt. He'd probably want to have sex just to prove he could do whatever he wanted with her. Nothing surprised her anymore. She crawled between the one-thousand-thread-count Egyptian cotton sheets Tanner preferred, rolling to her side. He flopped down next to her, slinging his arm across her belly, and pulling her close to him as though she were a piece of property belonging to him only. She felt his erection against her. Tears filled her eyes. Please God, she thought, not this. Not tonight.

She lay still, not daring to move. Slowing her breathing, she hoped Tanner would assume she'd fallen asleep instantly. Molly rarely slept a full night unless she took a sleeping pill, and she didn't like to take them often, but there were times when she had to simply in order to function the next day. Inhale. Exhale. Slowly and quietly. She counted in her head. When she reached fifty-nine, she felt Tanner's arm relax and loosen his possessive hold. When he drank, he sometimes snored. A low grumble came from him. She'd never been so glad to hear him snore in her life.

She had to get away from him. Soon. Her life was in shambles. If only she hadn't accepted his job offer all those years ago. If only she hadn't married him almost a year later, but then she wouldn't have Kristen. All the mental and physical abuse was worth it when she factored her daughter into the equation. She'd never loved anyone as much as she loved Kristen. What would she do when Kristen went to college? She would go completely insane. It frightened her to think of life without her daughter close by every day.

Carefully, so as not to wake him, she eased his arm aside, then carefully scooted, an inch at a time, toward the edge of the bed. She stopped to listen to his breathing to make sure he was still sleeping. The continuous rhythm assured her that he was out cold. Not giving herself time to overthink her situation, she sprung from the bed and hurried down the hall to Kristen's room. She didn't bother knocking for fear Tanner might wake up. Since the door opened when she turned the knob, either Kristen had not locked the door when she was told to or had unlocked it before she went to sleep, confident that her father was too busy with her mother to bother her. Inside, she closed the door as quietly as possible, then locked it behind her.

"Mom," Kristen asked in a sleepy voice, "are you okay?" She pushed the covers away and sat up in her bed, fully awake now. "Mom?"

Molly placed her finger to her lips. Kristen nodded, then moved over so Molly could get in bed with her. "I can't talk about this right now, Kristen, not in this house."

"Mom," Kristen whispered, a tone of urgency in her voice, "what did he do to you now? I know he hits you."

Molly was stunned by her daughter's words. She thought she'd kept Tanner's abuse secret. It wasn't like he hit her all the time.

"Your father gets angry sometimes. He's . . ."

She wouldn't make excuses for him, not even to his daughter. "There's something wrong with him. He's always been a bit of a loose cannon. At least with me." Molly stopped as she tried to recall others who'd been victims of Tanner's temper. That included almost everyone he came into contact with on a daily basis. She knew he had the reputation of being a slave driver. If you worked for Tanner, in any of his clinics, you worked. There were no fun times, no employees forming friendships. No paid holidays, no parties, and Tanner worked all holidays except Thanksgiving and Christmas. If he could have persuaded—rather, ordered—his employees to work on those two days, he would have worked then also.

Molly felt a chill and realized she was wearing nothing but her bra and panties. She pulled the sheet up to her neck.

Kristen got out of bed and quietly made her way over to her chest of drawers. She opened the top drawer and removed a long, flannel nightgown. "Here, put this on." She climbed over her mother and slid beneath the covers.

Grateful, Molly put the gown on, yet still she was chilled. Nerves, she thought as she pulled the covers up again. She needed to think. She could not continue living like this. Once Kristen was away at college, it would be open season for Tanner and the twins. The odds of their finding a job and their own place to live were slim. Why bother to leave a house where there was no discipline and you could abuse your father's wife to your heart's content?

And even if they did move out, she didn't want to be alone in the house with Tanner. Sally was in and out, but Molly didn't expect her to come to her defense every time she needed her. Sally's situation was much like her own, economics be damned. She used to think money could solve any problem—well, almost. She hadn't been, nor was she now, that naïve. However, now she knew better. Money might pay off the mortgage and allow one to freely shop whenever the urge hit, but money couldn't fix people who were broken. Nor could it make a disaster of a marriage into something else. Her and Tanner's marriage had been a disaster for a very long time.

"Mom, do you want me to tell Charlotte I can't go? Because if you do, I will." Kristen placed her head on her mother's shoulder. Molly embraced her, breathing in the clean scent of her freshly washed hair.

"Sweetie, I would never ask you to do that. This is your high-school graduation trip. I want you to go. See the world, make memories. Life is too short. I want you to do all the things I dreamed about but didn't get to experience."

The room was quiet except for the sounds of their breathing. What was a cheerful, typical teenager's room in daylight was now filled with dark shadows, hulking creatures, and wispy ghosts. Molly was letting her imagination take hold of her. Of course there were no creatures or ghosts. It was simply the large chest of drawers, the desk, and the white-lace curtains billowing in the breeze. Kristen always left her window open in the summer. The ghosts and creatures were in her mind, had always been there lurking, waiting to be heard, to be rediscovered, to be found.

"Mom," Kristen asked, her voice filled with concern. "What's wrong? You're too quiet."

Molly took a deep breath. There were so many things wrong on so many levels, it would take a lifetime to put them into words. "I'm upset with your dad. I wish there was someone he would talk to. He's just so . . . private."

She really knew very little about Tanner's past. His parents had been killed in a house fire when he was six. After their deaths, there'd been no family members to care for him, so he became a ward of the state. He spent most of his years in one foster home after another. She knew he'd been a difficult child from the stories he told her, though she never admitted this to him. After he told her the story of the fire, he refused to talk about it whenever she'd broached the topic. Tanner had gone into a rage the last time, right after Kristen was born.

That was the first time he hit her. She'd just had his child, and she'd wanted to know about Kristen's grandparents, her history. A punch in the gut said the topic was off-limits forever. She never asked him anything about his past from that day forward. The only positive outcome was that he never asked about her own past. So it was convenient for both of them.

Tanner was fond of saying, "My life began the first time I saw you," especially when they had guests. Molly had never believed him; she was much too smart to fall for any of his false endearments, especially one so over-the-top. Tanner had courted her with the lure of a better life, never doing without, and a ready-made family. Looking back, she realized how important those things had been to her. Security. A family. Normalcy. He'd tied an attractive bow around the package of rotten goods that he was really offering, and she'd taken the bait.

She'd spent the best years of her life with Tanner. She really tried to be a good mother to Holden and Graham, and it had worked for a while. But as the boys aged, Tanner's verbal abuse increased. And the way he treated Molly in their presence only encouraged them to treat her as if she were some sort of servant, not their stepmother, much less their mother.

Yes, he would smack her or shove her around, but only when they were alone. But then came the plate incident. And Molly feared him even more now. If she were totally honest with herself, she was afraid of the boys, too, especially now that she knew drugs were involved. She was thankful Holden hadn't killed himself by overdosing, but she knew there would be other times. This was only the beginning.

Kristen adjusted the covers, arranging herself so that she lay on her side, with her head in her hand. "Mom, there's something I think you need to know, but I don't know if I should tell you. Especially now."

Molly rolled to her side to face her daughter. "Kristen, please, whatever it is, I'll deal with it. And why wouldn't you tell me now?"

Though she knew the answer. Kristen didn't want to burden her. She was like that.

"It's about Holden," she whispered.

If he's touched her, I will kill him!

"Okay," she said, letting Kristen tell whatever it was in her own way.

"This is so horrible, I hate to say the words. You know he's into roofies, big-time?"

In fact, she hadn't known that, not until tonight's episode. Apparently she had been walking around with blinders on. "Go on," she encouraged.

"You remember Charlotte's cousin, Lucinda?"

Molly nodded. "Wasn't she here last year for Christmas break? Seems like I remember her being here with Charlotte."

"Yeah, she was, but she wasn't here just to hang with me and Char." Kristen had started calling Charlotte "Char" way back in elementary school, and the nickname had stuck. "She really wanted to see Holden. They were at Harvard together."

Molly had no clue where this was going, but she knew her daughter well enough to let her tell the story in her own way. Kristen could be very wordy at times when she wasn't prepared.

"I didn't know that," she said, hoping it would encourage her to get to the point. If Holden was involved, she knew that it couldn't be good.

Kristen took a deep breath. "Lucinda's best friend"—she paused—"her friend Emily, said Holden attacked her."

It took a few seconds for Molly to absorb her

words. When she did, an ice-cold fear twisted in the pit of her stomach. She remained silent, trying to gather her thoughts, yet all she could think of was what had happened to her all those years ago. On prom night. And now this. Surely, this Emily was mistaken?

"Mother, aren't you going to say anything?" she said more loudly.

Molly sat up in bed, pulled her knees to her chest, and rested her head on top of them. She swallowed, but her mouth was as dry as desert dust. Flashes of that night played out like a movie reel. The dress. Her car. The rape. The accident. After all this time, what if she'd killed her twin or one of his friends? She could be a murderer and not even know. And now her stepson was being accused of the lowest crime in the world.

"Mom!" Kristen said, this time not bothering to whisper.

Jolted out of her nightmarish thoughts, Molly spoke. "Shhh, I don't want to wake your father." There would be hell to pay. "I'm sorry. Tell me again. What happened?" She spoke in short, choppy sentences.

"It's nauseating, Mom, really. I don't like to think about it, but you know, I'm going to Europe and all. I just want to, you know, tell someone, just in case." She was hesitant as though she were afraid to speak.

"Kristen, whatever you tell me will remain between the two of us. You can trust me," she said, hoping to loosen her tongue a bit. Kristen was extremely loyal to those she cared about. It was more than obvious that Holden was not in that category.

"Lucinda wanted to confront Holden about it, but he'd left. I don't remember where he went, but she wasn't here for the tea and cookies. She was totally pissed about what Holden had done to Emily.

"Sorry, but that's the only way to describe it. I don't know what she'd planned to do, just that she was mad. So she says Emily and Holden were both at Racer's, you know, the club?"

She nodded. Molly had never been there but knew it was quite popular with the college crowd.

"Holden has a nasty rep, truly. No one likes him. I'm almost ashamed—no, I *am* ashamed—that he's my brother. I'm just thankful he's just my half brother. Anyway, he's got this rep with the girls, you know? Not a good one, either. He's a real male chauvinist pig."

Like father, like son, Molly wanted to add, but held her tongue. Kristen did not need to hear her say such a thing about Kristen's father.

"He has this weird sense of entitlement with girls. Holden thinks all women want him, and that no means yes." Kristen stopped. "You know about that, right?"

She shook her head. "If you're talking about sex, of course I know." *Very well.*

"So Emily meets Holden at the club, they hang out for a bit. Lucinda said he bought several drinks for Emily—three or four, she wasn't sure, because they were there having fun, and she figured Emily was an adult and she didn't

need to look out for her. She said that a couple
hours later, when it was time to leave, she
started searching for Emily and couldn't find
her. She looked in the restroom, asked the bar-
tender if he'd seen her leave, and no one had
any clue where she'd gone. Lucinda told us
she'd been a little drunk but sobered up when
she realized that Emily was missing. They'd
taken Emily's car, so she figured she was outside in the parking lot waiting for her. Lucinda
saw her car, and when she tried to open the
doors, they were all locked. She thought maybe
Emily had gone home with someone, but she
told us that Emily always tells her if she's gonna
hook up."

"Go on," Molly said, though she knew where
the story was heading.

"So she hears this sound and realizes it is
coming from the trunk, and she freaks out.
She tries to get in the car, runs around again to
make sure all four doors are locked, and when
she realizes that it is *Emily* she hears in the
trunk, she calls the cops, and they call the fire
department. They were able to unlock the
trunk. Lucinda said Emily was totally nude, her
clothes nowhere to be found. The cops tried to
write up a report. Lucinda said no, this was a
college prank, told them she was sorry for the
call, blah, blah, blah. When Emily was sober or
whatever, you know, when she wasn't stoned
from the dope, she told Lucinda that she'd
been roofied by Holden and he raped her."

Kristen hesitated, then went on. "Mom, he
needs to go to jail for what he did to Emily."

Molly was stunned. She took a deep breath, then another. "Who else knows about this?"

"I don't know, but there's more," Kristen said. "I guess Emily is pretty tame, if you know what I mean? Later, she told Lucinda that she was pregnant, and that the baby was Holden's."

"Dear God! What . . . where is the baby?" Shocked by the news, Molly broke out in a sweat, and her hands were shaking so badly that she tucked them beneath her so Kristen couldn't see how upset she was.

"That's just it, there is no baby. Lucinda said that Emily had a miscarriage."

"Did she report this to the authorities?"

"I don't think so. They would've questioned Holden, and with his big mouth, the entire city of Goldenhills would've known by now."

She was right about that. Holden did like to boast. Just like his father. It was one of the reasons he'd invited his doctor pals over for dinner last evening. If he had an operation big enough to attract investors, it would make him feel worthy and important. He once told her the only reason he wanted to become a doctor was to impress people. Doctors were highly respected.

He'd also explained to her that being a dentist was, hands down, the part of the medical profession where money could be made without the hassle of being on call and opening the door to lawsuits. Dentists were a much better breed, he'd said.

She might have thought so at one time, but not anymore. Tanner was so self-centered.

She'd spent the better part of her life with a man she barely knew. And raised his sons. But, of course, there was Kristen. When had her marriage turned so sour?

"Is Emily all right?" Molly knew firsthand how one vile act could change a person for the rest of her life. Emily would never be all right.

"According to Lucinda, she's okay, but Lucinda told Charlotte that Emily wasn't the same person since the attack. She said the only time she left her apartment was to go to work. She said she refuses to go out socially anymore. I think Holden's dangerous, and he should be punished for what he did to Emily. Guys who force themselves on women make me sick."

Had she come full circle? Is this what that phrase meant? She didn't know, but she knew that now wasn't the time to try to figure out idioms.

How she wished she could speak as frankly as her daughter just had. Had she been able to, her life might have taken a different course. But it was what it was, and she could only go forward. She needed to think. Maybe she could tag along with Kristen and Charlotte, act as a chaperone. She'd keep her distance, and it would give her time to think and plan.

"Don't you think Dad needs to know about this?"

Hell no! she wanted to shout, but didn't. "Not now. I need time to digest this. It's tragic, to say the very least. Possibly I could pay for counseling for her. Has anyone reached out to help her?"

"You don't get it, Mom. She can't prove anything. It's her word against Holden's, and where Holden is involved, Dad's involved. So basically, she is screwed. Dad's solution would be to pay her off."

"As much as I hate to, I agree with you. Your dad isn't very forgiving. Holden and Graham are his trophy sons. You know how he is with them."

"Yeah, and it disgusts me. I'm glad he doesn't treat me like a twelve-year-old mentally challenged kid, the way he does them. Of course, I don't act like those two. They're bullies, and I'll be glad when I leave for college."

Molly's heart broke a little more with Kristen's words. She wanted Kristen to see the world, but she also wanted to keep her close by. She wanted to keep her safe, and she wanted to keep her secrets safe.

"I think you should tell Charlotte to try to convince the girls to report this to the police. I don't know how it works"—*and by all rights I should*—"but it's the right thing to do. Maybe they could remain anonymous.

"I hate the thought of your leaving, you know that?" She offered up a halfhearted smile. Molly secretly hoped Kristen would invite her to tag along.

"I know, but I promise to Skype every day, just like we discussed," Kristen said. "It's only eight weeks, Mom. You could spend the time in the kitchen with Sally. I'll need lots of goodie boxes once I'm at Vanderbilt."

Kristen wanted to be a doctor and had been

accepted at Vanderbilt University in Tennessee, her first choice. Molly was so proud of her. However, she hated the thought of her daughter being so far away. She could've gone to Harvard but was adamant when choosing colleges her junior year. She didn't want to attend college in Massachusetts. She'd received several small scholarships, and Tanner had volunteered to foot the bill, the same as he had for Holden and Graham. Molly felt sure Kristen would use her degree. She wanted to study pediatrics. She was so proud, yet sad, too. Again, Molly's life was changing. She would go with the flow, but she, too, was about to make a major life change.

"Charlotte's meeting us at the airport. Promise you won't tell her you know about Emily?"

"I wish they would go to the police, but for now I'll respect their privacy." And Molly wondered if she would ever be able to look Holden in the eye again. Just thinking of what he was accused of made her sick. Knowing how it felt to be a victim made her even angrier. She wouldn't speak of this now, but in the future, she would do her best to see that Emily reported the rape. If she didn't, it would haunt her for the rest of her life. She knew this from personal experience. And she wanted to see Holden in jail, where he belonged.

"Thanks, Mom. I knew I could trust you."

"I'm reluctant, but I'll keep it between us for now, though I wish they would report this to the authorities. What if it happens to another girl? I don't think I can look at Holden now." She shouldn't have said that, but it was the truth.

"Graham isn't much better. I don't think he's attacked any girls, but he's got a bad rep, too. His temper. He's been in a lot of bar fights. I don't know how those two keep all this crap from Dad, or you. They give me the creeps," Kristen said.

What to do? Molly lay next to her daughter, her mind running in circles. Should she confront Tanner? Or Holden? Maybe if they thought she knew, Holden would be a bit more careful? Graham, too?

No, she answered her own questions. If Tanner knew, and if he knew that Kristen had told her, Kristen would pay the price. Knowing Tanner as she did, he would most likely refuse to pay for her college education. No, she had to keep this secret safe. As safe as the secret she'd carried with her for just over twenty-one years. No secret was safe forever, though she'd been more than fortunate to keep her past in the past. Even now, even with the Internet, her secret remained hers.

As tempting as it was to log onto the Internet and search, she'd never Googled her former name because not knowing what had actually happened on that dark road all those years ago is what kept her from losing her mind. Besides, Tanner had a habit of checking her Internet history. She couldn't risk his finding out who she had been. There would be too many questions.

And if he were to discover the truth, her life

as she now knew it would be over. Which wasn't a bad thing when she thought about it, but she had Kristen to consider.

When she married Tanner, she vowed she would never look back, that she would always look to the future. Now she wasn't so sure about that decision. One day at a time was her mantra.

She took another deep breath. "I'm sorry you feel that way about your brothers. It shouldn't be that way, really. They need help, the kind that I can't give them. I've tried to talk to your dad about their behavior, and he just gets angry. I'm sorry. I wish there was something I could do, but I've tried to understand them, too, and I can't. I guess blood is thicker than water in this case."

"It is for me, and I don't care. They're assholes, Mom," Kristen said. "I know you hate cursing, but they would make a saint turn evil."

There was nothing more to say. Molly and Kristen now both carried the burden of Holden's crime.

"I think we need to focus on your trip," Molly said, forcing herself to smile. "You're all set to go?" she asked.

"Yes. There wasn't much to pack since we'll be wearing biking shorts most of the time. I can't wait to see Europe." Kristen's enthusiasm was music to Molly's ears. She wanted this trip to be special for her, something she could look back on in the years to come.

Seeing the time, Molly forced herself from the bed. "You're going to have a blast, I just know it. Now, if I'm taking you to the airport, I need to shower and dress." She dreaded returning to her room. Tanner would be up by now, and hopefully last night's *incident*—she couldn't come up with a better word—would already be forgotten. He'd have a hangover, but she could deal with that. She really didn't have much choice.

"Okay, I'll be down as soon as I shower," Kristen said, then continued. "Mom, are you going to be okay when I leave?"

Was she?

"Of course I will, I'm a big girl," she said, then wrapped her arms around her daughter. If only she could keep her close and protect her from the evils of the world, all that she'd suffered would've been worthwhile.

Chapter Eleven

Traffic exiting Logan International Airport was horrendous this early in the morning. Molly's eyes were red-rimmed, her vision still a bit blurry from crying. She had sworn that she wasn't going to cry when she dropped Kristen off, but she did. Kristen cried, too, but hers were happy, excited tears. Molly would be on pins and needles waiting for her daughter's call as soon as they landed in Paris. It was a long flight, and she knew she'd have to keep herself busy all day in order to maintain her sanity.

Fortunately, when she'd returned to her bedroom earlier to shower and dress, Tanner was nowhere to be found. When she saw that his car was gone, she'd breathed a sigh of relief. Then she remembered that Holden and Graham were still upstairs, asleep in their rooms.

She wasn't sure what her reaction would be when she came face-to-face with Holden, but it was inevitable, so she decided she would act normal, as though she had no clue about his attack on Emily last year.

It would be hard, but she'd been through this kind of situation before. Sweep it under the rug, close the door, don't acknowledge what's right in front of her face, deny, deny, deny. She could do this. She'd had a lifetime of practice.

A horn blared, and she glanced in her rear-view mirror. "Sorry," she said out loud.

She'd swerved over into the right lane, cutting off another driver. He must've been in her blind spot. She gave a slight apologetic wave as she took the Goldenhills exit. Molly hated driving on the interstate, but she'd wanted to see Kristen off to the airport. The next two months were going to be the longest of her life.

Twenty minutes later, she was pulling into her driveway. She didn't bother parking the Mercedes in the garage. With Sally off for the next few days, Molly feared she would be bored to death, but as Kristen suggested, she was going to need a lot of goodie boxes. She could start preparing them today, and a possible trip to the market might be in order. She'd freeze whatever she made and ship it to Tennessee when Kristen was settled in her dorm.

She entered the house through the side door that led to the kitchen. Not sure what to expect, she quietly dropped her purse on the counter. She scanned the kitchen, searching for signs that either Tanner or the twins had been here, and saw nothing. The coffeemaker was freshly washed from last night. The dessert plates she'd promised Sally she would wash were still stacked neatly in the dish drainer. Other than the plates, all traces of last night's dinner were gone. She checked the formal dining room. It, too, was as she'd left it before Tanner's tirade last night. She saw that the bar was immaculate, no empty glasses or liquor bottles lying around, nothing to indicate she'd neglected her household duties. She peered into the formal living room, and all was as it should be. Funny, she had no memory of cleaning up, though given what she'd been through last night, household chores hadn't been uppermost in her mind.

Seeing nothing that indicated they'd had a fairly large dinner party, she returned to the kitchen and poured herself a glass of orange juice. She would stay busy, just as Kristen suggested. Tanner would come home tonight and act as if nothing had happened. She'd play the game, at least until Kristen returned. She wasn't sure how she would be able to remain civil to Holden, but she would figure out how to play that game, too. She did have quite the résumé when it came to avoidance behavior.

Before she dwelt too much on the horridness of his crime, she went to the pantry to search for baking ingredients. She'd make a few loaves of banana-nut bread. It froze well, and she'd play nice and ask Tanner if he wanted to take some to the office. He would, but he'd never share with his employees. He was becoming more and more selfish as the years passed. She took out a five-pound bag of flour, a canister of sugar, and a bag of walnuts. She then removed a large mixing bowl from the cupboard, preheated the oven, and took four loaf pans from a drawer and sprayed them liberally with cooking spray. For the next half hour, she dumped flour, sugar, butter, and overripe bananas in her giant mixing bowl. She filled each loaf pan with batter, then carefully placed the four pans on a large baking sheet, put the bread inside the oven, and set the timer for one hour.

Molly liked poking around in the kitchen, but today it hadn't relaxed her as it normally did. She knew the recipe by heart, but her thoughts were anything but soothing. If anything, she felt even more stressed than she had earlier. She was tense as she waited for Holden and Graham to come storming downstairs. Unsure what her reaction to Holden would be, she filled the sink with hot water and a squirt of dish detergent. She tossed her mixer parts and bowl in the sink to soak. She could not face Holden, not yet. Her hands were sweaty, and again, her mouth was dry as a bone. Nerves, she thought. She checked her watch, then grabbed her purse, and was about to head upstairs when the telephone rang.

"Crap," she said out loud, but then remembered it could be Kristen. Maybe her flight had been delayed or canceled.

"Hello," she said a bit breathlessly, expecting to hear Kristen's voice. When she heard nothing, she spoke again. "Hello, Kristen, is this you?"

Still nothing. She was about to hang up the phone when she heard an odd, high-pitched squeal, kind of like the sound her old car radio made back when she drove that red Mustang.

"Whoever this is, we have a bad connection. I can't understand what you're saying."

"I know who you are. And I know what you did."

What?

The room began to spin. She blinked, then whispered, "Who is this?"

There was laughter, then the squealing sound again. "I said, I know who you are, and I know what you did."

"This isn't funny," she said softly. Taking a deep breath, she raised her voice. "Okay, then tell me, who am I, what have I done?"

More laughter. The voice was definitely male. "You're Maddy Carmichael, Marcus's twin sister. And you know exactly what you did."

Then the line went dead.

Oh My God!

Her breath came in rapid gasps, the room tilted, and her throat felt like it was closing. She struggled for air. Her heart felt like a thousand hummingbird wings were beating against her chest. She threw the phone across the room, and it smashed against a wall. She managed to drag herself over to the sink. She turned it on, and with trembling hands, she splashed cold water on her face. Over and over until she was calm enough to think.

Someone knew her name. Her birth name. Full circle. She was coming full circle.

Chapter Twelve

Molly was virtually paralyzed. A sheer black fear swept through her, and she began to shake as images of the past came back to her. After twenty-one years, why now? On the day Kristen left. Was there a connection? Had someone from her past been watching her all this time without her knowledge? Taking several deep breaths, she tried to calm herself, but found that the deep breathing only caused her to be light-headed. She closed her eyes and counted. Sometimes this helped to relieve her anxiety.

It wasn't working.

Her body felt limp, as though she were made of liquid and would dissolve at any moment. She managed to slump into the chair she'd just vacated.

What to do? She'd never planned for this.

After so many years, she thought her secret was safe; but then, she acknowledged, there were no safe secrets. Maybe one could keep them at bay for a while, but somehow, some way, secrets always returned to haunt, taunt, or torment, whichever was the case. Each of those words accurately described what she was feeling at that exact moment.

Inhaling, trying to calm herself, she focused on what to do. She tried to retrace her steps, where she'd been, and with whom she'd had contact. Surely, she couldn't remember back over twenty years, so starting at the beginning was impossible. No, this unknown man who had just called her would have made himself known if he had had knowledge of her past. Possibly, he would have tried to blackmail her. Tanner was a very wealthy man, and this fact alone would be tempting if someone from her past knew who she was.

Possibly, she was being watched this very moment. She jumped out of her chair so fast that the room began to spin. Clutching the back of the chair, she closed her eyes and waited for the vertigo to pass.

But who? She'd never met anyone in Goldenhills who had any connection to Blossom City. At least none that she'd known of. Another deep breath. She sat in the chair, trying to clear her head. She needed to think.

She and Tanner didn't have much of a social life outside of the dinner parties they held. Given Tanner's difficult personality, their personal friendships were practically nonexistent, to say the least. Indeed, socially speaking, Tanner was pretty much of a pariah, someone to be avoided at almost any cost. They had acquaintances, but as far as she knew, no one she'd known from her past. While Tanner was big on showing off his home and his wealth to others in the medical profession, she couldn't name anyone who could be considered his close friend. And, sadly, other than Gloria, she didn't have any real friends, either. She'd remained in touch with Teresa and Lou throughout the years, but being in actual contact was rare—a Christmas card, the occasional phone call. She remembered when she'd told Lou and Teresa she was going to take the job Tanner, then Dr. McCann, offered. They'd both begged her to stay on at the diner, but she'd been adamant. The salary he'd offered had been too hard to resist.

If only she'd listened to them. Again, she thought of her daughter. All the pain and heartache had been worth it. Or at least that's what she'd always convinced herself of after a particularly nasty fight with Tanner. But they were all nasty, and more often than not, when they were alone, the arguments turned physical.

She realized now that she had to know, had to discover who'd tracked her down and threatened to expose the past she'd successfully hidden for decades. It was time, she realized. Kristen was leaving, and her marriage was such a sham that it was too late even to think about salvaging it. While she had loved Holden and Graham as toddlers, first as their nanny and then as their stepmother, and during their early childhood years, she could honestly say, at least to herself, that she now feared them more than anything else. Whatever maternal feelings she'd had before they were teenagers had been destroyed by their disrespectful and cruel ways.

No, it was time to engage her backup plan.

On shaking legs, Molly went upstairs to her room. Her hand trembled as she dialed the number of a local cab company. "I'll be ready in twenty minutes," she said after giving them her address, then placed the phone back in its receiver.

She took a small suitcase she'd purchased a few years ago from the top shelf in the closet. Inside were a few items she'd bought at a secondhand shop years before. With time at a minimum, she hurriedly tossed in a few basic necessities. Jeans, a couple of blouses, underclothes, and a nightshirt. In the master bath, she grabbed her toothbrush, toothpaste, and makeup kit.

She located the picture frame that held a picture of the kids at the beach, on a rare trip to Maine. Kristen was three, she remembered. It'd been one of the most memorable of the few family vacations they'd taken. She'd been happy then. She looked at them, remembering the woman who'd offered to take their picture. It'd been the only picture taken of them as a family on that trip. Carefully, she pushed aside the metal clips that held the back of the frame in place. Next to that was a thick gray piece of cardboard. Taped to the front of this was a single key. She removed the key and dropped it in her purse.

Without glancing behind her, she raced downstairs. She was about to step outside to walk down the long drive to wait for her ride when she remembered the banana-nut bread. She went over to the stove and turned the oven off. She was about to leave when she decided to take the bread out of the oven. She placed the baking sheet on the granite countertop. When Graham and Holden came downstairs, they'd simply think she'd stepped out for a trip to the market if they even realized that she wasn't in the house. Checking to make sure there was nothing suspicious about the way things appeared, she remembered the phone she had tossed across the room. She quickly gathered the broken pieces and found the two batteries. She dropped them in her purse, then walked out the side door, not bothering to lock it since she knew the boys were inside. Once they discovered her car in the garage, they might be curious, but not enough to do anything about it. Maybe they would be too stoned or hungover even to bother. She looked at her watch. She had five minutes.

Chapter Thirteen

"**M**s. M, haven't seen you lately," said the young girl behind the juice bar.

Molly gave up a phony smile. "Been busy, you know how that is." She doubted it, but it seemed the right thing to say.

"How was the class today?" the girl asked as she placed an olive-green smoothie on the counter.

"Rough, it's been a while," Molly said. At least that much was true. She'd been a member of All Night Fitness for ten years. No one in her family, at least as far as she knew, was aware of this. While she didn't attend the rumba class or any others with any degree of regularity, she did try to show up at least once a month to keep up appearances. Just in case.

And today was the day she'd thought about all those years ago when she'd joined the gym.

She took a few sips of the grass-tasting smoothie, left the girl a two-dollar tip, then headed for the showers. She had to make her visit to the gym appear normal. Though she wasn't a regular gym rat, the manager knew her, as did a few of the instructors. She never discussed anything personal, other than telling the few members she conversed with that her job didn't allow for a regular schedule. No one questioned her, and for that she was glad. Today was just like any other day as far as they were concerned. She'd made her appearance known in the class, just in case, though it really didn't matter. It was just that she was hesitant to vary her gym routine.

Inside the locker room, she quickly showered, dried her hair, and added a bit of makeup to cover the bruise forming on her cheek. Keep it normal, she kept saying to herself, though inside she felt anything but normal. A million thoughts skittered through her mind. Kristen was safe for now. She would be back before she returned from Paris. Maybe. She had no clue what the future held, but Molly was going to make things right. For Kristen's sake. She risked the possibility of Kristen's distrust and anger, but she felt that she no longer had a choice.

The phone call had been the final nail in the coffin. It was time to right the wrongs of the past. The nails had to be removed before she suffocated in her own lies. And she knew it was very possible that she would lose her freedom. But she had to do this now—she didn't have a choice any longer. It'd been taken away when she received that phone call from a man who knew that she had been Maddy Carmichael.

Finished with her makeup, she twisted her long blond hair into a topknot, then added a Boston Red Sox baseball cap. She wore a pair of faded men's Levi's she'd purchased from a secondhand store years ago and a black men's T-shirt. As soon as she was outside, she'd add the generic sunglasses she kept in the locker. She gave a final glance in the mirror before exiting the shower room. She looked like shit. She could still see the outline of the bruise forming on her cheek, but once she was out of here, it wouldn't matter.

She pulled her small piece of luggage behind her and went to the room where private lockers could be had for a monthly fee. She took the key out of her purse and opened her locker. She removed a large manila envelope from the top shelf. She looked inside to make sure of the contents. Satisfied, she put the envelope under one arm and dropped the key in her purse and headed for the exit. When she'd prepared for this ten years ago, when the boys were twelve and had begun, encouraged by their father, to show the disrespect that had become the norm as they entered their teenage years, she'd planned out as many details as possible, and though a lot had changed in ten years, she felt confident her plans were as concrete today as they were then. Once a month she made this same trip, checking for new surveillance cameras, anything or anyone that might possibly identify her. She walked three blocks to the bus stop. Fifteen minutes later, she was on her way to Boston.

She sat in the empty seat behind the driver, as this made her feel safe. She remembered how she used to ride the bus when she worked at the diner. She'd sat behind the driver then, too.

Images of her short time at the diner flashed through her head. She'd loved the six months she worked there in spite of the reason that had sent her running from Blossom City. When she and Sarah found that dingy little basement apartment, she'd been giddy. Her first real home. She and Sarah had established a routine and become as close as they could despite the fact that neither wanted to share her past. They lived in the moment. When Molly told Sarah she was taking the job with Dr. McCann, the girl had been devastated. Molly had tried to explain her financial situation, and how she, too, hoped to save up for college. Sarah hadn't understood why she couldn't work for the doctor and stay at the apartment, but that had been part of the job. Twin toddlers needed around-the-clock care. She'd been a bit afraid of losing Sarah's friendship, but they'd stayed close for a while. When Sarah was able to attend Harvard full-time, then continue on to Harvard Law, she'd rarely had time for Molly, so Molly had stopped calling her. She wondered if she'd finished law school, and if she'd done all those things they had talked about when they'd been in that small room with the twin beds. Did she have a family now? A successful law practice?

She took a deep breath. It didn't really matter, she thought, as she grabbed her luggage and got off at her designated stop. She glanced around. The place hadn't really changed all that much, but she knew that already. Molly made it her business to know it. It had offered her a sense of protection, a backup plan. She'd often thought of her escape, and she'd planned for Kristen to accompany her, but now she was glad she wasn't here. It would've been too hard to explain to her then, though she doubted it was going to be any easier when the time came— and it would come, that was guaranteed. There was no way around this, and she would be honest. It was highly probable things would turn out for the worst. She accepted this, but she couldn't avoid the past any longer.

Today's phone call had frightened her, and she was still scared because she didn't know who he was, or how he had found her. Before the proverbial crap hit the fan, Molly had to return to Blossom City. She had to return to the life she'd left behind all those years ago, and though she never imagined she would feel this way, she almost welcomed the challenge, the change. Though she was petrified at the thought of what awaited her there, she was no longer the frightened seventeen-year-old who had run from a situation that had spiraled out of control.

She walked the few blocks to the storage company, which was pretty much the same as it had been more than twenty years ago. The office décor had been updated a bit, a computer system added, along with a soda machine and a few plastic chairs that didn't look as beat-up as they had the last time she'd been here.

A glass partition separated a female clerk from the reception area. She leaned forward and spoke into a microphone. "I need to open unit 76," she said to the back of a girl who continued to type at lightning speed with hot-pink-painted fingernails that were at least an inch long. She held up one bright-pink nail, indicating she needed a minute. Molly rolled her eyes and tapped on the glass, trying to get her attention. The girl stopped typing and whirled around to face the glass. From behind, she'd looked like a young girl, though face-to-face she had to be in her mid to late forties. Her long black ponytail and slim figure would've fooled anyone, Molly thought. "I need to open unit 76."

"You's need it now?" the woman asked in a thick Boston accent.

"Yes," she said.

"Pedro's gonna be a few minutes, so have a seat." She nodded to the plastic chairs.

She should've called ahead, but hadn't thought about it until now. *Her cell phone.* Quickly, she rummaged through her purse, praying she hadn't left the phone behind. She'd told Kristen to call her on her cell phone the minute her plane landed in Paris. She breathed a sigh of relief when she found the bright-yellow case covered with daisies hiding the iPhone's emblem. She checked the battery life and saw she still had a full charge. She'd left the house without remembering to bring her charger. She'd purchase one as soon as she was on the road. She scanned the phone for missed texts or calls, but there were none. Molly was about to drop her phone back in her purse when she remembered that damned Friend Finder app that Tanner had insisted she install. It was basically a GPS tracker, and anyone she'd added to her friend list could locate her immediately. She thumbed through the apps until she located it, then held her thumb on the app until a wiggly black X appeared. She tapped the X, and the app asked her if she wished to delete it. She hit YES and tossed the phone back in her purse. Thank goodness she'd thought of that. Tanner was super tech savvy, so when she didn't come home tonight, it would be the first thing he would do to search for her. After that, well, she really wasn't sure. She doubted he would go to the police to report her missing because of the physical attack he had made on her last night. He could not afford the police finding her in her present condition, and he damn well knew it. While there were no witnesses, other than Kristen, who was on her way out of the country, it was possible the twins might've heard something—but no way would they go against their father. Would he hire a private investigator? She wasn't sure of that, either. He would probably weigh the pros and cons of the cost and chalk her up as a loss, at least until she came home. Then he would beat her to death, of that she was sure. Again, she was reminded of Elaine, the twins' biological mother, who'd died when she fell down a flight of steps. Molly had always suspected there was more to the woman's death than a mere accident, but she'd always kept those thoughts to herself.

Tanner wouldn't worry about her yet. She'd done her duty, and with Kristen starting college in the fall, he really had no use for her. Other than someone to host dinner parties and occasionally have sex with, she was of no value. And she sure as hell had no use for him.

She'd never been madly in love with him. Even in the very beginning, when their relationship went from employer/employee to dating, he hadn't caused any bells and whistles to go off. She remembered the first time she had slept with him. It had brought everything she'd tried to forget back, and in time, she'd learned enough to pretend she enjoyed it when he touched her. Now, the thought of his hands on her made her cringe with disgust. She'd sold herself to him all those years ago, and now she realized she'd been screwed, royally. Except for Kristen. It was worth it, for her daughter. But Kristen was older now, and Molly was taking a huge chance, going back to Blossom City. But she really had no other choice.

She had to return before Tanner learned of her past. If it cast a shadow on his prized reputation, he would not let it slide. No, he would most likely beat her to death. So she'd take her chances in Blossom City.

Chapter Fourteen

The Mustang's interior smelled of new leather and pine, an air freshener courtesy of the storage company where she'd managed to store the old beater for more than twenty years. She'd had the interior redone, along with a new engine and a bright cherry-red paint job, years ago, all unbeknownst to Tanner. For now it was untraceable, and she hoped it stayed that way. While it didn't have all the luxuries of her Mercedes, she found she actually liked driving the Mustang more. She'd had the air conditioner replaced but chose to roll the windows down and let the evening breeze blow through the car, snuffing out the fake pine smell.

As she drove out of the city, it seemed appropriate that she was leaving in the same vehicle in which she'd arrived, though it was in much better condition. And she had a working radio and CD player this time around. She remembered the old radio, the AM/FM selections, and how she could only pick up WBLO, the local AM station in Blossom City, and even that had been sketchy at best.

Once she was on the interstate, she relaxed a bit. She checked her watch and realized that Kristen would be arriving in Paris soon. She'd wanted to get farther away from Goldenhills before she stopped for the night, but she couldn't. When Kristen called, she wanted to be settled in for the night, so they could talk. She'd spent the last hour coming up with a story and hoped that Kristen would believe her.

She hated lying, but it really wasn't a total lie when she thought about it. Molly had decided to tell Kristen that she was leaving for a few days because she needed time to think about her relationship with her father, and she'd refer to the fight she and Tanner had the night before Kristen left. As much as she hated to admit it, Molly was glad that Kristen wasn't all that close to Tanner. She'd never been a daddy's girl. From the very beginning, Kristen had been Molly's daughter, and in her mind, Tanner was nothing more than a sperm donor, though she'd never voiced this to anyone, including Kristen.

Seeing a huge sign for a hotel, Molly took the proper exit and made a few sharp turns before she found the hotel she'd chosen: All Traveler's Inn. She'd never heard of it, and most likely it was privately owned, which to her

meant no security, no cameras in the parking
lot. She hoped. She parked away from the entrance and planned to try to hide her vehicle.
A classic restored red Mustang would draw attention. For a second, she questioned her decision to take the car, but what the hell, it was
what it was, and there was no turning back now.
She was no longer that immature young girl
who'd dared to escape her past; but really, was
she any different now? It had taken a lot of
courage to do what she had done when she
was seventeen. No, she hadn't been immature;
she'd been smart. And afraid. And now she was
stupid. Stupid to believe she could hide her
past from Tanner, Kristen, and the twins, though
she honestly didn't care about the boys. They'd
been so cruel to her, it was hard to remember a
time when she'd loved them as much as she
loved Kristen.

She took the manila envelope and stuffed it
inside her purse. She removed her baseball
cap and let her hair down. She saw her reflection in the hotel's glass door and decided she
looked ridiculous. Inside, she saw a young
man, probably in his early twenties, behind the
counter. He appeared clean-cut, which was unusual these days, when strange body piercing
and tattoos were the norm. He didn't bother
looking away from whatever held his attention
as she approached the counter. She waited a
few seconds, then cleared her throat. "Excuse
me," she said.

He jerked up and grinned. "Oh, sorry. I was
about to defeat the King of Orion. What's up?"

He said this as though she knew exactly what he referred to, though she knew it had to be a game he was playing on his cell phone. She couldn't help but smile. Kristen was addicted to Candy Crush, so she understood. Sort of.

"I need a room for the night," she stated in her best mom voice, hoping he didn't hear the fear and uncertainty in it.

"Sure thing."

He clicked a few keys on a keyboard, then asked to see her driver's license. She reached inside her purse for the small square of plastic, took it out, and placed it on top of the counter.

The boy repositioned the license so he could read the information. He never took his eyes away from the license as he typed her information into the computer.

She'd known this day would come and tonight she was thankful that she'd prepared herself. Years ago when she moved in with Sarah, she had applied for and received a Massachusetts driver's license as well as new license plates for the old Mustang. Throughout the years, whenever she received renewal notices, she'd trudged downtown to the Department of Motor Vehicles and paid the fees so everything was up to date.

"Okay, ma'am, you're in room . . ." He wrote the number on a small envelope containing the key card and slid the envelope across the counter so she could see her room number. Clerks were reluctant to say the room number out loud. She was thankful. You never knew who was listening, just waiting to pounce on you. "We have a free continental breakfast from six until ten if you're interested. Checkout time is noon, so have a good night." He pushed the key card toward her. She was a bit stunned at the use of her maiden name. It had been so long since she thought of herself as Maddy Carmichael. She thought of her trip all those years ago, and her stay at the Wilkins Motel in Georgia. She'd been terrified then.

It'd been fairly easy to change her name once she realized she had to have proper documentation if she were truly going to change it. It had taken several trips to the library and hours of research. Though it was risky, she'd applied to the court to legally change her name. The process required publishing your intention to do so in a local newspaper. If there were no objections within a thirty-day period, then the name change became legal. She still used the same date of birth and Social Security number.

When she first escaped, her real name had been published in the *Fort Myers News Press* as a missing person for the required thirty days, yet not a single soul had noticed. Her mother never read the paper, and Marcus, well, she wasn't even sure if he could read. So she'd felt fairly confident when she'd changed her name that there would be no objections from her family. Even though she'd been Molly McCann for most of her life, she had never forgotten her birth name.

Madeline "Maddy" Carmichael was going home.

She took the key and returned to her car.

Normally, she preferred hotels with inside entrances to the rooms, but tonight she wished for a room where she could come and go unnoticed, just in case. But it wasn't to be, so she'd make the best of it. She looked at her watch as she pushed the elevator button for the second floor.

The doors made a soft, swishing noise as they opened. She stepped off the elevator and quickly found Room 216.

The room was typical, and the stink of stale cigarette smoke clung to the heavy fabric of the chairs. A sweet floral scent did little to mask the underlying odor. She pulled the comforter off the bed, placing it on the chair. Who knew what kind of germs it contained? She pulled the top sheet up, fanned it a bit, then looked to make sure the fitted sheet beneath it was clean. Seeing nothing suspicious, she sat down on the bed, where she dumped the contents of her purse on the starched white sheet, checking to make sure she had her phone where she could locate it the minute her daughter called. If she did not answer, Kristen would call her father, wondering where her mother was. No, she couldn't let that happen. While the thought of lying to Kristen sickened her, she had to do what she could to protect her now.

She leaned against the headboard, her thoughts returning to the phone call that had sent her running. Who could it be? And why now? Why not five years ago? Ten? Whoever knew this had to know of Tanner's wealth, his status. Or was it possible that this mystery man

didn't care about money? Maybe he just wanted
to frighten her; if so, mission accomplished. If
it was anyone from her past, she knew that
blackmail would be the motivating factor. Why
hadn't he asked her for money? Or did he simply want to drive her insane with worry?

The timing was actually perfect. With Kristen leaving first for France and then shortly
after for college, Molly's life was bound to
change anyway. She would have a lot of free
time on her hands. She seriously had doubts
that Holden or Graham had anything to do
with this. They spent too much time focusing
on getting high. And what about Holden's raping Emily? It was impossible to think he would
do something so vile, but she hadn't thought
Ricky Rourke or the rest of Marcus's gang
would resort to this sick behavior either, and
she knew from firsthand experience that no
one could be exempt from an accusation so
vile. "Trust no one" was a motto she'd lived by
most of her life.

Her cell phone blasted with the loud cymbal
tone that Kristen suggested she use, telling her
this way she would know it was her.

"Hey," Molly said.

"Mom, this place is so freaking unbeliev-
able, I can't believe I'm here."

Molly's heart filled with relief. She was safe.
For now. "You'll get to use your French for real
now. How was the flight?"

"Long, but Charlotte and I watched movies,
and read, so it wasn't that bad."

She'd never been to Europe, but maybe

someday. She'd thought of Ireland in all its green glory. Maybe she would visit when she'd cleaned up the mess that was her life, but most likely she would be locked up, and travel would be the furthest thing from her mind.

"Good. Kristen, I hate to bring this up now, but it's important." She took a deep breath before continuing. "I'm taking a few days away from your father. That argument he and I had last night—"

"—finally made you realize what an ass he is? And an abuser?" Kristen said. "Mom, you should leave him. It won't hurt my feelings one little bit."

Kristen was making this too easy for her. "Your father has problems; we both know that. I just wanted to let you know. I don't want you to call him or the boys until I've had a chance to think things through. Are you okay with that?"

"Yeah, right, like I'd waste my minutes on them anyway. I'm not calling them, Mom, no way, so do whatever you need to do."

"I'm sorry you feel that way, but I understand. I didn't bring my laptop, so we won't be able to Skype, but you can FaceTime me if you want to."

"If I can, I will. There'll be a few areas where cell coverage is crappy, but you know that, so if you don't hear from me, don't freak out. I promised to stay in touch, and I will. You have enough to worry about."

How did I get so lucky to have such a mature and intelligent daughter?

"I won't worry, but promise me you'll be careful," Molly said, missing her daughter already, and she hadn't even been gone twenty-four hours.

"All the rides are supervised, Mom. The barge is, too, remember?"

"Of course I do, I wouldn't have let you go otherwise. I'm still your mom, and it's a mom thing," Molly explained, smiling at her own words.

"I know, and I promise to watch out for sexy French dudes, and women who smoke." Kristen had told her smoking was all the rage in France.

"I don't think I need to worry about you smoking. I know how much you detest the smell. Now, when will you call again?"

"Tomorrow?"

"That's perfect. Don't worry about the time difference, just call when you can," she added.

"Be careful, Mom," Kristen said, her tone serious.

"I'm always careful," Molly assured her. If Kristen only knew, and she would in time. But now was not the time to tell her. "I love you, sweetie."

"Ditto, Mom. Talk to you tomorrow," Kristen said, then clicked off.

Neither one was big on long phone conversations, so Molly didn't expect to hear a day-by-day account of her bike and barge tour, but she needed to hear her voice just to make sure she was okay. She couldn't even think about what she would do if anything happened to Kristen.

She looked at the charge on her phone and checked the time. It wasn't too late to hit a CVS or Rite Aid. She needed a charger, and she'd pick up a few snacks for the road. She was surprised that Tanner hadn't called, but maybe after last night, he'd decided to give her some space. She doubted he was home because he would've noticed her car in the garage and tried to call her, or maybe he was doing that now. Maybe he was checking that stupid GPS tracker app that she hated so much. She looked at her phone again to make sure she'd deleted the app. It was gone. Let him figure that one out. He would go into a rage when he was unable to find her, then he would plan on what he would do to her when she returned. She knew him fairly well after almost twenty years of marriage, or so she liked to think, but still there were so many things from his past that he refused to talk about. The fire that killed his parents, Elaine's accident.

She had wanted to know about his mother and father after Kristen's birth, but she soon learned that it was worse than pointless to ask. She often thought about Elaine during the first few years of their marriage, but again, after seeing how upset he became when she asked, she'd just stopped asking.

An idea began to form, and she decided to act on it before she dismissed it. She crammed the manila envelope back in her purse, along with her cell phone. She put the baseball cap back on and quietly slipped out of her room and downstairs past the desk clerk without being noticed.

Inside her car, she used her phone to Google the closest office-supply store. There was an Office Depot 1.3 miles from the hotel. She used the Google map to bring up directions. Five minutes later, she was parking the flashy red Mustang as close to the entrance as possible. She was really second-guessing her decision to use the Mustang. Right now, she needed to focus on one thing at a time. Inside the store, she took a shopping cart and cruised up and down two aisles before she located a phone charger for the hotel and one for the car. She also bought a throwaway phone, just in case. She grabbed a notebook and a pack of pens. At the front of the store, she saw several brands of laptop computers and quickly skimmed the stats and chose one that she was familiar with. She located a cheap case and grabbed three packages of flash drives. She didn't even know if she needed them, but she didn't want to make another purchase tonight. She pushed her cart to the front register and waited while the cashier asked the customer in front of her if she had an Office Depot savings card. Apparently she did, but she couldn't locate it. Molly wanted to scream and tell her to hurry, but she knew that would just draw unwanted attention to herself, and that was the last thing she wanted to do.

"Here it is," the woman said, holding up the card so the cashier could scan the bar code.

Molly watched as the woman made a chore out of counting out the required amount of change. She swore that if she could have, she would have pushed her out of the way. She was being impatient, and that wasn't like her. She took a deep breath and tried to slow her racing heart. Did she really believe Tanner would find her seventy miles out of Goldenhills in an Office Depot? The way her heart hammered, she actually considered it. What if he'd had her followed when she left the house today? No, he couldn't have. She'd called a taxi and had actually checked to make sure she wasn't being followed.

"Ma'am?" the cashier said.

Finally, she thought, as she placed her purchases on the counter. She left the laptop in the large box in the cart and positioned the box so the cashier could scan the bar code. "For thirty dollars you can purchase an extra year warranty."

"It's okay, I don't need it," Molly said.

"It's only thirty dollars, ma'am. You really should consider buying it, just in case," she said.

In case what, Molly wanted to shout but didn't. "I just want the computer. I don't need the warranty."

"It's your loss," the cashier said. She was probably around her own age, but Molly wasn't good at judging people's ages. She herself looked much older than her thirty-eight years.

"Then it will be *my* loss, okay?" she said in a smart-ass tone. What the hell? Did they get some sort of commission for selling the extended warranty?

"Yep," the clerk said as she scanned the rest of her items, tossing them carelessly into a plastic bag.

Molly was really ticked at this woman. How dare she make a frigging issue out of something that was none of her business? Again, in different circumstances, she would've asked to see the manager, but she didn't now as she couldn't draw any unwanted attention to herself.

"That will be seven hundred sixty-three dollars and fifty-five cents."

Molly thought she took great pleasure in stating the amount. If she only knew. This was peanuts. "Sure," she said and removed eight one-hundred dollar bills from the manila envelope in her purse. She held them out fanlike for the woman.

"Figures," the annoying woman said before she turned her back and picked up the phone.

Her tone sharp, Molly asked, "What are you doing?"

"I'm calling the manager. It's store policy when customers pay with this much cash."

Taking another deep breath, Molly did her best to appear as though she were calm, but she was anything but. What the hell was the world coming to when *cash money* was questioned? Though she rarely used cash, she'd spent years stashing this money away because she knew the day would come when she would need it. Maybe she should consider purchasing a gift card or two. She had almost thirty thousand dollars in that envelope, all in large bills. That was a mistake, she thought, as the manager approached the cashier with a look that said he didn't want to be bothered. *Tough,* Molly thought as she watched him run a scanner over the bills to make sure they weren't counterfeit.

"Lady, you might want to write a check next time," he said, then strode off down the main aisle.

And you might want to kiss my ass, she thought.

The cashier practically threw the change at her, but took extra time to tape her sales receipt to the top of the laptop box. "That's good," Molly said, then pushed the cart forward, leaving the woman no other choice but to step out of the way.

She breathed a small sigh of relief when she was in the parking lot. However, there was a part of her that was extremely paranoid, and rightfully so, given her current circumstances. She pushed the cart to the back of the Mustang and hurriedly opened the deep trunk and placed her purchases inside. Once she was in the driver's seat, she saw that her hands were shaking, and she felt light-headed, faint. She tried to calm herself before pulling out of the parking lot. An accident wasn't in her plans. Taking a couple of deep breaths, she released them, slowly. She waited another minute, then cranked the engine over and backed

out of the empty parking lot. Her stomach
growled, and she realized she hadn't eaten since
dinner last night. She'd been so nervous that
she hadn't eaten much, then add in the fight
with Tanner and the sickening knowledge that
Holden was a rapist, not to mention that this
trip might very well be her last hurrah as a free
woman, it was no wonder she was light-headed.

She spied a convenience store across the
main road and pulled into the parking lot. She
grabbed her purse, looping the long strap
around her neck, holding the purse close to
her chest. The last thing she needed was a
thief trying to rip her purse out of her hands.
Happened all the time. In her current circumstances, she was ripe for the picking.

Where did "ripe for the picking" come from? Are
my Florida roots returning already? She remembered that Marcus used to say that very thing.

With a death grip on her purse, she entered
the store, relieved when she saw an older man
and woman behind the counter. "Hello," the
woman said.

Molly smiled and took a blue basket from
the stack by the entrance. She might as well
load up for the road while she was here. She
went up and down the aisles, shocked at the
lack of any real food. Shopping at Gloria's all
these years had spoiled her. She put a loaf of
whole-wheat bread in the basket, a jar of
peanut butter, and a squeeze bottle of grape
jelly. A six pack of water, a box of cherry Pop-
Tarts, three Payday bars, and a large pack of
beef jerky. She tossed a large bag of cheese

puffs in the cart, figuring if this were her last few days of freedom, she might as well eat the garbage she'd spent so many years avoiding. She grabbed three bottles of Starbuck's coffee and three Cokes. She'd need the caffeine, as she planned on driving straight through, stopping only for gas and bathroom breaks.

She hefted her shopping basket onto the counter. Behind the register was a wall of cigarettes, and above that were several Styrofoam coolers.

"You need a cooler, young lady?" the man asked kindly.

Molly gave up a slight smile. "I was thinking about it. Do you have ice?" She hadn't thought about keeping her drinks cool, but now she decided it was a good idea.

"Yes, the machine is in the back. We fill it for free the first time," he said.

"Then I'll take one. Thanks for asking," she said.

The woman, short and a little roly-poly, managed to waddle out of her cushy chair. "Herman, get her ice, and I'll take care of the rest," she said.

Under different circumstances, Molly would've been quite amused at the elderly couple, but right now she just wished Herman and Wobbly would get a move on.

One by one, Wobbly removed her items from the basket, and with a bright-pink, pointed fingernail, she punched the keys on the old-fashioned cash register. Molly was shocked when she saw this. It reminded her of Blossom

City and her childhood, and even then, this type of register was ancient.

Molly could've written the figures down and added them quicker manually. The poor woman was so slow that when Herman returned with the cooler full of ice, she'd just hit the TOTAL button.

"Go on, hon, I'll finish up," Herman said when he saw his wife stooping for a shopping bag. She waddled back to her chair, and Molly swore she could hear an "ouch" sound coming from the chair as she sat down. She smiled to herself. She really needed to eat and get a good night's rest—if that were humanly possible. She had run out of the house without bothering to grab her prescription sleeping pills. She'd never sleep without them, but under her current circumstances, sleep was not at the top of her list.

After Herman bagged her items in a brown paper bag with handles, he offered to carry it out to her car.

"No, please, I'm fine. It'll just take me a minute." Molly grabbed the bag and was out the door before he had a chance to respond. She unlocked the door and tossed the bag onto the passenger seat. Leaving the door open, she went back inside for the cooler. She lifted it off the floor, surprised by its weight, and felt guilty that Herman had had to lift it in the first place. "Thanks so much. You all have a nice evening," she said, and raced for the door. Before she could use her hip to push the door open, Herman, ever the gentleman, was there opening it for her.

"Thanks," she said again, hoping he would take the hint and leave her to finish loading the car, but she wasn't that lucky. He followed her around to the passenger door.

He whistled in admiration. "Now this is a car. I haven't seen one this immaculate in years." He ran his hand over the top of the car, as if he were gently caressing a woman. He whistled again, though this time it was low and slow.

"Yes, well, thanks, but I have to go now," she said, hoping she didn't sound rude.

"You put a lot of money into her, huh?" he asked.

Of all nights, why now? When the last thing she wanted was to be noticed.

Preparing her answer, she decided to stick as close to the truth as possible, given her circumstances. "It was a gift," she said, hoping that would put any talk of money to rest. If he was as mannerly as she thought, he wouldn't engage in any talk of money where the car was concerned.

"Well, then I'd say that somebody sure has good taste. In gifts, of course," he added, and again, Molly thought the old guy charming, but now just wasn't the time.

"Thanks, I'll tell my . . . father, who is waiting for me, so thanks again," she said, closing the door and forcing Herman to move away from the car.

"Well, have a good night, then," he responded, as she slid onto the driver's seat.

"Sure thing." She gave him a big smile and a wave as she cranked the engine over. Shifting into REVERSE, she squealed out of the parking lot. "Damn!" she said out loud. For someone wanting to just get through the night without being noticed, she seemed to be doing everything but. Peeling out of a parking lot in a snazzy red Mustang wouldn't go unnoticed if anyone were to question Herman or his wife.

On the main highway, she breathed a sigh of relief. She needed to rethink her plans. She spied the hotel's sign and pulled into the parking lot. She parked as far away from the main road as possible, which meant she'd have to lug the cooler a bit farther, but she didn't care. She took the bread, peanut butter, and jelly, and two bottles of water, stashing them inside the cooler. She'd leave the rest of the food in the car since none of it needed to be refrigerated.

With her purse still slung around her neck, she managed to carry the cooler to the elevator, without being noticed. The door pinged open before she had a chance to get her key card out of her purse. She raced out of the elevator and down the hall to her room. Fumbling around in her purse, she located the key and slid it into the lock. When the green light flashed, she practically fell inside the room. She used her foot to push the cooler inside, then locked the door and slid the dead bolt in place.

An hour later, she'd eaten a peanut butter sandwich, washed it down with some bottled water, and taken a shower. Then she returned to her car to get her new laptop and two of the Cokes—she'd need the caffeine. She removed the computer from its box while it was still in the trunk. She knew how odd it would look if she were to be seen lugging a giant box to her room. Or maybe not. She wasn't sure of today's protocol when it came to hotels, motels, and inns. It had been years since she and Tanner had taken a trip together that required an overnight stay. She'd spent most of her time at home, raising kids and seeing to Tanner's needs.

Quickly, she had the computer up and running. The hotel offered free Wi-Fi, so she created a Google e-mail account and began her search.

Chapter Fifteen

"Where in the hell were you two when she left?" Tanner demanded. "I told both of you to watch her, and now look at this load of crap." He took one of the pans of banana-nut bread and hurled it across the kitchen, where it smashed into the cabinet, leaving a slight nick in the woodwork.

"Hey, she's not our responsibility," Graham shouted back. "Why are you just now getting home? Screwing that new hygienist, I bet."

"Man, you two need to lower your voices. My head feels like it's been stepped on," Holden complained. He was wearing nothing but a pair of light-blue boxer shorts. His hair stood up as though he'd purposely styled it that way, then sprayed it with hair spray.

With one sweep of his hand, Tanner cleared the remaining pans of banana bread from the counter and sent them flying through the kitchen. Seeing the mixing bowl in the sink, he picked it up, soap suds and all, and threw it at Graham. Lucky for Graham, he missed, but the sudsy water soaked the floor, and the bowl broke into dozens of pieces.

"What the hell is your problem?" Graham shouted. "Don't take your lousy excuse for a life out on me. I haven't done anything to you."

Tanner punched the wall, his fist making a nice round hole in the drywall. "That bitch, she's just like all women. You can't trust them, you two understand this?" he yelled, then went on, "Your mother was a whore. I bet you didn't know that! She was going to divorce me, but no way was that going to happen, I told her. That woman paid the ultimate price, too." Saliva dripped from his mouth, and his eyes bulged with rage, but he didn't care. No one walked away from Tanner McCann. No one.

"Dad, you need to calm down. You're gonna wake the neighbors." Holden laughed. "Oh yeah, I forgot. We don't have any neighbors!" He roared with laughter. "That's why we live here, isn't it? So we can rant and rave all we want without anyone hearing." He dropped to the floor, his back against the refrigerator. His laughter turned to sobs.

Tanner stood in front of Holden. "Get up!" He grabbed a fistful of hair, yanking his son to his feet. "You are a worthless piece of crap. You hear me?" Tanner raged, then spit in Holden's face. "That's what I really think of you." He whirled around just in time to see Graham start to leave the room. "Stop!"

"What is your problem, old man? Just because your wife isn't here to kiss your royal behind doesn't mean I'm taking her place." Graham's eyes flashed, a burning, faraway look in them. "You don't frighten me, *Dad*." He said *Dad* as though the title were poison. "You're a real freaking prize, you know that? You make me sick," Graham said, then turned his gaze on his twin.

"And look at you, man! What the hell are you on now? You've already made a total mess of your life with that slut."

Holden seemed to sober up immediately. "What are you talking about?" He pushed Tanner away from him, almost knocking the table over in the process.

"Yes, what is your brother talking about? I'd like to know. Who's pregnant now? I told you I wasn't going to spring for any more abortions for those tramps you seem to favor, you got that?" Tanner demanded. He'd calmed down a bit, his initial rage ebbing away as the reality of the situation began to sink in.

"No one is pregnant," Graham confirmed. "Right, Holden?"

"It's not anyone's business but mine, okay? And I'm not that stupid," he said.

"Sit down. Now." Tanner pointed to the chairs that remained upright. "You too, Graham. I am not playing games either."

Reluctantly, they did as they were told, knowing full well that their father could throw them out of the house and cut them off entirely if they pushed him too far.

"Something is up with your stepmother. She never leaves the house without telling me. If either of you had half a brain, you would've checked the garage. Her car is still there. The kitchen is a total mess. How hard is it to figure out something isn't quite right with this picture? Are you both so stoned out of your minds that you have no clue what's happening under the very roof that you sleep and eat under?" Tanner banged his fist on the table for emphasis. "Do you?"

Graham spoke up. "If there'd been anything going on, we would've heard it. What about Kristen? Where in the name of all that's holy is Daddy's little princess today? Why don't we ask her? She's around her mother twenty-four seven."

"She's in Paris, you stupid pieces of crud. If you weren't so messed up, you'd remember she is on her high-school graduation trip. She doesn't have anything to do with this, so just leave her out of it," Tanner said firmly.

"Maybe your lovely wife decided to join her?" Holden suggested, his voice dripping with sarcasm.

Tanner had thought the same thing himself, but he was positive that Molly would have asked his permission, as any wife should. And she would never leave the house in such a mess. She knew how he liked an immaculate house. He'd made his wishes very clear when they'd first married. So what she had done today, disappearing without permission and leaving the house as if she had been unexpectedly called away and would be returning to finish what she had been doing, was completely inexcusable.

"Or maybe she's been in an accident," Graham added, grinning broadly. The thought of Kristen's mother having been in a serious accident was a balm to his soul. He hated that woman and her prissy daughter so much.

Tanner hadn't considered that. It was possible, but how? Where? Her Mercedes was in the garage. She wouldn't take off on foot, at least he didn't think so. Unless she fell or something, and hit her head. For all he knew, she could be wandering around Goldenhills with a head injury. He considered this. Maybe he should report her missing. He could call Bryan Whitmore, a longtime patient who happened to be a detective with the Goldenhills Police Department.

But that could open up another can of worms. He needed to think. What if she was hurt and he made no attempt to find her? How would that look to his patients? The public? And any future investors?

"I want both of you to clean up this mess and get yourselves together," Tanner said, leaving no room for argument. "I'm calling the police to report her missing. Now get your act together, for once. And Holden, lay off the goddamn roofies, okay?"

When neither responded, Tanner lit into them. "I mean right now, this very moment!

The endless supply of money you both enjoy will be cut off immediately if you don't do as I say. And tonight will be the last night you spend under this roof. Do I make myself clear, boys?"

"Yes, sir," Graham said, giving a mock salute. "Your wish is my command. Come on, Holden, get your ass in the shower." Graham grabbed his brother by the arm and practically dragged him upstairs.

Tanner scrolled through his contacts, looking for Bryan Whitmore's number. He'd kept it in his personal contact list just in case he ever needed to call in a favor.

He located the number and was about to hit the CALL icon when he remembered that he'd installed the Friend Finder app on Molly's phone. He thumbed through his apps and clicked on Molly's name. A few seconds later the screen filled with "Molly is not available."

"Damn. What the hell does this mean?" he said to no one, then tried dialing her number. It rang several times before going to her voice mail. "Hi, this is Molly. Sorry I can't get to the phone, but please leave your name and a number, and I'll call you as soon as I can."

"That bitch," he said, and was about to toss his phone across the kitchen but thought better of it. He'd need it to call Bryan. Maybe Molly was in trouble. Maybe her cell phone was in its charger upstairs, turned off.

Tanner raced upstairs to the master suite. Molly always left her phone charger plugged in on the night table on her side of the bed.

The charger was there, but there was no sign of her phone. Before he changed his mind, he located Bryan's number and hit SEND.

"Dr. McCann, what can I do for you?" Bryan asked.

Tanner thought he must've seen his name before he answered. Sometimes a good thing, and sometimes not. "Bryan, hey, I appreciate your taking my call. I know it's late, but I have a problem, and I thought you might be able to help me out."

"Anything, Dr. McCann, I'm on duty now. What's up?"

Tanner took a deep breath, hoping like hell Molly was missing. Because if she wasn't, he was going to make her wish she was when he found her. "I need to file a missing person report. I came home, and my wife is missing."

"Man, I am sorry. Give me your address, and I'll send a unit out ASAP."

"That's just it, I'm not sure if . . . Bryan, we had a bit of a fight last night. You know how women are. Molly's ticked and just might be screwing with me, but I just can't live with myself if I don't do something. I thought maybe you could stop by. I need some advice, and I don't want to blow this whole marital spat out of proportion if I don't have to. You understand?" He spoke in the voice he used with other professionals. Smooth and calm, but just the right tone to indicate he was more than a little worried. He knew how the police worked. And he knew that if he played his cards right, Bryan Whitmore could start searching for Molly off the record. He'd promise braces for his homely daughter if he had to.

"All right. I'll be right over. I just need an address," the detective said.

Tanner gave him the address and began directing the cleanup to eliminate all traces of his earlier rampage.

Chapter Sixteen

Molly yawned and opened her last bottle of Coke, glad she had thought to toss them in the cooler with the water. There was a small coffee machine in the room, but she was saving that for the morning. She was a beast when she woke up and didn't have coffee, a habit she'd developed when she had worked at Lou's.

She wasn't sure where to start, so she decided to Google her name. Her *real* name. She typed "Madeline Rose Carmichael" in the browser. The wireless in the hotel was slow, or else there were too many users. It took a full two minutes before her results flashed on the screen. There were more than six hundred thousand hits. She scrolled through, searching for what, she wasn't sure, but when she saw it, she would know. After thirty minutes and twenty-three pages, she concluded that she wasn't getting anywhere. There were way too many Madeline Rose Carmichaels in the world. It was late, and she was tired, but she needed answers to questions she should have asked a long time ago.

Next, she typed in "Blossom City, Florida, June, 1994."

Her stomach was in knots as she waited for the results to appear on the screen. There were fourteen hits.

A fire in the early-morning hours at the tomato-canning factory. No injuries and minor damage.

Nothing new there, she thought. There were accidents at the factory all the time. She clicked on the next link.

Two graduating seniors had received college scholarships. Someone she didn't remember, Cindy Ann Burkette, had received a four-year scholarship to Florida State University. Good for her, she thought, and tried to call up a face to match the name, but couldn't. Maddy had been a loner, not too many friends except for Brett and Carla, and, of course, Cassie, but she'd moved away before high school. She continued to read the article.

Karen Clark had been granted a four-year full athletic scholarship to the University of Florida.

Oh my God!

She knew Karen, at least knew who she was. She'd been captain of the cheerleading team. Molly remembered how friendly she'd been to her on prom night. Not buddy-buddy friendly, but she'd waved at her that night when she'd walked into the gymnasium all alone.

Molly's heart rate increased a bit with this knowledge. Had Karen become a career woman? Or had she married and had a family? Or had she done both? It didn't matter, but Molly remembered her from a few classes. She hadn't been especially smart, but she had been very athletic. *Good for her*, she thought, as she clicked on the next link.

This article contained a photo, so it took a few minutes to download. She decided to take a bathroom break while the page loaded. She washed her hands and looked in the mirror. Bluish-purple crescents had formed beneath her eyes, and her skin was pale and dull. She didn't care at this point. She'd been scared out of her mind today, and add the beating from Tanner, the bruise on her cheek, and her lack of sleep, and really, she thought, given the circumstances, it's a miracle she looked as alive as she did. She saw her makeup case on the bathroom counter and dotted a bit of concealer on the bruise. She couldn't look at herself any longer. She returned to the small desk.

The link she'd been waiting to load was up. She rubbed her eyes, and began reading the article.

She began to shake as she read. Fear turned her stomach into knots, and a cold, icy fright gripped her heart like a sponge, squeezing out all thoughts of rationality. A panic unlike any she'd ever experienced welled in her throat. Her pulse beat so erratically, she feared she would suffer a heart attack. Her hands shook as she tried to scroll through the remainder of the article. She almost gave in to the tension that had been building in her all day, but she couldn't. Not yet. She took a deep breath, yet there was no relief. Her hands felt numb, and the tips of her fingers started to tingle. She swallowed several times. Her throat felt as if she'd sucked dust through a straw. She reached for the bottle of Coke and gulped its contents down. She had to calm herself before she passed out. She rolled the desk chair away from the computer and closed her eyes. Taking slow, deep breaths, she forced herself to focus on something calming.

Kristen. She would be leaving for her first bike trip shortly. Molly imagined her long, muscled legs as she pedaled through the French countryside. Her long blond hair would be in a braid flying behind her as she made her way through the small villages. Charlotte would ride alongside her, and they would laugh about a boy they knew or some silly gossip.

Yes, Molly thought, *I can do this.* She took a deep breath, and slowly released it. She mentally forced herself to calm down. She'd had a panic attack, nothing more. She'd had them off and on when she'd first arrived in the Boston area, but it had been years since she'd experienced a full-blown one. She took another deep breath, then another, and released it slowly.

Focus, she thought as she inhaled again. This will pass. Another breath, exhale. She leaned back in the chair and did her best to clear her mind. Molly needed to get a grip or she wouldn't be able to function. She was alone and had to take care of herself. She'd been in this same place many years ago and survived. She would do so again.

Determined yet still shaking, she rolled the chair back to the desk. Her screen saver, a beautiful mountain scene, filled the monitor. When she placed her index finger on the touch pad, the screen came back to life. The article she'd read flashed back at her like an evil serpent, daring her to continue.

She threw her shoulders back, stretched her arms out, then rolled her head from side to side in order to release the tension and kinks in her neck. Another deep breath, and she started reading the article again, from the beginning.

She read through it three times just to make sure she hadn't imagined the facts or the face in the picture. It made sense now. Though it had been more than twenty-one years, his features were still the same. He had aged very well, she thought now, as she focused on the photograph of a person who had only recently been in her home. She had calmed down enough to plot her next move.

Clearing the screen for a new search, she Googled his name and the city where he lived. Several hits came up. She opened the first link. Again, his smiling face, though this time his wife stood beside him as he received a humanitarian award from a charity that helped survivors of sexual abuse. The article went on to say that the son of a bitch and his wife were among the top financial donors.

Her next Google search was for similar organizations. The first thing that came up was RAINN.

The article stated that RAINN, the Rape, Abuse and Incest National Network, was the largest anti–sexual violence organization in the country and one of "America's 100 Best Charities," according to *Worth* magazine. It ended with a hotline number, adding that the hotline had helped more than one hundred thousand assault victims.

The organization was huge. She skimmed through the Web site, searching for his name, but it wasn't there. As she was about to click out of the site, another GET INFO link caught her eye. It offered information on several topics: statistics, how to reduce your risk of sexual assault, the effects of sexual assault, reporting the crime to the police, and the one that really grabbed her: the aftermath of sexual violence. The Web site explained how one might wish to receive medical attention and about making a safety plan if you were living in a dangerous home environment, but what caught her attention was the contents of what constituted a rape kit.

DNA evidence was collected from a crime scene, but the article went on to explain that it could also be collected from your body. But what interested her the most was that DNA could also be collected from clothes and other personal belongings.

Though she'd sworn that she would burn that ugly teal prom dress, she never had. She wasn't sure why she'd kept it all these years. She didn't need a reminder of the night that had changed her life, but nonetheless, she'd preserved the dress as best she could after she'd taken the job with Tanner. Until then, she'd kept the dress in the original plastic wastebasket liner until she had moved in with Sarah. Because she didn't want to see the ugly reminder, she'd then sealed the dress in a brown paper bag and kept the bag in a backpack she'd purchased. She didn't know a lot about preserving DNA, but there was a small chance that one of her attackers had left behind some trace of DNA. She remembered waking up, her dress tattered and torn, and she remembered the dampness between her legs. Thinking of it caused her heart to hammer, but she distinctly remembered using the front of the dress to wipe off the slime between her legs. She told herself it was highly doubtful that any DNA was on the dress, and even more doubtful that after a little more than twenty-one years, it could be identified.

The dress in question was now stored in a safe place.

Before she shut down her computer, she had another idea. While Blossom City wasn't much of a city, back in the day it had a weekly newspaper, the *Blossom City Banner*. It reported on church bazaars, births, deaths, weddings, and any crime, typically speeding tickets, drunk and disorderly conduct, and the occasional domestic call. Nothing that she now considered real news.

She Googled the paper and immediately came up with a hit. She clicked on the link, stunned that it was still in production, what with most small-town papers having succumbed due to the cyber world. She scrolled down the page until she came across the paper's archives. "Really," she muttered.

Amazed at the professionalism, she clicked on the link and saw that content went back as far as 1989. "Wow. Unreal." Her voice was dry and scratchy.

She took another long swig of her Coke and clicked on the year 1994.

She clicked on the month of June.

Apparently it had been a quiet month. A couple of weddings, typical for the month of June. She found herself looking at the obituary page even though she knew it wasn't a good idea. This could ruin her life. Given the woman she was now, she knew she would have to turn herself in for the crime she'd committed all those years ago, but she also knew that she had to know. She'd been in denial for all of her adult life. It was time to face the facts.

She surfed through the names of the deceased one by one.

Albert George Jameson, eighty-five.

Wanda Sue Goodman, sixty-seven.

Lenore Royer Carmichael, fifty-three.

She gasped when she saw the name. She was

shocked, and it took her several minutes to calm herself. That was her mother. She glanced over the obit to see if it listed the cause of death. Nothing.

Again, her hands trembled, but she had to know. She read the brief obituary, and when she saw that her mother was survived by her son, Marcus William Carmichael, she was stunned. There was no mention of her. She tried to drum up some emotion for the loss of her mother, but couldn't. While she'd been shocked at seeing her mother's name, she hadn't been surprised. She had most likely died of an overdose. And she'd only been fifty-three years old. Why had she thought her mother was much older? Because she looked twenty years older, given her years as a drug abuser. She hadn't even known her mother's real age.

Shaken, but not enough to stop, she continued searching the obits, looking for a name from that night long ago. There was nothing, but that didn't mean she hadn't killed one of those bastards. Not everyone put an obit in the paper, especially when they realized that there was a charge for doing so.

She continued to scan the archives, searching for car accidents, anything that would link her to that night, but she found nothing. She went back to the obits and read her mother's again.

Lenore *Royer* Carmichael.

When she realized the enormity of her discovery, she was shocked. Did this mean what she thought it meant?

Part Three

And where the offense is, let the great axe fall.
—William Shakespeare

Chapter Seventeen

Detective Bryan Whitmore didn't make a habit of going out on calls to file a missing person report, but he knew Dr. McCann wouldn't have called him unless it was a true emergency. He hadn't asked for details over the phone because it didn't work that way, and the doctor hadn't offered up anything other than that he'd had an argument with his wife and she was missing.

He looked at the address. Riverbend Road, one of the most exclusive neighborhoods in Goldenhills. The doctor charged a small fortune to crown a tooth, so he wasn't surprised at the ritzy address. He drove down the long driveway, parking his unmarked Ford as close to the front of the house as possible. He gazed at the McMansion and shook his head. *Some people.* He walked up the small set of steps and rang the doorbell.

He'd barely had a chance to remove his hand from the doorbell before the door swung open. "Detective, please come in," Tanner McCann said, stepping aside.

"Of course," Bryan said. He removed a pad from inside his shirt pocket. He patted around searching for a pen with no luck.

"Let's go into the den. We'll be more comfortable there."

Bryan wondered if the doctor was the one who felt more comfortable in his den, but he kept the thought to himself. He'd been to the doctor's office in Goldenhills several times. Dr. McCann was an excellent dentist. He was professional, and he always had a great manner with him and, he assumed, with the rest of his patients. He recalled his being a bit sharp with his dental assistant, but he wasn't judging him. Maybe his assistant was new to the job, who knew?

He followed him down a hall to a set of giant wooden double doors, the kind he saw in those old black-and-white movies he watched on Sunday afternoons when he was bored out of his mind. Since his divorce, weekends stunk. By mutual agreement, Paula, his ex-wife, had custody of their fifteen-year-old daughter, Marty. His job required him to be on call twenty-four-seven, while Paula's job as principal at Golden Elementary was pretty routine as far as hours went. He hated not seeing his daughter every weekend, but he and his ex had both decided that their marriage wasn't working and had divorced when Marty was eleven. Marty had been sad, but she made the best of the situation. As far as Bryan could tell, she hadn't been damaged by their divorce.

"Detective, can I offer you something to drink?" The doctor poured himself a drink from a minibar on the far side of the room.

"No, I'm on duty, but thanks. Now, tell me about your wife." If McCann had been that concerned, Bryan thought, there would be more of an emotional reaction, but as far as he could see, at least so far, the man acted like he'd invited him over to shoot the breeze. However, he knew from twenty years' experience that people reacted differently in stressful situations.

The doctor motioned for him to sit in a burgundy-leather wing chair in front of his massive desk. As soon as he was seated, Dr. McCann seated himself behind the desk. Putting himself in a position of power, Bryan thought.

"Here." The good doctor handed him a fountain pen. Apparently he'd been watching him.

"Thanks, now why don't you tell me about this argument you and your wife had." He flipped the small leather notebook open, preparing to take notes in a shorthand that only he could read.

Tanner smiled. "It's almost embarrassing, but I wouldn't be able to live with myself if I didn't follow the proper procedures. I'm—"

"Sorry to interrupt, but what exactly do you mean by 'proper procedures'?"

"As I was about to say, Detective, I'm quite familiar with the proper procedures when filing a police report."

"I don't understand," he replied. *Let the good doctor talk.*

"I lost my first wife, Elaine."

Bryan scribbled the name in his notebook. "How long ago?"

"When the twins were toddlers. Over twenty-one years ago. It seems like yesterday." He took a drink of the golden liquid in his glass.

"And you had to file a police report then?" he asked.

"Yes. She had an accident." Tanner shook his head. "It was the worst day of my life when she died."

Bryan rearranged himself in the uncomfortable chair. The doctor must've known how uncomfortable it was when he invited him to sit down. "What kind of accident?" he asked, wondering just how long the doctor planned on talking about his dead wife before he actually mentioned his current one, the one he claimed was missing.

"She fell down the stairs when the twins were just a few months old. I tried to revive her, but her skull was crushed. Still, I had to try. I just couldn't . . . it was hard with two babies. I hoped to save her life so they wouldn't grow up without a mother, but I met Molly when the boys were nine months old. When I met her, I knew right away that I'd met my soul mate. She's younger by ten years. We have a seventeen-year-old daughter, Kristen. She's in France right now. A high-school graduation trip."

"Doc, have you been drinking?" He had to ask. The doctor wasn't making sense, jumping all over the place.

He nodded. "I had a few drinks with a friend before I came home, and this." He held up his glass. "I'm not inebriated, if that's what you're asking."

"No, of course not. I just had to ask given that you're drinking now. I wasn't sure. Just want to make sure we're both clear on the details, that's all. Go on, you were telling me about your wife." *The dead one*, he thought, but didn't dare voice this.

"Yes, I was. She's great. Really. Cooks like a pro. You should see the dinner parties she throws. I met her in a diner where she worked. Hey, maybe we'll have you over some night. You can see for yourself."

Bryan thought the doctor was not only drunk but slightly off. He'd never been invited to dinner by one of his doctors, let alone one whose wife was missing.

"Yes, well then, let's talk about her. Her name is . . ." He looked blankly at the doctor "What did you say? I'm sorry, we're all over the place. My memory isn't getting any better with age." He liked to act like an airhead, kind of like Peter Falk in *Columbo*. It put people at ease. And that's when they let their guard down.

"Her name is Molly."

"Oh yes. Right. Molly. Now, tell me about the argument you two had."

"We had a few guests over for dinner last night. Doctors who want to invest in my fourth office. We're going to be nationwide in the future. People like pretty white teeth. It's a good investment if you're interested, though you probably don't have money to invest in a dental clinic." He laughed. "Sorry, I get excited when I start talking about the future in dentistry. We had dinner, then dessert. Molly served coffee, no, she didn't serve coffee. She set the pot on the buffet, and we served ourselves. She had some kind of cake she'd purchased at Gloria's, that organic market she can't seem to stay out of. Their prices are out of sight, too. Don't shop there, you'll go broke. As we were having dessert, Holden, my son, took a bad fall. He's the older of the twins by four minutes. I ran upstairs to see what the noise was. Graham was standing at the top of the staircase, scared to death. Apparently, Holden had tripped over the mess on his bedroom floor, hit his head on the corner of the bed, and knocked himself out. Cold as ice. I checked his pulse, and well, I am a doctor. After I determined he was okay, I told Molly to please ask our guests to leave since we had a family emergency. She did, but as soon as they were gone, she went crazy. She accused Holden of using drugs, she tore up a four-thousand-dollar dress, and, basically, she went ballistic."

Bryan nodded and continued to write in his notebook. "You didn't try to calm her down?"

"Of course I did, but as I said, she went crazy. She kept saying things about the boys that weren't true and told me she'd hated them since day one, and well, as a father, that's the last thing you want your wife to say about your kids, no matter how old they are. She took a nasty fall, smacked the you know what out of her cheek. Then, when Kristen saw how her mother was acting, she insisted that she come into her room. Molly stayed there all night. At least I think she was there all night. I'm sure she took Kristen to the airport this morning."

Bryan scribbled more information, but he had a memory like an elephant. If he missed writing it down, he'd remember it, no matter what. It was his best skill as a detective—at least he liked to think it was one of his best skills. "Are you saying you haven't seen her since your argument last night when she went to your daughter's room?"

"Yes, that's exactly what I'm saying."

Though this could be a typical case of a pissed-off wife who was staying with friends— or in this case, maybe some fancy spa—his gut told him otherwise. He'd learned a very long time ago to listen to his gut instinct, as he was rarely wrong when he did.

"Normally, we like to wait twenty-four hours before we start a formal investigation, but if we deem the circumstances appropriate, we will begin investigating immediately. Would it be possible to speak with your sons?"

The look on the doctor's face spoke volumes. Anger, Bryan could see it. Hell, on this man, he could smell it.

"No, that's not possible. As I told you, Holden suffered a head injury and wouldn't recall anything useful."

"And your other son? Graham, I believe. I'd like to speak with him." It was not a question.

"I'm afraid that's not possible, either. Graham wouldn't have anything to offer."

"Dr. McCann, why don't you let me decide what's useful and what isn't. You called me because you're concerned about your wife. I'm here to help. If your son Graham is here, I'd like to speak to him."

"He's out on a date. How in the hell did I forget that?" He laughed and stood up to pour himself another drink. "You sure you don't want something? A soda? Water? I might've had a bit too much to drink; I swear it completely slipped my mind. Graham called me this evening and told me he was going out and not to wait up."

"Did he call your cell phone? The number you called me from?" Bryan was curious what excuse he'd come up with now.

"Of course he did."

"Then you wouldn't mind showing me your cell phone, for when you received the call? Just procedure, but, of course, you know this." He laughed.

"Not at all." He removed his cell phone from his pocket and handed it to him.

"Thanks, what's Graham's number? The one he would have called from?"

"It's 617-555-0325."

Bryan pulled up the recent calls, making a note to remember the other numbers as he scrolled through them; he'd jot a few down if he had to. He went through them carefully, but didn't find the number. One more time, and he handed the phone back to Dr. McCann. "I can't seem to locate that number. Maybe there is another number he could have called from?"

"Shoot, I might've deleted it. Sorry."

"Okay, Dr. McCann. Let's talk about where your wife might be. Does she have a friend she'd stay with, a favorite spa, a hotel, someplace we can start searching. And what about her car. I'll need the make and model, and the license-plate number."

"That's the big mystery. Her car is still in the garage."

This is getting screwier by the minute, Bryan thought. "Would a friend have picked her up? How did she take your daughter to the airport this morning? Does she have another car?"

"No, she doesn't have anyone who would drive her to the airport when there is no need. Kristen has a car, but it's in the shop now. Barry's Automotive. You can check it out. It's a 2014 Honda Civic. She took it in for a tune-up

a couple of days ago. It should've been ready
by now. That's why Molly had to drive her to
the airport."

He knew Barry's; he took his own car there.
That would be easy to check. He jotted down a
few more notes, then closed the notebook and
laid the fountain pen on top of the doctor's
desk. He stood up and walked across the room
to the set of wooden doors.

"I thought you were going to write up a missing person report. What's the problem?" Tanner followed him to the door.

Bryan stopped at the exit. "Dr. McCann, I
can't see there's any cause for concern. You
had a fight. You're pretty sure Molly drove
your daughter to the airport, and your sons
have nothing to offer. I'm guessing—and humor
me, as this is an educated guess—your wife will
come home tomorrow full of apologies, you
will take her to some fancy place for dinner,
then come home and kiss and make up. I just
don't see any reason to start an investigation."

"So you're telling me I'm crazy? Is that what
you're saying? I know my wife, dammit! If I say
she's missing, she's missing. Get out of my
house! I plan on calling your superior the second you leave, so prepare yourself. If I have
anything to say, your incompetent ass will be
out of a job. Now get the hell out of my house!"

Bryan walked down the long hallway to the
front door and let himself out.

After hearing what Dr. McCann had to say,
Bryan had, with no compunction, lied to him.

He did indeed plan on starting an investigation, but it wasn't into the disappearance of the doctor's wife, at least not yet.

No, he planned to start an investigation into the doctor's background.

Chapter Eighteen

Molly spent what was left of the night tossing and turning. Images of Sunday mornings spent in Pastor Royer's church had taken on a whole new meaning since reading her mother's obituary.

It was still early, but she couldn't sleep and didn't see any reason to stay in the hotel any longer than necessary. She packed up her laptop, dumped the water from the cooler into the tub, and stuffed her makeup kit and old clothes inside her luggage. She left her key card on the desk, following the instructions for those guests who wished to check out without stopping at the front desk. She checked the room, making sure she hadn't left anything behind. When she was satisfied, she hefted the cooler to a spot on top of her luggage, hung her purse around her neck, and slung the computer bag over her right shoulder.

Being up and out so early was to her advantage. No one saw her leave. She opened the trunk and placed her luggage inside, along with the cooler. She could've filled it with ice from the hotel's ice machine, but right now all she cared about was heading south.

As she was about to open the driver's door, she heard an odd sound, almost like a baby's crying. She leaned closer to the front of the car, where she thought the sound came from.

There it was again.

"Crap," she muttered as she stooped down to look under the car. What she saw broke her heart. She opened the door and grabbed the bag of beef jerky. She opened it and squatted, holding out a piece to the little kitten huddled beneath the car. "Come here, baby. It's okay." Not sure if the little fur ball was feral, lost, or abandoned, she patiently waited for the cat to take the piece of jerky. Slowly, the cat made its way to the jerky. Molly tore the food into bite-size pieces and watched as the cat devoured it. She repeated the process two more times. Hesitant at first, she gently rubbed the cat between the ears. "Did someone kick you out?"

The cat meowed and rubbed against her leg. Before she could change her mind, she scooped the cat up in her arms and set it down in the passenger seat. "We're going for a long ride," she said, closing her door.

The cat meowed and settled against the seat

as though he or she belonged there. Molly plugged the phone charger into the old cigarette lighter and put the charging cord into her phone. Again, she brought up Google. She typed in "pet store." A Pet Supermarket was 2.3 miles from the hotel. Repeating last night's process, she hit the Google map and followed the directions. At this rate, she was never going to get out of Massachusetts. If Tanner sent someone searching for her, they would have no problem finding witnesses.

The cat was completely black except for its paws. They were white. She ran her finger beneath the pad of his or her paw. This cat had been declawed. Probably belonged to someone, but there was no collar. She knew some veterinarians could scan for a chip in lost pets, but she wasn't going to go that far. She fluffed the cat between the ears.

"Meow."

She smiled. "I think you're my new best friend." Kristen had always wanted a cat, but Tanner refused to allow an animal in their home. Bastard. If she were truly honest, and there was no reason not to be, she hated him.

Yes, she hated his guts with all of her heart and soul, and not only did she not care, but if she could, she would shout it to the world. If she were to cross his path again, and she was sure that she would, she planned to tell him exactly how much she hated him. Slowly but surely, she was becoming more gutsy in her thoughts and deeds. She'd been gone for more than twenty-four hours. Tanner was either planning to have her killed or telling some outrageous story about her disappearance.

She saw the sign for the Pet Supermarket and pulled into the parking lot. Knowing that most pets were welcome in pet stores, she scooped up the cat and carried him inside.

"Meow, meow."

She grabbed a large shopping cart and headed for the sign hanging from the ceiling that read CATS. Having never had the pleasure of being a pet owner, she needed a bit of help. She wasn't too happy about bringing attention to herself, but she needed advice.

"Excuse me," she said to a man who was unloading boxes. "I need some help with this cat." She smiled, hoping she didn't sound too silly.

"Sure thing." The man was about her age. His name tag read GREGG, STORE MANAGER. He scratched the cat between the ears.

"Meow."

Gregg laughed. "Good cat. Now what can I help you with?"

Here goes yet another lie. "A friend couldn't keep this little . . ." she wasn't sure of its sex and didn't want him to know, so she said, "Fur ball. An apartment thing. I volunteered to give it a home, but stupid me forgot to bring the supplies. I need everything."

"I can help you with that. Now, does this little guy like dry or wet food?" Again he fluffed the cat between the ears and received a hearty "meow" in response.

She had no clue, so she said, "Both."

"Most cats do, so I can take care of that. He looks a bit on the thin side, so let's give him something to bulk him up a bit. That okay?"

"Absolutely."

Twenty minutes later, Molly had a cart full of all the essentials. The cashier rang her up without any trouble, and before she knew it, she and Ace were in the car. She'd decided on the name when Gregg had commented that he was as black as an ace of spades. Continuing the ruse she said, "That's his name. Ace."

"Good name," he'd said.

Before leaving the parking lot, she put Ace's new bed on the seat next to her. On the floorboard was a small dish filled with dry food. She had a water dish, too, but he'd had plenty to drink before they left, so she hadn't refilled it. She'd placed a litter pan on the back floorboard, hoping he'd know what it was for when the time came. All in all, she was settled in for the long drive ahead, and her new companion seemed to be as well.

Once she was on the interstate, she thought about her mother's obituary. What did it mean, *Royer*? Were they related to Pastor Royer, and her mother had neglected to tell her, or was it something more? Molly decided that most likely it was something more. Her mother's family, what there was of it, lived in Texas—at least that's what she'd always been led to believe. If Pastor Royer had been a distant relative, she was sure her mother would've taken advantage of him. He had never mentioned they were related when she helped out on Sundays after the service. Surely, he would've said something to her. Molly had so many questions and, so far, very few answers.

Of course, by now she knew exactly who had called her yesterday, knew who it was that had almost scared the life out of her, but she had a plan, and she intended to see it through to the end. On her Internet search last night, she'd learned that the Florida statute of limitations specifically addressed the use of DNA to identify suspects. Specifically, it said prosecution for rape could be commenced within two years of the use of DNA evidence to establish or confirm the identity of the accused. And now she was putting her hopes on a twenty-one-year-old prom dress and someone else from her past.

Sarah Berkovitz-Fine, Boston's top assistant district attorney, who just so happened to specialize in sex crimes.

The crime had taken place in Florida, but Molly would bet her last nickel that her old roommate Sarah could advise her on how to achieve her goal of seeing as many of her attackers as could be identified by the DNA evidence prosecuted. Molly had seen a picture of Sarah on the Web. She was stunning, and her bio said she was married and had one son. She'd accomplished what she'd set out to do. Molly was happy for her, and sorry she hadn't stayed in touch. As soon as she arrived in Florida, she planned to call her. She'd added her number to her cell phone last night.

She glanced down at the gas gauge. She still had half a tank. The Mustang did not get good gas mileage, but she didn't care. Unlike the trip she'd made all those years ago, money was the least of her concerns. She'd go another fifty miles or so, then stop to fill the tank. She needed some caffeine anyway. And Ace was probably getting thirsty, too.

She hadn't heard from Kristen, but with the time difference, she hadn't expected to. Right now she was probably pedaling away on some country road in France. Molly was happy her daughter was experiencing all the joys a girl her age should. Her one regret: Kristen had no idea of her past. Sadly, she would learn about it, and, most likely, it was not going to be pretty when she did. If not for Kristen, she wouldn't care. However, last night when she'd read about the low-life bastard—at least one of the low-life bastards—who'd ruined her life, a spark had ignited deep in her gut, and she wanted to do whatever it took to see to it that they were all punished. If she'd killed or maimed any of them that night, she would accept whatever punishment a court of law meted out to her.

Ace stretched, his back arching in a U shape. He circled his new bed a couple of times, then lay back down, curling himself up in a ball. Gregg from the pet store had guessed he was at least six months old when she'd asked. While an animal was not in her plans, she found she kind of liked having him with her. She would say something, and he would look at her and respond with a meow.

For the next hour, she listened to a talk-radio

station based in Boston but then switched to a classical music station that also had news on the hour. She despised the news, but she thought there might be a chance that Tanner had reported her missing. She highly doubted he would, but in case he did, she wanted to know in order to prepare herself. She might need to adjust her plans. Not that he had a clue where she was headed, but one call to the taxi service and it wouldn't be too hard to follow her trail from there. The gym, the bus, the storage unit. Even though she'd been somewhat disguised, a good detective could find her.

She kept her fingers crossed that Tanner wouldn't call the police.

Chapter Nineteen

After leaving Dr. McCann, Bryan Whitmore returned to the station, where he spent the rest of his shift investigating the dentist. He did not like what he learned. He almost feared for the current Mrs. McCann, but a quick call to airport security confirmed that her Mercedes had been there yesterday morning, just like the doctor said. He'd checked the flight manifest, and, sure enough a Kristen Renee McCann had boarded a flight to Paris. So where was the doctor's wife? Though he'd only walked down the hallway leading to the doctor's den, he hadn't seen any signs of a struggle. Of course, how much would he have been able to see in a long and dimly lit hall? He hadn't realized how dark the hall was, as he thought about it just now. Had the dentist been hiding something? Blood? Flesh? Evidence of a gunshot?

He didn't know, but he planned to find out. He'd spent the remainder of his shift reading the accident report on Elaine McCann, and he didn't like that either.

The officer who took the report had retired, but the medical examiner, Vikki Kearns, hadn't. He planned to visit her as soon as he'd collected all the evidence from that old case from storage. He'd called for it to be picked up an hour ago. Misty, the officer in charge, promised him she'd have it ready for pickup by eight o'clock. It was quarter till, and if he knew Misty, she would've trudged downstairs to the basement, where old evidence was stored, and brought it up right away. It didn't hurt that she had a thing for him, but he wasn't interested. She was way too young, and from what some of the guys said, she loved to party. At forty-three, he was way over his partying days. He'd never been much for parties in his youth. He didn't see this changing anytime in the near future.

He entered the evidence room and signed in.

"Hey, handsome," Misty said. "I've got your box of goodies. What gives? This case was ruled an accident," she said as she signed her name next to his.

"It was, and I'm probably wasting time, but it's just one of those gut-feeling things I need to check out. I appreciate your being so prompt, kiddo." He added the last word in the hope, probably vain, that she would catch his drift.

"You're welcome, old man." She grinned, revealing a mouthful of silver braces. Definitely too young. His own daughter, Marty, was ready for braces. He could see him introducing Misty to his daughter. He shook his head. "Old man, my ass," he said, hoisting the banker's box onto his shoulder.

"See you, Bryan," she called as he made his way upstairs. He waved in return.

What he wanted to do was take this stuff home, but with Mrs. McCann still unaccounted for, he'd work at the station.

He wasn't tired anyway. The night shift had been fairly quiet. The Goldenhills Police Department consisted of fourteen blue suits and six detectives, plus the crime-scene gang, as he referred to the group of four. Add the medical examiner and her two assistants—well, it wasn't Boston—but they had a good team, and Bryan respected the entire force, no matter what their position. It was a good group, and he'd never regretted joining the force. There wasn't much crime in the area, just enough to keep them on their toes.

He dropped the box on top of his desk and called Vikki, the medical examiner. "What?" she asked. "Don't you realize I'm busy?"

Bryan laughed into the phone. Vikki was a top-notch medical examiner, and a good friend. In her late fifties, she looked ten years younger, and if they weren't such good friends, at one time he might've considered asking her for a date. "You know why I'm calling. I just wanted to make sure you had time to chat. I've got an old case I want you to look at. It's simple, and before you ask, yes, I have the autopsy report. I'll be over in five," he said.

The medical examiner's office was in a typical redbrick building with no parking, located directly across the street from the police department. He froze every time he entered the place. He walked down the hallway, then made a left and a right. He tapped on Vikki's door.

"Get your ass in here," she said. She was seated at her desk, a grin as bright as the sun on her face. With her short blond hair and light blue eyes, and with the sensuous set of her lips, she was a very attractive woman. She motioned for him to sit down in the chair across from her.

"You're a shitload of grace, you know that?" He tossed the autopsy report on her desk. "You remember this?"

Vikki picked up the sheaf of papers and took her time flipping through them. She went back and forth between several pages before passing them back to him. "I remember this case. I hadn't been the medical examiner very long when it happened."

"Tell me what you remember, and not what's in your report."

She took a deep breath, clasping her hands together. "Her head injury was intense. I remember there were several lacerations on the back of her head, just as the report stated. Guys on the scene thought there was more blood than there should've been. Her body was found in a position that I felt was inconsistent with

the fall she took. I remember the husband saying he'd moved her, tried to give her CPR, and
there was blood evidence to prove it, but I've
always suspected there was more to this. Why,
you working a cold case or just nosing around?"

"No to the cold case. I turned the position
down. I like being out in the field too much.
Maybe someday, but not now. Actually, the husband is remarried, and his new wife is currently missing. He's my dentist, do you believe
that?" Bryan gave a wry laugh and shook his
head.

"He called me last night, sort of as a favor.
Said he and his wife had had a fight the night
before, and he hadn't seen her since she spent
the night in their daughter's bedroom. The
daughter is on a high-school graduation trip in
France, which checks out, and the boys, twins
from his first marriage—well, let's just say he
doesn't want me talking to them."

"Were they at home when the argument
took place?" Vikki asked.

"Yes, and according to the doctor, the argument was over the boys. I think they're around
twenty-one or twenty-two now."

"Go on," Vikki prompted.

"The guy was all over the place. He even
asked me if I'd be interested in investing in his
dental clinics. I hate to say it, but he's a great
dentist. I've seen him a few times. Not much
patience with the hired help, but he might be
one of those doctors who has a God complex.
Talked about his first wife as though she were
an idol he worshipped. His story was iffy, to say

the least. I had Tom Riser at the airport look at the security tapes going in and out of the airport. Just like the doc said, she drove her daughter to the airport in her Mercedes, and he says no one has seen her since."

"What did he tell you about the argument, the boys? I don't get it," Vikki said.

"Apparently, and this is according to him, Molly—that's the wife—accused one of the boys of using drugs. Then he went on to say she hated the two of them. He said that she was drunk, and fell and slammed her face against the bed frame. He even had the audacity to tell me he knew proper police procedure. A real wacko.

"And he'd been drinking. When I asked again if I could talk to the sons, he got angry. Though he swore he'd talked to one of them earlier that night, when I asked to see his phone and the incoming call, again, he was a total jerk. Like I said, all over the place. So, given this"—he nodded at the sheaf of papers on her desk—"and now the other wife is nowhere to be found, I think it's suspicious."

"Yes, it sounds that way. So, what can I do?"

He took a deep breath and raked his hand across his face. "I just wanted to hear your take on his first wife's death, that's all. Plus I wanted to see your beautiful face," he said, laughing.

She rolled her eyes. "You and a dozen others. Seriously, though, I do remember the case and having misgivings at the time myself. You think it's worth reopening, taking a second look?"

"Maybe on the sly. I doubt the district attorney is going to open a case that was ruled an accident."

"What about the missing wife? What if she turns up dead? Think the DA would reopen the case then?"

"Too little, too late, as the saying goes. I'm concerned."

"So did the husband file a missing person report?"

"He tried, but I haven't officially decided if she's a missing person or not. You know me and my gut. It's telling me there's more going on with the good dentist and his wife than he told me. He was angry, and I would bet my last nickel he's violent. Maybe he hits her, who knows? To answer your question, I haven't formally filed the report, but I'm going to as soon as I go back to the office and make it official, so I can get a search warrant to check out that mansion he lives in on Riverbend Road."

Vikki whistled. "Those houses carry a pretty high price tag. Maybe I should've gone to dental school instead."

"Nah, your patients like you too much," he teased.

"Actually that's why I decided to go into the field. The dead tell stories, as we all know. Sometimes, there's a story to tell *before* they die, and that's your job, to arrest the perps."

Bryan noticed the change in Vikki's tone. "Something happen to you, Vik?" he asked, using the pet name he'd given her years ago.

"Not to me. To a kid in the neighborhood

where I grew up. Four-year-old boy. He was the cutest kid ever. Silver-blond hair, and the bluest eyes." Tears filled her eyes, and she wiped at them with the sleeve of her white jacket.

"And?"

"His stepmom found him dead in the living room. He'd sucked in some plastic from a dry-cleaning bag. Mom took him to the hospital, but it was too late."

"Okay, I get the four-year-old kid was innocent, but why did his death affect you?"

"His sister was my best friend. Her mom had died when she was little, and her father remarried. She hated her stepmom and always swore that she'd killed Billy. That was his name."

"And this is why you wanted to be a medical examiner?"

She nodded. "Twenty years later, I ruled Billy's death a homicide. The stepmom is serving a life sentence with no parole."

"Whew! That is some story, but how did you become involved twenty years after the fact?"

"The stepmom murdered my friend's father, her husband, and a damned good investigator did his job. Twenty years later, Billy's body was exhumed, and I was the acting medical examiner. And the rest, as they say, is history."

"Son of a bitch," was all Bryan could say.

Chapter Twenty

Molly drove all day and through the night, stopping only for gas, two bathroom breaks, and to let Ace take care of business. He knew what his litter pan was, but she decided he preferred doing his business outdoors.

It was just half past six when she took the exit off I-75 to Blossom City. It seemed like only yesterday, she thought, as she headed down Carroll Road, the highway on which she had run over those bastards who had raped her. She rolled down the window, and the blast of hot, moist air took her breath away. *Hotbed of hell*, she thought as she cruised toward her destination. Pulling off to the side of the road, she got out of the Mustang, taking Ace along. It was too hot for him to stay in the car. There was no traffic at this hour, nothing to set any alarm bells ringing. She crossed the median and looked at the strip of road facing north. She walked about fifty yards ahead and stopped.

This was it. The scene of the accident. She knew it was because this was where the road curved, and just beyond this point, her rapists had been drunk and standing in the middle of the road. She looked to the west and saw miles and miles of orange groves. This is where Ricky Rourke had parked his bright-yellow Camaro that night. She took in her surroundings, waiting for a reaction. A panic attack, maybe her heart racing a bit, but she felt nothing. This was simply an old road flanked by orange groves. If you inhaled, you could still smell the tomato-canning factory. Molly was surprised it was still operational, but she knew that back in the day, it had employed a third of the town. Probably still did, she thought, as she crossed the median and returned to her car. She took a bottle of water from the cooler she'd placed in the backseat and filled Ace's water dish. He lapped thirstily, then settled back in his bed. She ran her hand along his spine and then tugged his tail. "I should've named you Lucky."

She had just pulled back onto Carroll Road when her cell phone rang with Kristen's familiar cymbal sound. "Hey kiddo, what's up?"

"*Tu me manques.*"

"I didn't study French," she said, a smile on her face. "What's it mean?"

"It means 'I miss you,' and I do. Are you okay?" Kristen asked.

"I miss you, too, sweetie, and I'm fine. I have a surprise for you when you come home."

"Mom! You know how I hate it when you do that. What is it? You know I'll go nuts thinking about it."

"Don't go nuts, but it's something you've always wanted."

"Are you with Dad?"

"No," Molly said, hearing the anger in her voice. "Why do you ask?"

"You sound happy, so I knew you weren't with him; I just had to check. Okay, Mom, we are about to head out. I'll call tomorrow. Love you," Kristen said, then hung up.

Molly placed the phone on the passenger seat and headed to her next destination. She knew the route by heart, and she felt a sudden sense of loss. She turned off Carroll Road and made the turn onto Orange Park Way. She slowed down as she drove past her old high school. There were a few cars in the parking lot, but school was out, so she knew there would be no students around. On a whim, she made a U-turn and pulled into the parking lot. The teachers' parking lot. Everything looked the same. Old and tired, with secrets that she knew weren't safe anymore.

She got out of the car, again taking Ace as the heat was horrendous. She needed to see for herself, needed to look at the exact location where her life had changed. Without giving it a second thought, she hurried toward the football field.

She stopped when she reached the bleachers. Taking a deep breath, and holding Ace so tight he meowed loudly, she walked around to the back of the bleachers. The ground was covered in dirt; the grass had long since dried up. Soda cans, empty cigarette packages, and other unidentifiable debris littered the shadowed area under the bleachers. She tried to find the exact location where she'd been brutally raped all those years ago, but time had softened her memory, and she'd been unconscious for some of it. She remembered waking up under the bleachers, but she had no way to pinpoint the spot. She walked the length of the old wooden bleachers twice, but she still couldn't pick out any definite place. All she recalled was that she'd been dragged under the bleachers. The lights from the football field had shone between the bleachers; she remembered that. She looked at the lights on the field, their positions, and had no memory of it since the lights looked new and most likely had been placed a few feet, give or take, from their original spots. She saw nothing that triggered a memory. Just as the place on Carroll Road was just a local roadway, this was just a high-school football field.

Heading back to her car, she felt disappointed, not knowing what, if anything, she had expected to find. However, she knew what she was really doing.

Avoiding the most obvious thing.

It would be outright insane, but she knew she had to do this. She'd traveled many miles, and now she realized there was really no purpose in her returning to her hometown. What had she expected to find? Her rapists lined up in a neat little row with handwritten apologies? Of course not, she thought, as she put Ace on his bed. She sat on the seat and remembered this was Florida, the Sunshine State. Where the sun bore into the seat of your car seats and you burned your legs if you weren't careful.

She hated this place. She'd never liked living here, even though, at the time, she'd had nothing to compare it to. Still, she had hated it. The heat. The bugs, the sickening smell of the canning factory. This was her past, her history, but not her future. She would never bring Kristen to this place. Never.

Angry at herself, she left her old high school and headed for the place she'd called home. That hot tin can. *It was probably scrap metal by now,* she thought as she drove to the edge of town.

The old trailer park on Seahorse Road was still there! Shocked, she drove through the entrance, counting the tin boxes. One. Two. Three. Four.

And there was number five.

She pulled off the dirt road and put the car in PARK. Molly got out of the car and walked to the only home she'd ever known for her first seventeen years. The goddamn place hadn't changed one bit. The aqua siding had faded, and where once it had been white, it was now rusted and broken. The wooden porch was new. Their old porch was gray with age and rickety on the third step. She remembered how she'd hated hearing that sound when Marcus and his buddies were running in and out. This porch had a handicapped ramp. She supposed

the tenants—that's what they called them then—
were wheelchair-bound. The park was quiet,
unlike how it had been in her day. No teenagers roaring in and out of the lots, spinning
dust in their wake. No women watching small
kids run around in nothing but diapers. No
clotheslines draped with the dark-green uniforms from the canning factory. There had
never been a breeze.

The place looked like the end of the world.
Dead. Dried up. She had a thought, and it sickened her, but she realized now that it was the
truth.

*Had I not been raped, I might still be living here
in this death camp.*

She was about to get back in the car when
the door to her old place swung open. Molly
couldn't help herself. She turned and stared as
a man in an old wheelchair pushed himself
onto the porch. He sat there for a few seconds,
then reached in his breast pocket, pulled out
a pack of cigarettes. His hands were atrophied,
almost clawlike, as he arranged the cigarette
between his lips. With the same deformed
hands, he removed a lighter from the same
pocket. He used his thumb, and she could see
that it was difficult for him to light his cigarette. She thought she should offer to help him,
but she hated the smell of cigarette smoke, so
she remained rooted to her spot by the Mustang, with Ace fast asleep in her arms, as she
watched the man take a long drag after he finally managed to light the cigarette. He blew
the smoke out in circles. She remembered kids

in school doing this but couldn't recall what it was called. He took another long puff, and again, he slowly blew the smoke out from his lungs in perfect white circles.

Something about the act brought back memories of her mother. And her twin brother. She gasped, rooted to the ground. It couldn't be! But her eyes told her it not only could be but was.

She stepped away from the protection of her car and slowly walked toward the trailer, where the man continued to blow white circles of smoke from his mouth.

As she came closer to the trailer, she saw an oxygen tank fastened to the wheelchair, with a long, clear hose wrapped around the base. Beneath that was a clear bag filled with dark yellow liquid. *Urine.* A drainage bag for a catheter.

Good Lord, she thought, as she openly stared at the man. Curiosity was like a magnet, its force drawing her toward the tin can and the man. She couldn't have stopped herself if her life had depended on it. Slowly, she crossed the dirt path leading to the home she'd left a little more than twenty-one years before.

She stood at the bottom of the ramp, sweat dripping down her face, her back, and beneath her arms. Ace felt like a heating pad against her skin, but she held him closer.

Her throat was dry, and she wished for a bottle of water from the cooler. Frightened, but not the way she used to be, she stepped onto the porch.

"Marcus?"

Chapter Twenty-one

Bryan rode in the patrol car with two uniforms, Jaime Rodriguez and Alex Craig.

"This guy must be rolling in the bucks," Craig said.

"He's a dentist. Worked on my teeth a few times. Actually, he's pretty good, but he charges out the ass," Bryan said.

"Think he'll give us any trouble?" Rodriguez asked.

"I doubt it, but that's why I dragged you two along." Bryan laughed. "Two of Goldenhills' finest."

Craig was built like a prizefighter, muscles with muscles, but not very tall, maybe five-seven. With his shaved head and piercing, dark eyes, he was intimidation at its best. Rodriguez stood six-foot-seven, lanky, and lean, with the prowess of a panther. On one occasion he had wrestled three suspects at once to the ground and not broken a sweat. Bryan had known exactly what he was doing when he asked the pair to accompany him to deliver the search warrant.

The patrol car inched down the long drive as though they had all the time in the world. The tactic was used in the hope of catching recipients of search warrants, whoever they might be, in the act of either running or hiding something. Give the bad guys enough rope to hang themselves.

When they reached the edge of the drive, Bryan asked Rodriguez, who was driving, to pull up as close to the front of the house as possible. With luck, the good doctor would allow them to search the premises and be on their way. Bad luck, and they'd all be earning their pay.

They got out of the car. "Hang back for now," he instructed the uniforms. "You'll intimidate the hell out of the doc. Hell, you intimidate the hell out of me."

Bryan rang the doorbell. He knew the doctor and his sons were home because someone had been watching the house. No answer. Bryan rang the bell again, this time holding his finger on the button without removing it.

The door was yanked open by a young guy wearing nothing but a pair of green boxers. "Hey, dudes, what's up?" he singsonged cheerfully.

"Holden, get your damn ass back upstairs. Now!" someone yelled from within the house.

The guy, obviously Holden McCann, held both palms up in surrender before backing away from the door and turning to speak to his father, who had come up behind him. "Okay, Dad. You need to cool it, totally," he said, and anyone who could hear him had to know that he was as high as a kite.

Tanner McCann stepped outside. "What can I do for you, Detective Whitmore? I was about to leave. I have an appointment in Boston."

"You might want to cancel it, Dr. McCann. We have a search warrant." Bryan handed the warrant to him for his perusal.

"Exactly what is it you're looking for? My wife? I'll save you the trouble. She isn't here. Now, if you will be on your way, I can be on mine."

Craig and Rodriguez walked closer to the door.

"So you are giving us permission to search the premises without your presence?" Bryan questioned.

"Hell no, I'm not! What gives you that idea?"

"Dr. McCann, we have a search warrant. We are authorized to search your home with or without your permission. Remember, you wanted to file that missing person report? This is just the beginning. So, if I were you, I'd take the easy way out, let us do our jobs, and if you're lucky, you'll make your appointment in Boston. If not, we'll have to have Officer Craig restrain you so we can do our jobs. The choice is yours entirely," Bryan explained

He'd never been so excited to see a grown

man squirm in his life. The emotions that danced across the doctor's face were that of a child about to throw a temper tantrum. He couldn't help himself, and he laughed out loud.

"I don't see the humor, Detective. I bet if I report this to your superior, he won't see any either."

"I thought you had already tried that, speaking to my superior. Strange, he never mentioned it to me. And I'm afraid that you're wrong. He would. Now, permission to enter?" He jerked his head toward Craig and Rodriguez.

The two officers stepped behind Dr. McCann and pushed the front door open. "Where to start, sir?" Craig asked Bryan, all formality now.

Molly McCann liked to cook, Bryan remembered. "Let's start in the kitchen."

"I haven't given you my permission," McCann yelled to their backs, as they walked inside.

Bryan hung back, hoping to quiet this idiot so they could do what they were here to do. "We don't need it, Doc. So let's just get this over with, okay. Remember, you called me? Your wife is missing. We want to do everything within our power to find her. I'm sure you do, too. I certainly would hate for you to lose another wife to a tragic accident. I know you're worried, and you're just acting out, but you do want us to find your wife alive, right?"

A shadow fell across McCann's dark eyes. He turned away, so Bryan couldn't see his face.

Good reaction, he thought, but he knew that he had this sick bastard's number. He'd play nice. For now.

"Of course I do," Dr. McCann said through gritted teeth. "What do you think I am? Some kind of maniac?"

That's exactly what Bryan thought. He couldn't have said it better himself. He grinned. This son of a bitch was hiding something, and Bryan was going to find out what it was or die trying. His gut rarely failed him, and it was jumping, big-time.

"Of course not. Now let's go inside, so you can show me around. I'll want to look through Molly's things. That way you can tell me if anything is missing." Make him feel like he was doing *them* a favor.

"All right," he said, and headed back inside the house.

"This is a beautiful home you have, Dr. Mc-Cann. I promise we'll be careful not to break anything, though it does happen occasionally."

"If you break anything, I will hold the police department personally responsible."

Of course you would, you jerk. "As I said, we're careful." Sometimes they weren't. Especially when they were dealing with an ass like Tanner McCann.

"Dude, what the hell? I mean, Dad, what the hell are the cops here for?" It was the same guy in the green boxers.

"Dr. McCann, this must be one of your sons."

"Lucky for him," said the guy. "I'm Olden, I

mean Holden." He held out a limp hand to Bryan. Bryan reached for the young man's hand and shook it, though his palm was so sweaty that Bryan could barely get a grip. Definitely a doper.

"Pleased to meet you, Holden." Before the obviously stoned young man's dad had a chance to quiet him, Bryan pounced. "Holden, we're here because your father reported your mother missing last night. Were you aware of this?"

Holden's eyes doubled. "Wow, no, man I didn't know. She dead?" he asked in his drug-induced haze.

"Goddammit, Holden, go upstairs! You're drunk."

"No, Dr. McCann, I want to speak to him. And I'm not sure that he's drunk, though we can do a Breathalyzer test if he consents. He is over eighteen, correct?"

"I'm cool, dude, but I need to get some clothes on."

Bryan followed him. "I'll just hang behind."

"Sure, dude."

Bryan knew that both sons, though he'd yet to meet the other, had recently graduated from Harvard. Amazing what an Ivy League education could do for one.

Holden's room was at the top of the stairs and to the right. When Bryan stepped inside, he almost gagged. Piles of clothes smelling from sweat were everywhere. Pizza boxes, plates with something no longer edible were on the hardwood flooring. Little packets of bubble wrap with pills inside littered the floor. Bryan would make a call to the narcotics squad. They'd have a field day in this room, but he wasn't here to bust the guy.

Holden picked a pair of jeans from one of the many piles and a black T-shirt. "Do I need shoes?" he asked Bryan.

What a waste, he thought. "Only if you prefer."

"What's that 'spose to mean?" he slurred.

The words "Harvard-educated" kept playing through Bryan's brain. He'd make a point to tell Marty that Harvard wasn't all it was cracked up to be.

"Let's talk for a minute before we go downstairs. You okay with that?"

Holden nodded, then dropped down on the unmade bed. The sheets were filthy and stiff. How in the hell could a person do this to himself? But that wasn't for him to decide. No way was he going to sit down in the filthy room, so he crammed his hands in his pockets and began pacing. "So you didn't realize your mother was missing? Do you remember the last time you saw her?"

He doubted he would gain anything from this so-called talk, but it was worth a shot.

"Nope, not today. She's not our mom. Just the step one. She's nice, though."

Great.

"So she's your stepmother, then?"

Holden nodded.

"Do you remember your biological mother?"

"Nope. She's dead. Fell downstairs, but Graham said Dad really pushed her. 'Cause she hated him, too."

Bryan stopped pacing. Were these the words of a stoner, or were they true?

"Why do you think she hated your father?" Bryan asked him.

"Everybody hates him."

The door to the room filled with a presence. Bryan turned to see who it was and was a bit surprised when he saw a cleaned-up version of Holden.

"You must be Graham. I'm Detective Whitmore."

"I know who you are," Graham said.

Sober and a smart-ass, just like his father— at least the smart-ass part.

"Then you know why we're here. You're father reported your mother missing last night. We are here to search for anything that might give us an idea where she went, who she's with, that sort of thing. Do you remember the last time you saw your mother?" Bryan asked. He wasn't going to pussyfoot around with Graham. He was sober and could answer the questions.

"They had a dinner party the night before last. She was in the kitchen, with Sally, the maid. I haven't seen her since," Graham stated. "Is that all?"

"I'm not finished, son."

"I'm not your son, and I would appreciate it if you didn't refer to me that way."

"Sorry. You aren't my son, you're right. But

if you were, I can guarantee you wouldn't talk to me like some smart-ass middle schooler. So, let's continue, *Graham.*" He put extra emphasis on his name. "Were you home all night after the dinner party?"

"Yes."

"Did you hear your parents fighting?"

"Man, *I* did. Dad was sooo pissed," Holden shot out from his perch on the bed.

Bryan directed his gaze at Graham but spoke to Holden. "What did you hear, Holden?"

"It was bad . . ."

"Shut up, Holden," Graham said to his twin.

"Are you afraid he might say something he shouldn't?" Bryan asked Graham. The look on the younger twin's face said it all. Of course he was.

"I'm finished with you now, *Graham.* You can leave the room. I want to speak with your brother. Alone."

"My dad will have your badge," he said, then left the room.

What a little jerk. Like father, like son.

He directed his attention back to the lump of humanity on the bed. "So, Holden, you were saying your dad was pissed and that it was bad. What does that mean?"

"Dad was, man, he was so pissed. The kitchen was baked in. Molly, dude, she can bake good stuff. And Dad threw the pans. She wasn't here, but I saw her go, she, man, she wanted to go. But she's not driving 'cause that taxi got her. That pink thing. I seen her go, man. She had her bags all dragged behind her. She didn't wanna get tossed, like down them stairs, like Mom. Like before, Graham says."

Though Holden was stoned, he wasn't as bad as he'd been when they arrived. If what he said was true, then Molly McCann hadn't gone missing. She'd left of her own free will.

"Okay, Holden, you rest up, and I'll talk to you in a bit." He knew he sounded like he was talking to a child, but in all the ways that were important, he was. A child that just happened to reside in the body of a man.

He left Holden lying on the bed and hurried downstairs to the kitchen, where Craig and Rodriguez were taking their good old easy time as they searched the kitchen. It was huge. It could take hours.

"Sir, I think you might want to have a look at this," Craig said. He was standing with a top-of-the-line dishwasher open. Inside, it was full of pans used to bake bread in. He knew this because he liked to bake. He'd never admit it to the guys, but on his days off he was known to make a hearty loaf of rye or two.

"What's so interesting about loaf pans, Officer Craig?"

He took one of the pans from the dishwasher; they were clean, which might not be a good thing in this case, and walked over to the kitchen cabinet. "See this?" He took the pan and placed its sharp corner in a large nick in the wood door on the cabinet. "It's a perfect fit."

"It is. Let's get some pictures. Bag the pan, and let's take the door off the hinges."

At that moment, Dr. McCann and his younger son both forced their way into the kitchen.

"You are not taking one item out of my house, and you are certainly not going to remove a very expensive door from custom-made cabinets. It's not going to happen," the doctor said.

"We are, and it is. If you don't calm down, Dr. McCann, I'm going to have you arrested for verbal assault, and before you tell me I can't, I can. And while I've got your attention, I think your wife left. Willingly. And I think you know it, too. I want a complete guest list from your dinner party. I want names and numbers, and don't you dare try to tell me you don't have them. You got that, Dr. McCann?" Bryan all but snarled. He'd had enough mollycoddling for one day. "Now, not later."

He wasn't going to sit on the information Holden had revealed another minute. Everyone in Goldenhills knew the pink taxicab company. It was known by the not-so-original name of Pinky's.

Chapter Twenty-two

The boy with the golden eyes. Molly looked at the man in the wheelchair. "Do you know who I am?" she asked, her voice a whisper.

He looked at her, up and down, an evil grin lifting the corners of his mouth. "Should I?"

Dear God, he was as sick now as he'd been as a teenager.

"Marcus, look at me."

He rolled his eyes but did as she asked. Her skin crawled as his gaze traveled the length of her body, stopping at the V between her legs, then her breasts. "Turn around. I always remember a nice ass." He laughed, the sound hoarse. He began to cough, hacking so loud that Ace stretched his neck in order to see where the noise was coming from. When he stopped, he hocked and sent a glob of mucus flying across the porch. Molly couldn't help but look. Piles of slimy gunk were all over the porch. She wanted to throw up.

"I'm going to ask you one more time. Look at me. And I don't mean look at my . . . private parts, you pervert. Look in my eyes, you filthy son of a bitch!" She couldn't help it. Twenty-one years of rage were erupting, and she couldn't stop.

"You nasty, filthy piece of trash! Don't you recognize me?" She screamed so loud that she startled Ace again, and he was no longer resting peacefully in her arms.

Marcus wheeled the chair around so that he could look more closely. He inched as near as he could without knocking her backward. Molly almost gagged at the odor. Urine, feces, and something else she couldn't put a name to. She took a step back.

At that moment she truly understood the meaning of hate.

"Did I screw you back in the day?" he asked, then laughed. "Is that how you know my name?" His teeth, what was left of them, were brown and rotten, each tooth no more than a sliver.

This was the odor she couldn't identify. Rotted teeth. The thought flashed through her head: Tanner would have had his work cut out for him.

If she'd had a weapon, she would've used it. This man was vile, gross, and repulsive. She couldn't come up with enough adjectives to describe his foulness.

"It's me, you perverted son of a bitch! Maddy. Your twin sister. Remember prom night? You took money from those low-life sons of bitches who were your friends so they could look at my body! Do you remember, Marcus?" She screamed so loud, a woman in the next trailer came out and stood on her porch, watching.

She saw his reaction as recognition dawned on him.

He looked at her again, only this time he squinted those golden eyes that their mother had been so proud of. "Well, I'll be a son of a bitch, it *is* you!" He struggled to get a full breath of air. "You fucking whore, you did this to me! You ruined my life. Why you comin' home now? You knocked up? Got one of them sexually transmitted diseases? You killed Mom, you bitch! When you left, ya killed her!"

"Screw you, Marcus." God, it felt good to say that after so long. "I hate your guts, and you know what? I think it's hysterical you're in that pissy-smelling wheelchair. I bet you can't even get it up anymore! Well, can you, you nasty piece of garbage?

"I only wish you'd died that night. I've prayed for it all these years. And something else, you nasty piece of work. I am glad that our mother is dead. I hated her, almost as much as I hate you. I ought to do the world a favor and put you out of your misery this very second!" Rage burned deep in her gut, and she wanted to hurt this worthless piece of humanity—no, that was too good a word for him, this worthless piece of whale crap.

"You came back thinkin' you're gonna get my disability check! Ain't no way, whore. It's deposited directly in my account every single month." He smiled at her as though he had just offered her Donald Trump's wealth.

"Disability? You think that's why I came back to this godforsaken hole? You're out of your mind. Apparently, you're not getting enough of that oxygen to your brain, but wait, do you actually have a brain?"

She pulsed with an anger so deep, it shocked her. Words she'd never thought she knew came out of her mouth. "Did you ever learn to read anything besides *Hustler*? Oh wait, you didn't need to read *Hustler*, you just looked at the pictures!" She couldn't hold back any longer. She leaned forward and spat in his face, then kicked the wheelchair so hard it rolled across to the opposite side of the porch. But she wasn't finished. Not caring that she'd have to touch his filthy skin, she gripped Ace in her left hand as tight as she could; then, with her right hand, she swung as hard as she could, her fist landing on his filthy mouth.

"Get off my property before I call the cops. They hear you're in town, they'll be coming after you like flies on shit, *sissy*!"

She gritted her teeth so hard that it hurt. "Call them now! Go on, do it! I want you to call them. Tell them what your damned sick friends did to me on prom night! *CALL THEM NOW!*"

"Get outta here, you whore!"

"Is that all you can do is call me a whore? You must have me mistaken for *our mother*! She was the whore! Or don't you remember? You sicken me. When I leave here, I am calling the police! I'm going to report the crime that I should have reported twenty-one years ago!" She turned to leave but decided she wasn't finished yet.

She walked the few steps to where he sat. She reached inside his filthy shirt pocket, took his cigarettes and lighter out, and smashed them in his face. "I hope you die and go to hell, and choke on our mother's ashes, which I am sure are still smoldering in the pits of hell!"

She looked at the rage on his face and slapped him as hard as she could. "That's for ruining my life!"

He screamed at her then, but she ran down the ramp and to her car so fast, she had no memory when she looked up and saw she'd arrived at the church. Her hands shook so badly, she wished for a drink to calm them. Ace was in his bed, sleeping, and she had no memory of placing him there, either.

The church. Her second-to-last stop before she left.

Pastor Royer.

According to the sign out front, the one that announced the times for Sunday service, he was still the pastor.

Good, she thought, as she kicked open the Mustang's door. She grabbed Ace and headed for the entrance. If the present was anything like the past, and she felt sure that it was, the good pastor would be in his office planning this Sunday's sermon.

She practically ran down the sidewalk leading to the church entrance. Father Wink would not approve of the thoughts she was having. She'd have to say so many Hail Marys, she would die before she finished. Never in her thirty-eight years had she felt such rage, even when Tanner hit her. She'd been afraid of him but hadn't felt rage, only hatred and resignation.

She had been afraid her entire life. Today she was putting those fears to rest, burying them, and she made a promise to herself: she would *never* allow another human being to mistreat her again.

"Can I help you?" a female voice called out from behind the piano.

"No, Bobbie Lou, you can't. What you can do is find Pastor Royer for me."

"Why, he's busy plannin' the Sunday sermon and can't be disturbed. Who are you, anyway? And how do you know my name?"

Molly felt the woman stare at her from behind the piano. The woman could see her, but Molly couldn't see the woman, though she recognized Bobbie Lou's nasally voice. She wanted to holler and cuss but had enough respect not to do so in a church.

"Go. Get. Pastor. Royer. Now. Do. Not. Say. Another. Word. GO!" she screamed, putting emphasis on her last word. Bobbie Lou saw her and raced down the aisle. She would've laughed had the situation not been so revolting.

Seconds later, Pastor Royer, with a shaking

Bobbie Lou cowering behind him, walked down the long aisle.

"You have scared my pianist, young lady. I'm asking you to leave peacefully. If not, I will have to call the authorities." He sounded just like he used to. His high-pitched voice sounded like that of a female. She remembered the Sundays when she would help clean up and replace the hymnals, and a few times she would hear some of the well-known church ladies making fun of his voice. One had said she suspected he was homosexual. Well, she thought, they could put that thought to rest because she was here in the flesh, and somehow, she just knew she wasn't created by Immaculate Conception. More like no *contraception*.

"Call them," she said in a voice so commanding she surprised herself. "And when you do, I want you to explain to them why the pastor of their church, the *only* church in Blossom City, is a phony and a pervert. Tell them all about your private life, *Pastor.*"

He looked at Bobbie Lou, his beady little eyes reminding her of a rat's. "Bobbie Lou, give us a moment."

As soon as she was out of earshot, Molly spoke. "Pastor, I have a question—"

"May the blessings of—"

"Shut up! I neither want nor need your blessing. Especially not *your* blessing. You have already given me more than enough.

"Now, I said I have a question, and I want an answer when I am through speaking. I don't want to hear a word out of that hypocritical mouth of yours until I finish what I came here to say."

His mouth opened, and Molly walked toward him, her right hand raised. "Don't speak until I tell you to!"

His mouth moved up and down like a puppet's, minus the voice.

She sat down in one of the pews because her legs were shaking. "Pastor, please." She waved her hand in front of her. He stared at her, but did nothing. "Sit!"

He dropped to the pew so fast, he stirred up a small breeze, causing a page in the hymnal to flutter. *Coward*, she thought.

She didn't say anything, but waited. She wanted him to feel the fear, to second-guess what was about to happen to him. Molly took a deep breath, and for show, she ran her hands up and down Ace's spine.

"Meow."

"Good kitty," she said, in a voice that was worthy of a starring role in a horror flick.

"I suppose you're wondering who I am and why I'm here," she said in her horror-movie voice.

He nodded his head up and down but didn't say anything. Good.

"Remember that little girl, Maddy Carmichael?" She watched for his reaction. His face turned as white as the wafers Father Wink offered up at Mass.

He nodded.

"She used to clean up after church services. Do you remember that?"

He nodded again.

"And you paid her twenty dollars. She tried to refuse, but you always insisted it would be stupid of her to refuse."

She didn't speak for a few minutes. She watched him, never took her eyes from his. He turned away.

"Now listen to me. You're a deadbeat dad. You married my mother, who just so happened to be a whore"—she held her hand up to prevent him from interrupting—"and you married her. When she gave birth to twins, you divorced her, deciding you'd devote your life to a higher calling. Well, *Daddy*, I'm that higher calling, and I have a proposition for you. Actually, it's more of a demand, but either way, you have no choice. Just like I had no choice when I had to work three jobs, study, and hope for a better life, only to have all of my hopes and dreams destroyed by your son. My brother. My twin brother. The boy with the golden eyes.

"Mother loved him, never me, but the past is prologue. Now, to the future. You are going to resign as pastor of this church, effective immediately—"

"I can't do that—"

Molly pointed her finger at him. "Don't interrupt me when I'm speaking. You can and you will. I am not leaving this church until you've written a detailed account of your life. When I have that, I'll make sure it's published in every newspaper in the state of Florida.

Then I want you to take all the money you've saved and donate it to a children's home. I also want to know about Marcus's accident."

"He was in a car accident on the highway . . . a few months after graduation. His friends died."

"Tell me their names."

He looked at her as though she'd lost her mind.

"Don't look at me that way, *Daddy*. I am Maddy Carmichael, or should I say Maddy *Royer*. And if need be, I'll insist upon a DNA test. It's not fun to be at my mercy, is it? Now go on, tell me the names."

"Ricky Rourke, Dennis Wilderman, and Troy Bowers." He hung his head.

Then she hadn't killed anyone! Nor had she been the cause of Marcus's accident. That lying bastard. It was another car accident that got them. It was as though fate was gunning for them, as they escaped that night only to be killed shortly thereafter. But there was still Dr. Kevin Marsden. She would see that he was prosecuted to the full extent of the law, that he would lose his license to practice medicine and end up in jail.

"It's time we head to your office, so we can get started on your memoir."

Three hours later, she left the church with exactly what she had come for. As soon as she returned to Goldenhills, she would send his story to all the newspapers in the state, just as she had promised him she would do. She'd also made him sign an agreement stating he wished to donate all of his savings to an orphanage.

She had one more stop to make before she left town. It wasn't far from the church, and she was glad. She was so emotionally drained from the rage, she thought she would pass out. Maybe her life would have been different had she done this years ago, but it is what it is, and she was making changes that would affect her and Kristen for the rest of their lives.

The Blossom Hill Cemetery was just down the road from the church. It was the only cemetery in town. Or it had been twenty-one years ago, and as with most other things in this town, she was sure that hadn't changed either.

Sure enough, there it was in the middle of a dried-up field without a single tree. Florida's scalding sun probably cremated the bodies as soon as they were in the ground.

She knew she sounded horrible, but she didn't care. A lifetime of hurt and anger was being expunged today. Almost. Now to get this over with. She parked the Mustang at the cemetery's entrance. It wasn't large, so she knew it wouldn't take her long to find what she was looking for. She left Ace in the car with the windows down and the air conditioner running full blast.

Three rows down, under the next-to-last marker, she found her mother's grave. She looked down at the brass marker, the engraved letters stating her name, date of birth, and date of death. She wanted to feel sad, a sense of loss, but she didn't. Molly couldn't force what wasn't there, and for that she was sad. She'd come here with the intention of telling her mother exactly what she thought of her, but as she stared down at the small marker, Molly decided she just wasn't worth it.

Chapter Twenty-three

Craig and Rodriguez stayed at the McCann house, taking statements from the doctor and the two boys. Bryan didn't expect to learn anything more than what he already knew, but it was enough.

As soon as he was back at the station, he put the wheels in motion. He immediately called Pinky's. "This is Detective Whitmore, Goldenhills Police Department. One of your guys picked up a fare on Riverbend Road a few days ago. I need to know where they dropped her off. This can't wait. Yes, I'll hold."

Sometimes being a cop got things done. Today was one of those days.

Pinky's came back on the line. He grabbed his pen and wrote down the address. All Night Fitness. He grabbed his badge and gun, and within twenty minutes, he was showing Molly McCann's picture to a young girl at the juice bar.

"That's Ms. M. She's been coming here forever. Is she in trouble? She's super nice. I'll get the owner—she can tell you more than I can."

Bryan was greeted by a woman a few years younger than he, and she would give Craig a run for his money in the muscle department. She introduced herself as Becky.

He showed her a picture. "That's Ms. M. She's been coming here for over ten years. Just once a month or so. She in trouble?"

"No, nothing like that. Actually, her husband has reported her missing, and, of course, we're following all leads."

Becky shook her head, her short brown hair moving from side to side. "I had no idea she was even married. I thought she was a career woman. She'd mentioned something about her job not allowing her much time at the gym. I hope she's okay. She's a very nice lady."

"Yes, so it seems. Did she ever meet anyone here? A man? Woman? Did she ever bring her daughter?" Bryan continued his questioning.

"This gets more surprising by the minute. I never saw her with anyone. She kept to herself, attended a few classes when she showed up. She would always get a smoothie and tip the gals, even though it's not required. I figured her as a class act. No clue she had a daughter, or even a husband."

"It seems Molly kept to herself."

"Her name is Molly?" Becky asked, though it was more a statement than a question. "We all called her Ms. M."

"Do you remember the last time she was here?" Bryan knew this was the most pivotal question, as this could turn his investigation around, either way.

"I do because she left here pulling an old piece of luggage behind her. And she was walking. I thought that beyond odd because for the last five years or so, she always drove a Mercedes. A silver one. Again, she was a class act. It was two days ago."

So she'd taken a taxi to the gym. Why here? Why not a hotel? A spa? Something a woman does when she's pissed at her husband.

If she hadn't met someone here, there had to be another reason. All he had to do was find it. For some strange reason, he felt it was his special duty to bring this woman home, safe and sound. Not that he didn't feel this way about all the citizens he'd sworn to serve and protect, but there was something that nagged him about this case, and right now he couldn't put a finger on it, but he would.

"Becky, this is going to sound insulting, and I want to apologize before I ask this question. This is a super cool place, and if I didn't have a home gym, I'd join in a heartbeat, but I do, so let me just spit it out. Why would Molly, Ms. M., come here if she were trying to escape or get away? Why not a hotel or a spa? A friend's house? You're a woman, so help me get inside her head."

"If I had to wage a guess, I would say she came here to empty her locker."

Bingo!

"Excellent. I had no clue gyms provided lockers other than the usual kind where you bring your own lock and just find what's empty or convenient, and switch out every time you go to the gym. Is that what we're talking about here?"

"No. We have permanent lockers. You want to see?" she asked.

"Absolutely."

He followed her through a maze of fitness equipment, past the smoothie bar, then to another room. Becky had a ring of keys around her arm, one of those rubbery bracelet styles that could double as jewelry. "First, you have to have a key to get into the room." She unlocked the door. "For a monthly fee, you can have a permanent locker, and while we have a few clients that choose this method, Ms. M., Molly, was the only member who has had a locker from the very beginning of her membership. We use keys, not combination locks. A bit more secure."

Here comes the hard part, he thought, but he was a police officer, it was his duty. "Can you open her locker? Or would you require a court order? I know it's an invasion of the client's privacy, but this could be serious. As in life-or-death serious."

Becky took a few seconds to consider his request. "I don't need a court order. I'll open it for you, but I don't think you'll find anything inside. She emptied the locker when she left."

"You saw her do it?"

"Not exactly. I couldn't swear that she emptied out everything, but I saw her coming in, and I saw her leave. Given the fact that she's missing, I'm just assuming she came here to remove something important. Just a guess, though."

"Let's have a look inside," he said.

"I'll have to check her locker number in the office. Give me a minute." Becky whirled out of the room, returning a couple of minutes later.

"It's 524."

Again, she fingered through her keys, and when she found what she was searching for, she slid the master key into locker number 524.

The door opened without any resistance.

"Can I?" he asked. "Just in case there is evidence."

She nodded and stepped away from the locker. Bryan peered inside the locker, which was much larger than one would normally expect. There were two hooks, but nothing was hanging from them. He felt around, and there was nothing there.

"The top shelf," Becky said.

Bryan stretched to see what she was referring to. There was a small metal shelf, its depth about five inches. Enough to store a handbag, or something else. He reached in and was stunned when his hand felt something. He hadn't really expected to find anything since

Molly had made a special trip here just to remove the contents from this locker, or that's
where his thoughts were leading him. He
pulled a brown paper bag from the shelf, careful to use the tips of his fingers just in case this
had to go to the print lab.

He set the brown bag on the long bench in
front of the lockers. He took his cell phone
from his pocket and took pictures from every
angle before returning it to his pocket.

"That's a super old bag," Becky said, and
they both laughed. "You know what I mean."

"No, tell me."

Without touching the bag, she pointed to a
faded logo that read LOU'S DINER. "They're still
in business, but I know for a fact these bags
aren't what they use now. They're located in
Cambridge, near Harvard. Believe it or not, I
actually attended college there. Studied medicine, but dropped out in my second year. Too
gory for me. My father is a doctor. It was expected," she offered as a way of explanation.
"Their take-out bags are plastic now. I've been
there a few times since. They have the best
corned-beef hash in the state."

Bryan took his phone out again and used
the flashlight app in order to read the logo
more clearly. "I think you're right, Becky. It
does say LOU'S DINER, but it's faded. I'm going
to have to take this with me. Evidence. Do you
have a garbage bag? I need to keep this as secure as I can."

"Sure, you want a giant one or kitchen-
sized?"

"A kitchen-sized bag should work if you don't mind getting me one."

Again, she made fast work of getting him the bag. He carefully placed the Lou's Diner bag inside. Something was in the paper bag, and it was a bit heavy, not deadweight heavy, but something more spread out. Fabric, maybe. As soon as he secured the bag, he took a few more pictures, then took several of the locker, both inside and out.

"Becky, I appreciate your cooperation. And because of this I have a buddy I'm going to send your way." He grinned. "He's a cop, and he's got more muscles than Popeye. We call him by his last name, Craig. You'll know him when you see him. And I will make sure he stops by. He may have a few questions for you." He nodded, then made his way to the front of the gym.

Becky trailed behind. "Tell him the first thirty days are free. You don't like, you don't buy." She was smiling.

"I'll tell him. Thanks again," he said. He put the bag in the trunk of his unmarked car and looked around. Where would a woman pulling a suitcase behind her go? At least from the gym. He walked down the street, heading south. He thought this was the most obvious direction, since north led into the business district.

What had she been wearing? "You're kidding," he said to himself and hoofed it back to the gym. Becky was talking to a woman at the smoothie bar. She smiled when she saw him.

"I forgot to ask the most obvious question. What was she wearing when she left? Do you happen to remember?"

"She always dressed classy. Nice jeans, a pretty blouse. Her hair was always in a French braid or a neat ponytail. She wasn't one of those gym pigs. That's what we call folks who come in their gym clothes and leave in their gym clothes. Ms. M. always showered before she left, and this last time, she showered and dried her hair, which she always does. She really stood out when she left, and I could tell she was trying to make sure no one saw her. She wore her hair up under a Boston Red Sox cap, and she had a pair of faded Levi's on. Men's, because I saw the red tag, and a black T-shirt. I didn't see what kind of shoes she wore, but I assume she had on sneakers."

"If you ever want a job, the police department could use someone like you. You have a good memory and an eye for detail. You're great, Becky, but now I have to get my ass off to work."

She waved, and for the second time, he headed south. He walked four blocks when he spied the bus stop. He needed an afternoon bus schedule, which he had back at the station. Running now, he was out of breath by the time he returned to his car. Inside, he took a few minutes to make notes, then he headed toward the station.

Holden had been absolutely right about his stepmother. He wondered if everything else he said was true as well. Though he'd been stoned, he knew what he was saying; Bryan would bet on it.

On his way back to the station, he called Vikki. He replayed his visit with Holden.

"I don't know if the DA will fall for it, no pun intended, but I can put a bug in his ear."

"It can't hurt. Thanks, Vik, I'll keep you posted."

Back at the station, he took the bag from the gym and did all the paperwork required to record it as evidence.

As soon as he was at his desk, he called Boston PD. His ex-wife's brother was a detective, and they were still friends. He called his cell number, yawning as he waited for him to pick up. Bryan hadn't slept in twenty-four hours. The day was catching up with him. And the night.

"Bry, my friend, what the hell is up?" Thomas finally answered as he was about to hang up.

"I need a favor," Bryan said.

Thomas laughed, the sound deep and throaty. "You's always needs a favor. What now?" He spoke with a heavy Boston accent. Bryan thought some of it was for show, but now wasn't the time to rag him about it. "There's a diner by the college. Lou's. You heard of it?"

"Hey, everybody's heard of Lou's. It's a freaking institution around Harvard. Why? You hungry?" Thomas laughed, and Bryan did, too.

"Ever the comic, I see. Nothing's changed.

Actually, it's about a case I'm working on." For the next ten minutes, he filled him in on as many details as possible.

"I'll send someone over now. As soon as I have any news, I'll call ya, and Bry, don't be a stranger."

"Same for you," he said, then clicked off.

Next on his list was the bus schedule. He pulled a copy from his drawer and found three possibilities that worked within the time frame Molly left the gym. He called the supervisor— he couldn't remember his name, but they had spoken a few times in the past. He explained what he needed.

"That'll be either Ron, Keith, or Stu. I'll call 'em now and get back to you."

"Thanks," Bryan said, amazed how cooperative people were. But there was a missing woman, a mother, and if that didn't touch your heart, then as far as he was concerned, you didn't have one.

Bryan stood up, stretched, and yawned. He needed java. In the break room, several of the guys coming on duty poured paper cups of coffee. The room reeked of cheap cologne and masculinity. Any other day, he'd hang out and shoot the breeze, but not today. He waved and hurried back to his desk. Something nagged at him, as usual, something the doctor said the night he'd called to report Molly missing.

He took great pride in his memory, but it failed him now. He raked his hand through his hair. He needed a shower and a shave, but it would have to wait. He sipped the coffee, the

bitter brew returning as acid. He took a roll of
Tums from his desk, popped two, and chewed
them. They were almost as bad as the acid, he
thought as he took another sip. The night he'd
gone to the McMansion the doctor had ram-
bled, was all over the place. He couldn't put
his finger on it, but he would. He always did.

He turned around just in time to see Craig
and Rodriguez heading his way.

"I can't believe you drink that toxic stuff,"
Craig said. "It's deadly."

Rodriguez sat on top of his desk. "I spoke to
the housekeeper a while ago. Sally. Nice old
gal. Said she's worked for the McCanns since
the daughter was small; she couldn't recall
how long, only that it's been a very long time.
Her words.

"Says the doc is an asshole. Again, her words.
The sons are pricks, still her words. According
to her, and I have no reason to doubt her, the
doc beats the crap out of his wife. Said Molly
tried to act like it wasn't so, but she knew. Said
the twins were abusive, too. Verbally. She told
us about the dinner party, but she left before
the action started. When I told her the wife was
missing, she smiled. Said if she was missing, it
was because she wanted to be. Said she was too
smart for the doc, and he hated that. Made fun
of her because she didn't have a college degree. Sally said he always referred to her as
'that waitress from the dump.' "

"That's it," Bryan said slowly. "I've been trying to remember what it was he said that kept

nagging me. He said Molly was working as a waitress when he met her."

The pieces of the puzzle were slowly coming together. He would bet his last nickel, as always, that Molly had carried that brown paper bag from Lou's around with her for a very long time.

"The doc's story on the kid's car checks out. Barry's Automotive. Said it's been ready for days, and no one's picked it up. The mom and daughter dropped off the car for a tune-up," Craig said, his hands crossed over his broad chest.

"At least he's telling the truth about something," Bryan said dryly. "Before I forget, Craig, I met a girl today, actually she's a lady, a very nice lady. She owns All Night Fitness. Her name is Becky. I told her you were looking to join a gym. Said you needed to meet someone. Go there, ask for Becky, and tell her Bryan sent you. Don't ask. Just do it."

His cell phone went off. "Detective Whitmore."

"Hey, one of my guys remembers that woman. Ron. Said she sat in the first seat behind him. Thought she was a man at first, but when he saw her face, he knew better. Said she was pretty but paranoid, if you know what I mean? Dropped her off at some storage facility where they store classic cars. Said she went inside, and that's the last he saw of her. That help?"

"You can't imagine how much it helps. I owe

you one. You get pulled over, tell them to call Bryan Whitmore." He hung up. Both Craig and Rodriguez shook their heads.

"Don't say a word," he warned, grinning.

He relayed the bus supervisor's information to one of the patrol cars in the area. "Check the place out, and I'll meet you there in twenty minutes.

"You two keep an eye on the doctor, watch his place. If you see anything funky, I don't have to tell you what to do."

As soon as Bryan left the station, his cell phone rang again. "Whitmore," he said. He was tired, and it was starting to show. He was always courteous when he answered his phone.

"This is Officer Edwards. I have a woman here at the storage house who says she's got video footage of your victim leaving the lot."

Hot damn!

"I'm on my way."

Chapter Twenty-four

Molly was hot and sweaty and wanted nothing more than to take a hot shower. She needed to cleanse the filth from her body, and not just the physical kind. She needed to cleanse the images she'd just witnessed from her soul.

She asked God for forgiveness as she drove out of Blossom City. Words that prior to now had crossed her mind, but only just now spewed out of her mouth like a geyser. But, in a sad way, she felt as though she'd been purified.

Confronting Marcus had been the worst. His life choices had left him in a wheelchair, and his lack of parental guidance and education had turned him into nothing more than a dirty bag of rot. He used to be so handsome, and now he was barely recognizable. She felt no pity for him when she recalled what he'd done to her. He certainly hadn't felt any pity for her.

She hated him, truly. This was something she would have to live with, but she could. She had for decades.

But what freed her the most was knowing she hadn't killed any of those bastards. She had spent her entire adult life thinking she was guilty of a horrid crime, murder, or, at the very least, maiming those worthless bastards. And when she saw Marcus in the wheelchair, she'd at first felt guilty, believing she'd crippled him when she ran into them, but she hadn't. He had done it to himself. And the others. In a sick way, justice had been served. When she found out that all but one of her attackers had been killed in that car accident, she thought that Lady Justice had exacted her revenge.

And then there was Dr. Kevin Marsden. He was still alive. And living quite luxuriously, she was sure. But with only Marcus as a witness to what had happened that night twenty-one years ago—and she knew he would never come forth unless he were forced to, and even then he would probably lie—she had her hopes pinned on the dress she had worn that night. The dress she had sworn to burn a dozen times. But something always seemed to stop her. And now she knew why that was. Again, in mysterious ways, Lady Justice was at work.

She smiled and gave Ace a fluff between the ears. She couldn't wait for Kristen to meet him. She loved animals, and Tanner was such an ass that he would not agree to the kids having a pet growing up.

Tanner. Holden and Graham. She would have to deal with all of them when she returned, and she would.

First, she was going to contact her friend and old roommate, Sarah Berkovitz, to see if she could recommend a good divorce lawyer. Then maybe when life settled down, they could renew their friendship. Molly decided she would like that. Other than Sally, she had no real female friends.

The women she saw occasionally at the gym were just people she saw once a month. In ten years, she'd never really allowed any of its members to befriend her, and a few of them had tried. Tanner didn't like her having friends, didn't like it when she left the house. She would've loved to work for Gloria, even if it was just part-time. The homey smells, the environment, not to mention the food—all were so appealing to her. Trips to Gloria's were always the highlight of her week. Besides her daughter. She'd sent her a text message when she'd calmed down. She couldn't talk to her yet, but she'd been thrilled when Kristen answered her right away, telling her how much fun she and Charlotte were having and how much she missed her. She missed her, too, but Kristen needed to experience what a young woman her age should.

Sadly, Molly had missed out on so many things, but she was still fairly young. Her life was ahead of her now, and she could pursue anything she wanted. Maybe she would take Gloria up on her offer.

What she couldn't do was stay in that house that held so many bad memories. As she'd done in Blossom City, she would exorcise that house—from her past and her future. Something told her that when Kristen left for college, her life as an adult woman, an adult mother, would truly begin.

She checked the gas gauge and saw that the tank was nearing empty. She stopped on the outskirts of Haines City, at a Flying J's, a reputable truck stop. She filled up, checked her oil, fed Ace, and walked him in an area exclusively for animals, where he attended to his private business. Inside she paid for her gas and handed over an extra twenty dollars to use the showers they offered to truckers.

Unsure of what to do with Ace, she stuffed him inside her suitcase, leaving room for him to peek out. She pulled the suitcase behind her, but no one said anything about a cat's peering out. Inside the women's showers, she let Ace roam for a few minutes, then he curled into a ball and fell asleep on top of the suitcase.

As she scrubbed herself clean with the fresh-smelling body wash provided in a mounted container, she relished the feeling of soap suds running down her body. Using the shampoo in the container, she washed her hair, then washed it a second time. She lathered conditioner into her hair, massaging it all the way to the ends. She thought she might cut her hair. Tanner had always demanded she keep it long.

It was heavy and too much work. As soon as she could, she would get one of those new haircuts that were short in the back and angled sharply on the sides. It would look good on her, she thought, as she rinsed the conditioner out of her hair.

When she returned to Goldenhills, she would not be the same woman who had left. She'd shed that pitiful skin in Blossom City. She often wondered how such a dreadful, ugly city wound up with such a pretty name. There wasn't the first hint of a blossom, unless you considered the orange trees. Maybe that's where its name originated. It didn't matter anymore, she thought, as she let the warm water cascade down her back and legs. She couldn't remember when she'd enjoyed taking a shower this much. That fancy tub in the master suite couldn't hold a candle to this single-stall public shower. At least that is what she thought. Perhaps it was because, in a sense, this was the first shower she had ever taken as a free woman, as someone with no guilty secrets needing to be hidden.

She scrubbed down one more time just because she could, and let the hot water wash the last two days away. She would feel hot and grimy later, but right now, she felt as fresh and clean as a hothouse daisy, which happened to be her favorite flower.

Molly removed a pair of jeans and a red T-shirt from the luggage, Ace making it known she was disturbing him with a super loud "meow."

Hurrying so she could get back on the road,

she dried off with the towel they'd provided with the shower fee, dressed, and felt almost human. Until she looked in the mirror. She took her makeup kit out of the luggage. Blush and mascara, then a swipe of peach lip gloss at the very least, added a bit of color to her face. She combed out her hair and pulled it back in a ponytail.

She bought two hot dogs, a bag of pretzels, and a large Coke before she left. When she was back on the interstate, she munched on the food and cranked the radio up to a station that played happy tunes. For the first time in her life, she felt that the burden of guilt had been lifted, as though an angel had brushed it away. The emotional release brought tears to her eyes.

Happy tears. Like the radio station.

Epilogue

Two months later

Molly was so excited as she waited inside the terminal for Kristen's plane to arrive. So much had happened in the months she'd been in France. She'd told her bits and pieces over the phone, but sometime in the near future, before Kristen left for college, Molly planned to sit down with her and tell her all about her past. She had no reason to keep it from her anymore. She had every reason to let Kristen know who her mother really was, and now, since filing for divorce last week, she no longer had any reason to fear Tanner. They would always share a daughter, but that was the only thing they had in common anymore.

Tanner had gone insane when she had come home.

She'd pulled into the long driveway in her red Mustang, music blaring and Ace sitting on her lap. The driveway was full of vehicles, two of which were police cars. At first she had thought something had happened to Kristen, but she'd just spoken with her, so it had to be something else.

When she got out of the car, she was welcomed home by Detective Bryan Whitmore. Smiling at the memory of her confusion, she went inside with him.

Tanner had been his usual angry self. Holden was high, and Graham wouldn't even look at her.

"You've had a lot of people searching for you," Bryan had said, then proceeded to fill her in on the events of the past three days.

"You reported me missing?" she'd asked Tanner.

"No wife of mine leaves me," Tanner had shouted.

"And that's why we're here, Mrs. McCann. We have reason to suspect that your husband's first wife's death was not, in point of fact, an accident. We're here to protect you while you get your things. You can't stay here now."

"It's my home," she whispered, stunned.

"That may very well be, but when your husband learned that you were returning, he filed a restraining order."

"What?"

"He doesn't want you in his house. Those were his very words."

"You son of a bitch! I don't need you to speak for me. She's my wife, I can say and do whatever I please!"

Bryan walked across the room and got right in Tanner's face. "No, sir, you lost that privilege when you filed that restraining order."

Ace had meowed, and the look on Tanner's face when he saw him curled up in her arms was priceless.

"It's okay, Detective. I wasn't planning to stay here anyway as I will be filing for divorce," Molly said. Again, the look on Tanner's face was priceless.

Once she started, she couldn't stop. "I think you killed Elaine, just like you said you did. Oh, you were drunk when you said it, but you admitted to shoving her down the stairs. She wanted a divorce. I wonder if she despised you as much as I do?

"Detective, I want to report a crime. Twenty-one years ago, I was raped by a boy who is now one of my husband's colleagues. His name is Dr. Kevin Marsden. We went to high school together in Florida. I might have DNA evidence to prove it, too. There is a teal prom dress in my locker at All Night Fitness. You have my permission to remove it from the locker."

"We've got the dress, Ms. McCann. Forensics is checking it for DNA as we speak. Just get your things, and you can take care of your legal issues later." He looked at Tanner as though daring him to say anything.

"There is something else," she said. Hating to betray her daughter's trust, but unwilling to be a part of Holden's crime, she said, "Holden McCann raped a young woman at Racer's. Her name is Emily. He laced her drink with roofies."

This got Holden's attention right away. "That's a lie!"

Molly walked over and stood right in front of him. "You and your brother have mental issues, deep-rooted, just like your father. I'm sorry, Holden, but I don't believe you. The girl you raped got pregnant and suffered a miscarriage. I will do whatever it takes to see that she presses charges against you, you son of a bitch!"

And the accusations and the arguments continued until Bryan walked her to the door.

Now, two months later, with the divorce behind her, and the division of property from the divorce settlement making her quite well-to-do, as well as ensuring that Tanner would have to pay for Kristen's college education as he had paid for Holden's and Graham's, she had gone on her very first real date with Detective Bryan Whitmore. She'd met Marty last week. She was adorable. And now Kristen was coming home. So many changes—some good, some bad—but her daughter was tough, and like her, she, too, would survive.

Holden had been arrested for raping Emily. She'd convinced Emily that pressing charges was the right thing to do, going as far as telling Emily her own story, hoping to coax her into contacting the authorities. She had, and Holden was currently out on bail awaiting trial.

Graham had left Goldenhills when his older brother was arrested. No one knew where he was, and, sadly, Molly thought it was for the best.

She would always cherish the memories of the boys when they were little kids, but they had turned into spoiled, mean men, just like their father.

Vikki Kearns and Sarah Berkovitz were working day and night to reopen the case of Elaine's death. The last she'd heard, Tanner had hired a high-priced defense attorney. News of this traveled fast. Within weeks, Tanner had to close his dental practice in Goldenhills, and from what she'd learned, his offices in Ocean Orr were next. And he'd thought he was going to garner enough attention to warrant investors in an office in Boston. Hah!

He'd received enough attention, but it hadn't been the right kind. Along with his name opening the evening news with stories of the investigation into his first wife's death, Tanner was also being investigated for arson in the case of his parents' deaths.

She cringed when she learned this, but now nothing surprised her where her former husband was concerned. He was almost as evil as her mother and Marcus. Almost. His saving grace: Kristen.

A voice over the airport intercom announced that Flight 927 from France had arrived at Gate 14.

"You'll like her, I promise," Molly said, as Bryan squeezed her hand.

"I have no doubts. If she's like her mother, chances are good that I'll more than like her."

Bryan normally didn't get involved with the people he met while working on his cases, but there had been something about this case right from the beginning that had drawn him in. When he met Molly, he knew she had been placed in his life for a reason. She was good and decent and kind. Everything her ex-husband was not. She'd been through hell and back, more than once, and looking at her now, he couldn't believe she was smiling.

She started waving crazily at a young girl heading toward her. He followed her gaze, and for a minute he thought Molly had a twin.

Kristen was the spitting image of Molly.

"Hey, you," he said, "I have a question."

She turned to look at him. "What's that?"

"When you changed your name from Maddy to Molly, before you married Tanner, what was your last name?"

She raised her perfectly waxed eyebrows and swung her newly cropped hair around. "It was Hall."

"*Sixteen Candles*, right?"

She nodded. "It used to be one of my favorite movies."

Though he never would have admitted to anyone, and he meant *anyone*, it had been a favorite of his, too. "Same here," he said, laughing at her expression. "We'll talk more later." He eyed Kristen running toward them.

She grabbed her daughter and squeezed her so tight, she thought she might break her. But Kristen was tough as nails. "I've missed you so much, sweetie. I can't begin to tell you." She stepped out of their hug to look at her daughter. Her long legs were even leaner than they'd been when she had left, her skin was golden from days in the sun, and her long hair was streaked with sun-kissed shades of yellow.

"I can't believe you're finally home," Molly said, and hugged her daughter again.

Bryan remained silent as the two soaked each other up. He could see that Kristen was a good soul, just like her mother. Her eyes sparkled, and her hair looked like spun gold. Marty was going to love her; he just knew it. And if their relationship continued in the same vein, he would love her and her daughter. His gut told him that this was highly probable.

"I'm such a love hog," Molly said to him. "Kristen, I want you to meet Detective Bryan David Whitmore. Goldenhills' finest. And I do mean fine," she added, and they all laughed.

Kristen reached in and gave him a huge hug. "I've heard so much about you, but before I tell you all of Mom's secrets, I have to thank you for taking this case. Mom says if it weren't for you, well, you know all the stuff she's been through. I just think it's so cool that you two are dating." She kissed Bryan's cheek.

"Me, too," he said, thrilled with her uninhibited display of affection.

"Mom told me you have a daughter. Marty. I can't wait to meet her. Mom says she's fifteen. I've always wanted a little sister," she blurted out. Then when she realized what she'd said, she backpedaled. "Oh crap, I've stuck my foot in my mouth. Again. I do it all the time, right, Mom?"

She glanced at her mother, who was smiling like a happy child. She'd never seen her mother like this. She'd spent so many years on edge, but Kristen was putting all that bad stuff behind her, just like they'd discussed over the phone.

"You're seventeen, kiddo. You're supposed to put your foot in your mouth."

Bryan stood in the middle and wrapped his arms around both of them. As soon as Marty was with them, he would be complete.

"What's that look on your face?" Molly asked.

"I think he's in love," Kristen teased. "Oops! Foot in mouth again."

"I think this is the happiest day of my life," Molly said. "Except for the day I gave birth to you." They all hugged, and if anyone were watching, they would know people in this trio were as happy as anyone could ever hope to be.

Dear Readers,

I cannot know this for certain, but I think all of you out there know someone or have heard of someone who has been sexually abused. I know I have. Way too many, actually. The truth is, one person is one too many.

On the off chance any of you do know someone who has been abused, I ask you to, if you can, tell them about a wonderful organization called RAINN and to ask for help. As Molly learned in *No Safe Secret*, RAINN stands for Rape, Abuse and Incest National Network. This is a wonderful organization dedicated to helping women and children who have been abused.

RAINN has a National Sexual Assault Online Hotline. It is open 24/7 for crisis support. It provides one-on-one confidential support. Staff members are highly trained and are there to help you. The Online Hotline—the nation's first online crisis hotline—provides free, anonymous, confidential support services 24 hours a day, 7 days a week. It has been operational since 1994 and has supported over 2.5 million people online and over the phone, serving victims and survivors from all over the country. Two-and-a-half million is such a staggering number. I urge you, all my readers, to reach out to anyone you think might need this service.

Victims can call 1-800-656-HOPE (4673). They will be connected to a trained staff member who will put them in touch with a local center near where they live. They can also e-mail info@rainn.org.

All I ask is that you keep all of the above in mind and if you see someone who needs help, follow through. Don't turn away because it's an ugly thing you don't want to deal with. You or I could make all the difference in the world to someone's very survival by encouraging victims to seek the help that is available with a phone call or the tap of a computer key.

My last thought that I want to share with all of you is this: "WE'RE WOMEN!" We can do whatever we set our minds to doing and come out on top. YES-WE-CAN!

Thank you for taking the time to read this.

Fern

#1 New York Times *bestselling author Fern Michaels's new novel is a deeply satisfying and uplifting story of one woman's journey from heartbreak to triumph.*

SWEET VENGEANCE

Life Is Full of Surprises

Tessa Jamison couldn't have imagined anything worse than losing her beloved twin girls and husband—until she was convicted of their murder. For ten years, she has counted off the days in Florida's Correctional Center for Women, fully expecting to die behind bars. Fighting to prove her innocence holds little appeal now that her family's gone. But on one extraordinary day, her lawyers announce that Tessa's conviction has been overturned due to a technicality, and she's released on bail to await a new trial.

Hounded by the press, Tessa retreats to the small tropical island owned by her late husband's pharmaceutical company. There, she begins to gather knowledge about others in similar situations to her own . . . people who have lost their families in horrific ways, only to see the perpetrators walk away unpunished. For the first time since her nightmare began, Tessa feels a sense of purpose. She'll use the fortune at her disposal to track down criminals who have outwitted the law. Only this time, it'll be Tessa, not the courts, who determines what their sentence should be.

One by one, the guilty will be led to justice, and victims like Tessa can gain closure. But when it comes to her own case, will Tessa be able to learn the truth at last . . . and reclaim her freedom and her future?

Keep reading for a special look!

A Kensington hardcover and eBook
on sale now.

Tessa Jamison counted the time so that she might arrive at a restful place when Death's hand reached out for her own. Each second, minute, and hour, excluding those during which she slept, admittedly few, brought her closer to her inevitable meeting with Death. Surely, she would find peace, or possibly sheer nothingness, in death. If not peace, or a white noise of sorts, if the tenets of her Christian faith were as pure and true as she'd been brought up to believe, she would be reunited with the family she had slaughtered so callously.

Since her conviction ten years ago, the quote from the *San Maribel News Press* had haunted every single minute of her essentially lifeless existence in Florida's Correctional Center for Women.

Slaughtered so callously. A mantra of sorts. *Slaughtered so callously.* The words drummed in her head like a rapid heartbeat. Images of Joel's mangled body, the carnage, the horror of seeing her family.

Dead.

Joel's body unidentifiable by visual means, the coroner had stated.

Gone in the blink of an eye.

It wasn't until three years after her imprisonment for the murders that the memory of the aftermath of their savage deaths emerged from her safe place—the dark confines hidden deep inside the protective corner of her subconscious. For years, Tessa's mind refused to retrieve the image of their slain bodies. Lily pads. She recalled thinking of lily pads floating in the aqua-blue pool on the fateful day when she'd discovered their bodies. Like a fine French claret, sinewy ribbons spread throughout the aquamarine water, the tomb that held the last whisper of their lives. Their last thoughts. Their last heartbeats. Their last cries. Their understanding that this was indeed the end, that the finality of life was now death.

Tessa hated this part the most. She could not bear to think of their last moments as the dark shroud of Death engulfed them. Had they struggled? Had they cried? Or had they simply taken their final breaths, accepting what was to come as their fate?

These thoughts tormented her. Day and night, images of their bodies taunted her. Broken marionettes. Their limbs and arms askew, bloated, as decomposition began to set in. Later, she would recall the coroner testifying at her trial. Joel had died defending his daughters. His fingers and arms were covered in defensive wounds, and again, the fact that Joel was visually *unidentifiable*.

"It's as if the victim didn't even have a face," the coroner had testified.

The testimony still had the power to cause her heart to race.

Tessa struggled to keep the bitter prison coffee down as the images assaulted her. Catching her reflection in the small, steel-like mirror hanging above the built-in desk, Tessa no longer recognized the woman she'd become. Her blond hair was now streaked with thick stripes of silver, her once-bright blue eyes were now as dull as the mop-water-colored prison walls that stared back at her. Ten years living, if you could even call it that, in a seven-foot-by-ten-foot cell could do that to a person. She stared at the steel hinges that held her single bunk to the wall. Her bed was a thin, blue-and-white-striped dingy mattress atop rusted springs that creaked with every twist and turn. And the worn gray wool blanket on the bed, which she'd learned to make with military precision, was nothing more than a nighttime battle-ground. Underneath that blanket she fought the demons that haunted her dreams at night and tormented her days. She'd adjusted to life in prison as well as anyone could under the circumstances, but the anger that grew deep inside her with each day spent behind bars was now barely containable. Ten years of incarceration for a crime she had not committed, of complete and utter hell, had infested and darkened her soul.

The clank of metal against metal, a shrill cry, a moan from someone in the depths of prison passion, were so common now that she hardly noticed them. Each day was the same as the thousand next and the one before it.

In the beginning, she'd simply curled up at the corner of her bunk at night, fearful of what might happen if she fell asleep. Given the nature of her supposed crime, she was immediately ostracized by the other inmates. Other than former cops, baby killers received the worst treatment inside prison.

Dinnertime was the worst. The other inmates' chanting the words *baby killer, baby killer* greeted her as soon as she entered the utilitarian cafeteria each day. It wasn't unusual for a spoonful of food to fly across the cafeteria, smacking her in the face, or to have a glob of instant mashed potatoes smashed in her hair as though she were nothing but a thing to torment. As hard as it was, Tessa refused to fight back. After a few years, she blended in, just like the others. She was a number, an inmate, a convicted murderer. She would die here in Florida's Correctional Center for Women. No one would care; there would be no memorial service to honor the person she'd been. Nothing. She would be carted out in a pine box, and from there, she would most likely be buried in the state's cemetery, where all the other inmates who had died were laid to rest.

Stop, she told herself. *Stop!* It was these thoughts that would kill her. Not the other murderers and drug addicts. Not the child molesters and rapists housed in the men's prison across the road. No, she would not die at their hands, but her own, if she continued to allow her thoughts to return to that day, now almost eleven years ago.

She had died that day because since the moment she discovered the dead bodies of her husband and twin daughters floating in their pool, bobbing, up and down, like the red-and-white bobbers used by fishermen, she'd had no life.

Nothing would change the devastation of what her family had suffered. There was no going back. To this very second, she was as traumatized as she'd been the day the words *guilty of murder in the first degree* filled the court-room. Nothing would ever bring her a moment of happiness.

Nor did she deserve it. If only she'd stayed home that weekend instead of racing to the mainland to prepare for an indefinite stay with the girls.

The memory of that last day was all too clear to her now, very clear, having emerged in bits and pieces during her ten years in prison. If only she could turn back the hands of time.